D1083912

Campion Towers

ALSO BY JOHN AND PATRICIA BEATTY
At the Seven Stars (1963)

BY PATRICIA BEATTY
Indian Canoemaker (1960)
Bonanza Girl (1962)
The Nickel-Plated Beauty (1964)

Campion Towers

JOHN AND PATRICIA BEATTY

THE MACMILLAN COMPANY, NEW YORK

COLLIER–MACMILLAN LIMITED, LONDON

Designed by Margery Kronengold
Library of Congress catalog card number: 65–13594
The Macmillan Company, New York
Collier-Macmillan Canada, Ltd., Toronto, Ontario
Printed in the United States of America
FIRST EDITION

To
Alwyne Kirchhoff
and to
the memory of
Anne Hunter

Contents

The "Godspeed" Out of Bristol

I STOOD on the headland, the winds from the northeast warm upon my face and whipping my skirts, and it was I who first saw the *Godspeed*, a black speck upon the gray sea. She was past due.

The ship from England had come again to us in Salem Town, Massachusetts Bay Colony, this June of 1651.

There was no reason why I should keep watch. The coming of the Massachusetts Bay Company's ship meant little to me except that I wished to hear the latest news my father's old friend Captain Samuel Enderby had gathered from Bristol and Southampton. Now that I was fifteen and full grown, I, too, was interested in news.

I left the headland. Soon all would know that the Bristol ship was entering Salem harbor. The boom of the cannon from Fort Pickering in the north would signal its arrival. On Winter Island they would know it was the *Godspeed*.

Captain Enderly would come to my father's house tonight for supper. I would hear what news there was of an England

I

I had never seen, an England torn by nearly ten years of Civil War. Perhaps the captain's news could make me forget my own unhappiness for a moment or two.

Nothing ever came to me, to Penitence Hervey, on the *Godspeed*. I had no gold to order fine things from London or from the cities of France or Spain. Although our house was white-plastered and had three gables, the Herveys were not rich.

I would never see England. I was not so fortunate as my best friend, Amity Wrenn, who would sail on the *Godspeed*'s homeward journey to visit her father's family in Swindon.

I walked by the marshlike town common where the cowherd called to me and waved. No fine future awaited me as it might await Amity even here in gray Salem, a place of rocks and of dark forests marked only by the trails of savage Indians. I was but a servant in my father's house, a nursemaid to my half brothers and sisters, and misliked by my stepmother, Elizabeth. There was to be no dowry for me. If a man married me, he would have to take me for love alone—not wealth. Few men in Salem Town would be so foolish.

Now I heard the cannon from Fort Pickering. Everyone around would hasten to the wharves. The *Godspeed* came from our company. It was our ship. Amity Wrenn would be on the wharf waiting to tell Captain Enderby that she and her family sailed with him. My oldest half brother, Obedience, who was named after my father, would be there surely, hoping to be asked aboard.

Slowly I walked up crooked Essex Street to my father's house and cooperage. As I neared it, I heard no sounds of pounding or hammering and I saw no plume of smoke from the chimneys of the cooperage. It was as I had thought. No barrels were being made today. My father had few buyers and I knew he sat in his shop with his Bible, reading silently, while my stepmother made the house adjoining the cooperage unbearable with her sharp tongue.

As I passed First Church, Pastor Wrenn's church, I was afraid. Elizabeth would probably beat me because I had left the house that morning without her permission. I paused with my hand on the latch, hating my life. More and more often I had to escape Elizabeth for a time. Her blows were becoming more frequent as my father's trade fell off and money grew scarcer.

I opened the door and went inside. Our house was low and dim. The hearthfire and polished copper kettles were the only notes of color. As Puritans we dressed in black, gray, and brown. We had no laces and ribbons. There were no bows to my black leather shoes, only pewter buckles. Our homes and our meetinghouse were as plain as my white linen cap. I longed sometimes for color, for flowers and bright blue skies. They cost nothing but the longing was not godly.

"The *Godspeed* has come, mistress," I said to Elizabeth, hoping to avert trouble by my news.

My father's second wife, a tall brown-haired woman with a thin, hawk-featured face, stood near the little cradle my father had made long ago for me. She glared at me, but instead of taking up her stick by the door she bent and picked up the baby, Oliver. Oliver wailed loudly as she walked across the floor with him in her arms.

"He teethes," she told me. She frowned, her thick dark eyebrows drawn together. "Samuel Enderby comes at a poor time. You must see to supper, Penitence. Your father bids the captain to my house all too often. There are chars to be done. Get to them."

I nodded and went through the house to the shed in back where the tall wooden butter churn and the roasting hens waited for me. There was indeed much work to be done today. It would all fall to me, just as the smoking of the hams and the drying of the peppers which hung from the beams had been my task. I also made the soap, bleached our homespun linen cloth, and baked our bread.

The younger children were of little help to me, although they did help make baskets and brooms. Jonathan, who was seven, and Purity, who was six, came into the shed, too, to watch the milk turn to butter. They were like unto Elizabeth, already tall and, like her, brown-haired.

"Where is your brother, Obedience?" I asked Jonathan.

He answered me after a longing glance at the churn. "At the wharves. He took Ann with him."

I had to smile. Obedience loved the world of ships. He was nine and had not decided if he would be a sailor and fight against the Spanish in the West Indies or against Dutch and French pirates, or become a soldier. He yearned to be ten years old and begin giving his eight days each year to the militia. Already he could shoot an arrow straight and now he could hardly wait to be taught the handling of a half-pike and a musket. The tales of Captain Myles Standish's fights against the Indians fascinated him, but even more he worshipped Captain Enderby, who had sailed even to the East Indies. After all, Obedience knew Captain Enderby and he had never seen Myles Standish, for Standish's Plymouth was a goodly distance from Salem Town. And although Elizabeth and our father had come from England, we children had never left Salem except to go to Beverley or Marblehead, close by. We had not seen Boston, which was two days' journey.

"The *Godspeed* has come," I told Jonathan and Purity, hoping they, too, would go to the wharves.

They sat down on little three-legged stools and watched me as I churned. Nothing would make them leave me in peace, not even the mention of the ship.

Bedford, our mouser, a prettily striped gray, white, and orange cat, came to rub herself against my skirts, look up at me out of her amber eyes, and mew. She liked buttermilk, but I had none for her then.

"Later, Bedford," I told her, "I shall put down a bowl for you."

The shed door burst open with a crash and like a sleek gray trout Bedford fled to hide behind an unsalable warped barrel, now filled with autumn's salt pork. It was Obedience, of course, who held his sister's hand tight in his.

His cheeks were rosy. So were Ann's, while her hair was a pale tangle from the wind. They had been running. "It is the *Godspeed*," Obedience called out loudly, "she is in port!"

"I know," I said and I appealed to Obedience. "Please you, take Jonathan and Purity out to play. Captain Enderby will come to supper. I have work here, the baby is ill, and your mother is busy."

Obedience shooed the other children out with his usual authority, ordering them to go back to weeding our Indian corn and bean patch. Neither he nor Ann went out. I sighed. They were my favorites, sinful as it was of me to have favorites, and they took advantage of it. Now Ann seated herself on a stool and said happily, "They is a letter for you."

Obedience, who was eager to show me how strong he was becoming, had grabbed the dasher from me and had begun to make the churn dance about on the shed's uneven floor.

"Never tell falsehoods, Ann," I scolded the little girl whose face fell, making me want to hug her. Yet she must learn that lies did not lead to favor. Liars stood in our pillory before our church with their tongues put through a cleft stick. I did not like the pillory any more than I did the whipping post or the stocks but these were realities.

"It is not a lie!" Obedience defended his sister. "It is true. I saw Captain Enderby and he says he has a letter for you. 'Tis come from England. He wants you to go to the *Godspeed* to fetch it."

I would not believe it. "No, Obedience," I corrected. "It is a letter for our father. I shall tell him."

Obedience put his strength into the churning. It was difficult to hear him over the thumping sounds, but I saw how he shook his head. No, Obedience knew better than to lie.

"It is for you. I never saw it, but Captain Enderby told me right enough it was for you. You are to fetch it. He does not want to bring it here."

I was perplexed at this. Obedience must have bewildered the facts. A letter for me?

"Why must I go?" I asked him.

Obedience shrugged and took the cover off the churn.

I made up my mind. "Obedience, will you help me with the hens later?" I would have to go to Captain Enderby if only not to anger my father by disobeying his friends.

"Um," Obedience replied and I took that as consent. He would be there when I returned from the wharves. I should help Obedience if he helped me, so I caught Ann by the hand and we went out the shed door almost running.

Of course, Obedience was mistaken, I told myself. Who would write me? I hoped though that it would be a letter that brought my father good news for his business. Captain Enderby often put him in the way of a good cheap price for iron strips for barrel hoops so it would not do to make Samuel Enderby angry with us. I hurried along, my skirts flying about my ankles, Ann skipping to keep up. We rushed past the Pine Tree Tavern and the houses with their open-front shops.

I took Ann up and edged my way through the crowd at the wharf. Mostly everyone was there watching the sailors unload the barrels of malt for our beer, kegs of nails, boxes of books and shoes, and casks of wine marked with the names of strange cities, far from Salem Town—Roman Catholic cities with names like Bordeaux, Boulogne, and Cádiz. It was always a rare show to watch the cargo unloaded.

I saw the master of the *Godspeed* now. He stood on his quarterdeck speaking with his mate who was overseeing the unloading of the cargo, while a tall sailor kept the citizens of Salem off the plank.

Silvery-blonde Amity Wrenn, her cap awry with excitement, came out of the crowd to put her arm about me. There was a smile on her lips. Her round blue eyes were fixed greedily on the ship. I felt a stab of jealousy. Amity had much better luck than I.

"I shall sail with Captain Enderby in two days," she said to me for at least the tenth time. "Will you miss me, Penitence? I shall miss you sorely."

"I shall miss you, Amity," I told her. "But now I am to board the *Godspeed*. Captain Enderby has a letter." I was glad to get away from Amity. I had learned, since she told me she would go to England, that looking at happiness through another's eyes is the most difficult thing in the world.

I waved my arm and called out to the captain. It was unseemly and people stared at me. Even Amity fell back with a gasp at my forwardness, but I had no time to waste. I was relieved when Captain Enderby finally spied me out.

"Come aboard, Penitence Hervey," he called to me. "I have somewhat to interest ye."

Carrying Ann and aware that everyone was staring at us, I went up the plank of the *Godspeed* to be met by Captain Enderby. He took Ann from my arms and swung her high into the air, delighting her. Like many men who had never had a family, he adored children and they loved him.

He was not changeable. He was always the same little round man with sharp blue eyes, an inquisitive nose, bushy red eyebrows, a face as smooth and brown as a nutmeg, and curling reddish hair. Captain Enderby wore a black woolen coat and breeches and a plain steeple hat, but his garments were far richer than those of most of us Salem folk, for his broad white collar was edged with a half inch of Flemish lace as were his cuffs, and the buckles on his shoes were undoubtedly silver, not pewter. They were never tarnished. I reckoned that they were polished each day to keep them bright, for nothing tarnishes silver so swiftly as salt sea air.

"Ah, prettier than ever, Mistress Hervey," he said.

I made him a curtsy. It was not befitting for him to flatter me so. I was not comely. I despaired of my hair. It was the color of Indian corn and curled in paler yellow wisps about my face no matter what I did to control it and keep it under my cap. My eyebrows and lashes were near black and my eyes a gray-green with a strange gold-fleck shaggy pattern. My face was too broad and my forehead too high for true comeliness, Elizabeth told me while Amity agreed. I was like unto my mother who had come from England as a bride and who had died but a month after my birth. She had not been a Puritan always. Elizabeth told me this often and I perceived that Elizabeth had been no friend to my mother on the ship that took them all out of England in 1636, away from those who persecuted us for our religion.

"You have a letter, sir?" I asked.

"Aye, that I do." He reached into the deep cuff of his coat and drew out a piece of folded white paper.

I took it, hearing it crush in my fingers and, much interested, I looked at its heavy red scar of sealing wax marked with a shield bearing two fleurs-de-lis. On the other side I read my own name "Penitence Hervey" in a flowing script. It seemed truly a letter for me!

I asked the captain, "What does it say?"

He shook his head. "How should I know, mistress? I have kept it in my strongbox from Bristol to Salem harbor and only this morning fetched it out to give to you. Open it and find out. I was given payment to bring it to you and I am to take a reply back to Bristol with me."

I saw Pastor Wrenn coming now. Seeing him made me remember the chickens waiting to be plucked at home. It was sinful of me but I had always thought Pastor Wrenn was much like unto a plucked chicken, yellow, pale, and plump.

"Do you sup with my father tonight?" I asked the captain hastily.

"Aye, Penitence."

I dropped him a quick curtsy and took Ann's hand, dragging her away from an enticing coil of tarry rope. We went by Pastor Wrenn, both of us curtsying to him.

There was no time to lose. At any moment Elizabeth might find me gone. I stuffed the mysterious letter into my apron pocket. Perhaps I would find a free moment to read it before nightfall. I knew that I should surrender it to Elizabeth first, but it *did* bear my name. So I *would* read it even if it meant I was punished.

As we hurried back to the house, I touched the letter with my fingers. I had never seen my name on a letter before. I was excited, more excited than I dared admit.

The Aylmer Inheritance

OBEDIENCE had finished the churning. He joined me working over the hens for supper. And just as we finished, Elizabeth came into the shed.

It was time for our bread and cheese and small beer. I had hoped to have a moment between plucking the hens and feeding the children to look at the letter but it was not to be. I fed the children quickly from our everyday wooden trenchers and then I ate standing. I had called my father from the cooperage shop but there was no reply. He must have gone to the Pine Tree. Young Obedience had surely told him of Captain Enderby's arrival. Elizabeth seated herself on a stool, Oliver in her arms, her face dark with disgust. She was always angry when her children teethed or hurt themselves. She, too, ate swiftly. I was much too busy to read my letter—the trenchers had to be scraped, the two pigs, Henrietta and Maria, fed the scraps, and the hens roasted.

I threaded the fowls onto the spit and sat down by the hearth. This was the char I most fancied, watching for scarlet salamanders in the flames while I lazily turned the spit with the firehearth jack. I liked seeing the plump birds turn golden brown and hearing the drippings crackle as they fell onto the coals. Because we were to have a guest, I basted the hens now and then with a ladle of melted new-churned butter, wasteful as this was.

I was very aware of the letter. I wondered greatly about it as I sat at the hearth and when Obedience spelled me at the jack I hoped to get away to the pantry or to the shed to read it. But once more it was not to be. Elizabeth gave Oliver to me. The baby still howled and I rocked him, wishing he would stop. I hated to hear him wail. How I wished that we had some strong spirits in the house. I had seen mothers dip a finger in rum and rub it on a baby's gums. It helped ease the pain. We did have a bottle of heavy Madeira wine put aside for supper and, without asking Elizabeth's permission, I put a drop of it onto my finger and put it on Oliver's red swollen gums. Elizabeth came out of the pantry to scowl at me.

"Have a care of that, mistress," she said. "The wine is meant for your father's excellent friend from Bristol, Captain Samuel Enderby." She sniffed as she pronounced the captain's name. "Aye, we go without so Samuel Enderby may fill his belly with costly wines."

I had nothing to say. My father had few enough friends. Elizabeth's tongue had driven most of them away. When my father first came to Massachusetts Bay Colony I had been told, even our famous Governor Endicott had come to the cooperage to enjoy my father's conversation and company, but I could not remember ever having seen John Endicott except once when I passed the Pine Tree Tavern and spied him entering it.

In the middle of a wail Oliver yawned. Then he sighed

deeply, closed his eyes, and babelike slept. It was time for me to see to the supper. I put Oliver carefully back into his cradle and called Ann to sit by him and rock him gently.

I poked the hens with a toasting fork and watched the juices spurtle onto the glowing coals. The birds were done and it was dusk, so I spoke softly to Obedience. He would fetch my father and Captain Enderby from the Pine Tree.

Obedience flung out of the door. He loved going to the Pine Tree to see who sat at the innkeeper's tables. Whenever he could, he listened to the talk and brought us news. But Elizabeth and my father did not like Obedience to go to the tavern except on errands. It could be a dangerous place, often frequented by sinful people from the other colonies and from England. More than once I had seen sailors from the West Indies come out of the Pine Tree roaring drunk, filled with rum. Their golden earrings, knives, dark faces, and their short linen trousers—their strangeness—terrified me. I knew what they truly were. They were pirates. They preyed on the Spanish fleet that sailed to Mexico. In doing this they rendered England a service against Spain, her chief enemy, but still they frightened me. Other men, even more fearful than the pirates, had come to the Pine Tree. It was a well-known fact that Papists, Roman Catholics, from Maryland had supped there. Papists were friends to Spain—even if they bore English names. Papists were enemies to England and my faith.

Now I set up the trestle table for supper. It looked quite fine with my true mother's silver candlesticks and pewter plates. Our candles tonight were of costly wax, not tallow. The silver and pewter gleamed in the light.

"I wonder what news Captain Enderby brings this time?" I said, setting the third place. I would sup with the other children in the pantry and perhaps there would be a bit of hen left for us.

Elizabeth shrugged. "Who knows? We are many miles from England. It concerns me little."

I kept my eyes on the shining candles. It was true Elizabeth cared far less for news from England than anyone else I knew. She hated England and was pleased when our colony had abolished the Oath of Allegiance to the Crown eight years past. She had been a servant maid in England. I had heard this from Amity who had heard it from her father. The Civil War was nothing more to my stepmother than a sign of God's vengeance upon the wicked and the rich. I had rejoiced when I heard of the great Puritan victory at Naseby six years past, although I had been only Obedience's age. Elizabeth had not cared.

I put the youngest children to bed, but I still had not got to the letter. While I was busy in the pantry, Captain Enderby had arrived. I came out to find him in his usual place of honor in the finest chair beside the hearth, while my father sat across from him. Both men smoked father's long white clay pipes and pulled hard at them. No one was permitted to smoke in public. If he did, he was fined a shilling. Smoking was my father's greatest pleasure but he could not waste shillings. Elizabeth sat at the far end of the low-ceilinged, oak-beamed room knitting a stocking while she rocked Oliver's cradle with her foot. Obedience crouched on a stool near Captain Enderby.

The captain stopped speaking when he saw me. He gestured toward me with his pipe and gave me a long piercing look. I knew what he meant and shook my head. No, I had not read my letter yet. I seated myself on a second stool beside my half brother.

Enderby understood. He turned away to give his attention to my father, whose pale, thin face was alive with interest.

"What has come about since the battle of Dunbar, Samuel? On your last voyage you spoke of General Cromwell's fight against the young Charles Stuart's army in Scotland. Dunbar was a great victory for Cromwell."

The sea captain blew out a puff of smoke. "Aye, a lucky victory."

"It was God's will," Elizabeth muttered.

But Captain Enderby ignored her and went on, "I think you heard that the man the Cavaliers call 'Charles II'—Charles Stuart—was crowned at Scone in Scotland after he lost to Cromwell at Dunbar. Charles Stuart remained in Scotland. There has been peace in England since that time, but there are rumors that Charles will venture again for the throne his father, Charles I, lost when he was beheaded two years past."

"To gain the crown he will have to defeat Cromwell and his army," my father said grimly.

"Aye, and that is not very likely," Enderby agreed. "But young Charles will not forgive the Parliament—not the Parliament that chopped off his father's head."

"What is Charles Stuart like?" I asked, greatly daring. I knew the heir to the throne of England was not old, but twenty-one, my father had told me. My father was not offended as I had thought he might be at my interruption.

Enderby answered me. "He is a black devil of a man, or so they say, Mistress Penitence. Rumor has it that he flits about England, but wise men in London know from their spies that he skulks in Scotland. He is a devil with the wenches wherever he goes, I might add."

"That is enough of such clack before Penitence. The maid knows all kings are evil but she need not have the particulars," Elizabeth put in coldly.

Captain Enderby nodded, accepting the rebuke. Even if it had been spoken out of mislike it was just. My father shot a glance of warning at his wife, but she had her head bent over her knitting as if she had dropped a stitch. I suspected she was smiling for having scored off the master of the *Godspeed*.

"Is Charles Stuart now a Papist?" my father asked.

"They say he is not. But who knows?" Captain Enderby replied. "His mother, Henrietta Maria of France, is a Papist and he seeks a rich bride among all the Roman Catholic houses of Europe. The Stuarts are church-mouse poor."

"What does it matter if he takes a Romish wife?" asked my father.

It was not truly a question. He felt that no Stuart would ever again sit upon the throne of England. The Puritan Parliament would be on its guard. It would not permit Charles Stuart to return. We Puritans remembered all too well how Protestants had suffered and perished as martyrs in England under a Roman Catholic queen in the last century. England was Protestant now. Some of it was Puritan, like ourselves in the Massachusetts Bay Colony; most of it was Anglican, or Church of England. But the Anglicans, while less godly than we, were still Protestants. They too hated the Church of Rome.

"Penitence, it is time for supper," Elizabeth told me and I got to my feet. She rose, too, and filled the captain's glass and my father's glass with a dark red gush of wine. She poured none for herself, I noticed, as I took the hens from the spit, placed them on a wooden platter, and set them on the table. Then I motioned to young Obedience to follow me into the pantry.

"Take this to the table," I said to him as I gave him a trencher of new baked bread and yellow cheese. Captain Enderby would sup well tonight.

As Obedience left I took the letter from my apron pocket at last and put my fingernail under the wax. Swiftly I broke the seal and thread and by the light of a pantry candle unfolded the letter someone had addressed to me—to Penitence Hervey.

The handwriting was an elaborate one and not easy to read by the dancing candlelight. Somehow, I thought it was like to my mother's script that I had often seen in our old household accompt books. I glanced first at the signature and knew I shook my head in wonder for it read "Laurel Killingtree." What a strange name that was. How odd to be named after a tree and not a virtue! Why did she write me? Who was she? The letter was penned three months past and had been written from a place called "Campion Towers" in England. Slowly I read the letter:

My dear great-niece Penitence,

You may find it most singular that I write you at this time. However, I learned not long ago, after having made inquiries from the pastor of your father's church in Bristol, that my niece had left a child who survived. Your father years gone by wrote of your mother's death in a savage land and of your birth. None of us supposed a motherless child could survive. We presumed that you, too, had died.

Now your grandmother, that is, your mother's mother, has fallen ill. She is an Aylmer, not that I can believe you have been told of the Aylmers. Your grandmother, Philippa Aylmer, has the Aylmer inheritance. It is an inheritance that has been conveyed from female heir to female heir for more than a hundred and fifty years. Your mother was once to have been this heiress. Although you are but a child, we know your grandmother Aylmer wishes to see you and has asked me to write you requesting you to come here to us at Campion Towers before she dies. I found that the ship Godspeed *sails for Salem soon. I am sending a messenger to its master with this letter and with the money for your passage if you choose to come. I trust your father will opt your sailing for England on the return voyage of the* Godspeed. *Despite the fact that your father is not of our religious faith and bears us no affection, I pray that he will permit you to see your grandmother, who has spoken of you often since I learned in Bristol of your existence. As your great-aunt, your grandfather's sister, I urge you to sail with Captain Enderby. You will be met at Bristol by someone from Campion Towers.*

And the letter was closed with, "Most faithfully, your kinswoman and affectionate servant, Laurel Killingtree."

I held the strange letter in my hand. Who was Laurel Killingtree, I asked myself once more? "Aylmer" meant nothing at all to me. I read the letter again. It was surely mine. My mother had been a Killingtree. I had gleaned this even though my father rarely spoke of my mother or her family. Elizabeth did not relish hearing of my mother and my father misliked my mother's family. It was only when Elizabeth accused me of some vanity that I heard the name—as she said angrily, "What else could be expected from Nicola Killingtree's whelp?"

Slowly I went back to the hearth and sat down in the chimney seat. My elders would soon be finished. Fine food was rare in our house and quickly eaten.

"Penitence, have you read your letter?" Captain Enderby asked, surprising me.

I nodded, "Yes, sir."

He was pleased. "Ye'd been gone just long enough I thought."

My father was not so pleased. He put his wine glass down suddenly. "A letter you say, Samuel? A letter for Penitence?"

"Aye, I fetched her a letter from England."

My stepmother leaned forward now. "From England? A letter from England for Penitence? Who would write her?"

"Give me the letter, Penitence," my father said. We all sat silent as he read it. Tight lines formed at the corners of his mouth, lines I had never seen before. His voice was rough. "What do you know of this, Samuel? This letter should have come to me, not to Penitence."

The master of the *Godspeed* shrugged. "My cargo was aboard. I waited for the tide, to cast off in Bristol, when a man, a servant, I reckoned, came up to my ship on a lathered horse. He asked me if I knew a Penitence Hervey. At first I told him 'no.' I did not consider Penitence here in Salem Town until he asked if I knew an Obedience Hervey in Massachusetts Bay Colony. When I got my wits together, I said that I knew you both. He put a purse full of gold and that letter into my hands and demanded that I sign a paper stating that I had taken the money and that I would deliver the letter. Then he ran down the plank as if the devil were at his heels, leaped onto his horse, and rode off. The tide was with the *Godspeed*, I put the letter and the money into my strongbox, took my place on the quarterdeck, and sailed."

"But what does the letter say?" Elizabeth demanded. Folk did not often permit Elizabeth to remain in ignorance.

My father's tone was sharp. "It has come from Penitence's great-aunt. The Killingtrees wish her to come to England. They have sent her passage money to return on the *Godspeed*." Without rising he held the letter out to my stepmother, who reached across the table to snatch it up.

Elizabeth did not read easily. Her lips moved as she devoured the letter greedily. I had seen her eyes flash when she heard Captain Enderby speak of gold. At last Elizabeth came to the end of my letter. She looked at me now in a different way, almost as if she summed me up in her accompt books. "It would be a wicked thing, indeed, if Penitence does not see her grandmother before the poor old woman dies," she said to my father.

"No. It is a long and dangerous journey for a maid. I will not permit Penitence to go so far from Salem and to such people." My father was very brave tonight.

Elizabeth pursed up her lips as she did when someone crossed her and she glared, her dark forehead lowered like an animal's with anger. Then she must have thought of the gold again. "Come now," she said, "this business can wait. We shall talk about it later." Elizabeth caught up the wine bottle and refilled both my father's and the captain's glasses to the brim and as I watched she did an astonishing thing. She poured herself a glass of Madeira, too. She paused with her hand still about the neck of the wine bottle. "When do you sail, Captain Enderby?"

"In two days' time, Mistress Hervey." He smiled at me.

Once the door had closed behind Captain Enderby and Elizabeth had shot the bolt, she swung about to face the three of us. "You, Obedience, get to bed," she told my half brother, not looking at him. He wisely took up a candle holder and did as she bid. Elizabeth's eyes were on my father as she ordered, "Clear away the table, Penitence."

I hopped to it. She was determined to gain her way over my father. I had seen that look in her eye many times before. My stepmother's voice rose high and shrill as I left. "What of it? They sent money for the girl's passage. She is quite capable of looking after herself."

My father's words were slow. "You do not know the Killingtrees, Elizabeth. They are not of our faith. They showed no interest in Nicola once she had married me. They have shown no interest in Nicola's child until now. I do not know why Laurel Killingtree made inquiries about me in Bristol. It is most strange and I do not like it. They are not folk I would choose to have Penitence know."

Elizabeth raged at him. "Because they are gentlefolk and rich! What else do you have against them? You have never even seen them. You met Nicola Killingtree in London at a kinsman's house. You told me that yourself. In England you were a gentleman, not a humble cooper. Remember that. That letter bears a coat of arms. You have arms, too, but you will not display them here."

"Elizabeth," my father said wearily. "I was the younger son of a gentleman, a very poor gentleman. You know we have no use here for a coat of arms. It would much offend the men who buy my barrels. We have no fine coach door on which to carry arms. I have no land in England. My father's house and his debts went to my older brother. He was killed nine years past at the battle of Edgehill. The Hervey property fell to my family's creditors. The Killingtrees did not want Nicola to marry me, not only because I was a Puritan but also because I had no prospects as a younger son of a ruined family. They care nothing for Penitence. I do not know why they write such a letter to her."

"They cared enough to send her the passage money," Elizabeth flared. "They are rich. Think of the money. Think of the inheritance the letter mentions. She can have the Aylmer money! That will mean a dowry for your Penitence, not to mention what we need for my children. I ask something better than the dame school for Obedience and Jonathan. Penitence can make all come true. She need not remain long in England. The old Aylmer woman lies dying. The letter is clear enough on that point."

My father's voice rose to a height of rage I had never heard.

"Penitence is my daughter! If you do not care for her welfare, I do, mistress. She will not go to Campion Towers—to Worcester! The journey is long and dangerous."

Elizabeth was not finished. "Get to bed, Penitence. You can finish your work in the morning. It is late." She took up the quarrel again, her words drifting after me as I went out of the room, for she did not care if I overheard. "What danger? The Wrenns travel on the *Godspeed*, too. They can look after Penitence. If the Killingtrees can spend ten pounds to fetch her to England they will hardly neglect her welfare." I shifted my garments, hearing the unequal battle raging, but I could no longer make out the words.

Late at night I awoke as Bedford, the little cat, leaped onto my bed. I had forgotten and left the casement open. Now I got up and closed it snugly against the dangerous night air. Bedford curled up between Ann and me and began her usual soft purr of happiness. The house was quiet at last. Whatever had been determined was determined. I knew who had won, of course.

In the morning when I came out to make suppawn for the children I found Elizabeth up beforetimes, sitting on her tall stool, a small triumphant smile on her lips as she ripped out the seams of her second-best gray gown. There was no hum of the spinning wheel this morning.

I was to have a third gown to take to England with me, it seemed.

She finished as I watched and then picked up a needle, sighting at it while she poked the dark thread neatly into its eye. "When you have cooked the suppawn, you had best run to the wharves to tell Captain Enderby you sail with him."

As she bent her white-capped head to her sewing, she rocked Oliver's cradle with her foot. He wailed, but she would not hold him to comfort him. There was no time for that.

I made haste. I cooked the corn-meal porridge in the black iron pot over the fire and then I roused the children, dressing the little ones and scolding them into washing their hands and faces.

I would tell Captain Enderby. But first I would tell Amity Wrenn that I was going to England, too!

Amity was annoyed for a moment when she learned that she was not the only maid from Salem sailing to England on the *Godspeed,* but then she became very excited. We both sped to the wharves where I called out Elizabeth's decision to the captain. He only nodded. He had known how events would come about.

At dusk I unpacked my mother's old leather trunk, taking out the beautiful gowns she had brought from England. They were of sinful shining colors—none of them wearable in Salem Town by members of our church. My mother's sober-hued cloaks had been cut down for my half sisters and me. What else we wore had come from Elizabeth, her homespun castoffs.

There was no money for trumperies such as fine clothing even if we Puritans had worn such things. The plain truth was that my father was an indifferent cooper. His barrels were neither the cheapest nor the best. People did not clamor to apprentice their sons to him and pay fat masters' fees.

I had little to put into the sturdy trunk. Two plain wool gowns, two aprons, and three white caps did not make a brave show. I knelt beside the trunk, and held to my cheek a silk gown the color of the red-gold of the autumn leaves I loved so well. The glorious costumes my mother had worn always made me wonder about her. What had she been like? What sort of life had she led in England?

Lost in thought, I did not hear my father come up behind me. He had kept to his shop all day as if he avoided us.

Hastily I dropped the red gown.

He seemed to have grown older overnight. His eyes were sad as he gazed at the gleaming pile of brocades and silks. "I did not know your mother's family in England, Penitence," he told me, "they are not of our religion, as you know, but . . ." Here he faltered and seemed to change his thoughts in his next words. "Conduct yourself to them as you would to us in Salem. You are a good member of our church and will be a credit to our Puritan faith. If ever you can forward our cause, do not hold back to do so. Whatever you do, do not take on the ways of the Killingtrees. Remember always who you are and what you are, my child. You should know this. You were named 'Penitence' at your mother's request."

I was surprised. I had always taken it for granted that my father had named me.

He went on, "Your mother wished you to bear this name to make amends for her inconstancy and foolishness as a maid. When she died, she was of our faith—at last. She joined our church. We Herveys are gentlefolk, although I am now but a cooper. The Killingtrees are above us, I believe. Your grandfather is a knight, perhaps by now a baronet. Things seem to be changing swiftly in England these days. Yet no Hervey need feel inferior to a Killingtree. Be kindly to your grandmother and courteous to your mother's family—but no more than that. Come back to us soon. There will always be a place here for you. I shall miss you. May the Lord protect you on your long voyage.

We shall offer up prayers for you at meeting tomorrow. Do not bear malice to Elizabeth. Poverty has soured her. She was not always so."

With these words my father gave me some coins which I knew he must have borrowed. "Your passage home," he told me, putting the money into my palm and folding my fingers over it, "and there is a bit more, too. If the Killingtrees use you ill or attempt to corrupt you, leave at once. Go to Swindon— to the Wrenns. They will look after you. I have spoken with Pastor Wrenn. Penitence, remember what I have told you about your mother's family. They are not like us." And then, for the first time I could ever remember since I was very young, my father kissed me. He said something more but it was drowned out by a loud rapping on the door—one of the sailors from the *Godspeed* had come for my trunk.

I said my farewells to everyone in the family. Needlessly, Elizabeth urged me to be very kind to my grandmother Aylmer and to be very sure not to offend anyone. I nodded, embraced her swiftly, and then kissed each of my half brothers and sisters. I left home with a final curtsy to both my father and Elizabeth and, with young Obedience, went to the wharves on the heels of the sailor who carried my light trunk easily over the cartwheel ruts of Essex Street.

My half brother was the last person I saw as I stepped from the wharves onto the lantern-lit plank. Tears ran down his face in the yellow light of his horn lantern. Tearful, too, I called out to him, not knowing what to say, "Take care of your brothers and sisters and Bedford, too. Do not weep. I promise I will bring you a fine skinner's knife from England."

He gulped and shouted to me. "I will keep watch over 'em.

I promise, too. Get me a red plume for my hat!" He swung the lantern once and ran up the wharf, his shoes clattering on the planks.

I found it no great wonder he was my favorite. He wanted a spirit of humility as much as I. I went below to the tiny cabin I was to share with Amity Wrenn, the little cabin boy leading the way. It was a wood-paneled room with two hard beds. The door was open so I could see Amity inside, sitting on one of the beds, her hands folded in her lap. She wept, too.

"I am homesick," she wailed, "and we have not left Salem harbor."

So was I. I sat on my bunk thinking fondly of those who stayed behind. After a time though I dried my eyes with my apron and began the first of many nights' wonderings about the mysterious Killingtrees.

The *Godspeed* sailed at dawn. Neither Amity nor I saw Salem before the ship beat out of the harbor. We went out on deck to gaze over the gunwales at the hard black-gray coastline, all rocky beaches and coves. We expected nothing else, for we knew the way we took. We traveled northward to Newfoundland for a cargo of dried fish, prized in the Old World. Captain Enderby had taken on his Salem cargo in one day—the last furs of winter, mink, otter, and beaver to line the traveling hoods of fine ladies, to make muffs for their soft white hands, and to trim the garments of noble lords. The captain had also taken aboard Massachusetts Bay Colony pitch and turpentine, "naval stores," he called them. We people in the colonies had little to send to England as yet and we were painfully aware of it.

We put in at a barren little port in Newfoundland and Amity

and I looked on from the rail as the *Godspeed* filled her bottom with barrel after barrel of dried salt fish.

When Captain Enderby's mate pronounced the hold filled, we went to our knees on the deck along with the captain and the crew while Pastor Wrenn prayed. "Oh, Lord, if it be thy will, give us fair winds and a safe voyage over your bourne of waters. Look down upon thy humble servants. Preserve us from storms, pirates, Papists, and shipwreck, from evildoers and malefactors of other lands, and bring us safe to England."

As her father finished, Amity reached for my hand and held it tightly. I understood. I knew all too well where much of our Newfoundland fish would be landed—in Cádiz, the terrible port city in Spain, the city that we English had attacked and raided twice in a century, the city that surely hated us, the city of Papists, of the dreaded English-burning Roman Catholics.

I found the long voyage tedious. Amity was seasick much of the time, as was her father, so they kept to their beds. I walked about the deck, now and then with little Mistress Wrenn, who was a better sailor, and sometimes with Captain Enderby, who, as master of the ship, was even to me a sterner man. He had little time for his four passengers, but I was not offended. We Salem folk knew that captains at sea and captains ashore were two different persons.

We met few storms as we journeyed across the ocean to Spain, traveling southeast. Never having crossed the Atlantic before, I had no idea how fortunate we were not to be mewed up under hatches.

Pastor Wrenn's prayer had been heard. We saw no other sails —neither foe nor friend. I soon became weary of the gray-blue waters, the same food each day, the constant winds, the noises of the ship, and the calls of the sailors.

Although Mistress Wrenn did not say it, I felt that she was scandalized at my traveling alone to England to strangers. But one fine morning, as we sailed into warmer waters, I told her of the Aylmer inheritance. Her lips tightened and she spoke her mind. "So that is why Elizabeth sends you. I had not known of any inheritance. I might have guessed it though. Well, child, if you need us, come to us in Swindon, do you hear? This is what your father wishes."

I promised. To tell the truth I became more frightened with each day's passing.

Finally the sun shone brightly day after day, and as I sat one afternoon, carefully shielding my face from the sun to keep it white, I heard a sailor shout from the top of the tallest mast, "Land ho!"

The captain, proud of his powers as a navigator, was confident. "It will be Spain, of course," he told me. And so it was. I watched the purple-blue land ahead of us turn slowly greenish as we approached and then I spied the tall ships coming toward us sailing westward. The strange ships carried great crucifixes on their sails.

Captain Enderby looked at them through his glass and shouted to me. "Look at them, lass. They are a rare show. 'Tis the silver fleet bound for Mexico unless I miss my guess. Would our lads at Tortuga be interested in this!" I nodded, knowing he meant the West Indies pirates.

At the captain's shout a thinner Pastor Wrenn came out on deck. "I shall not give thanks for this landfall until we be safely gone out of this harbor. God save us all if we be at war with Spain again."

"Aye," said the captain gravely, "but they seem peaceable enough to me. There has been grief enough in England with a Civil War, but ye never know. Mayhap young Charles Stuart stirs up the Spanish against the Parliament." And I knew he spoke of the young man who had newly been crowned King Charles II. Captain Enderby went on, "I never enter Cádiz harbor without asking myself if there be a Spanish prison readied for me." He shook his head. "But trade is trade for all the danger. Cádiz is nigh to famous vineyards. Spanish wine sells well in England."

The silver fleet sailed westward under a blazing sun while we struck canvas to wait. We sailed on then. Just outside the harbor we waited again while our sailors, who had cursed under their breaths at the sight of the Spanish ships and who eyed the greenish-brown Spanish waters with loathing, three times fired one of our small cannon as a signal to the harbor pilot.

A little boat came skimming toward us, bright in the hot sunshine, and before long a dark-complexioned, sharp-featured man, dressed all in black velvet, came climbing up our ship's ladder. It was the Gaditano pilot who bowed to Captain Enderby, calling him "El Capitán Inglés." We all breathed deep sighs of deliverance. We were not at war with Spain. The pilot bowed in turn to Amity, who had come on deck, too, to her mother, and finally to me, sweeping off his purple-plumed hat. He spoke to Captain Enderby in his soft language while our English sailors kept silent, their eyes wary, watching the pilot's small boat and the pilot, himself.

"When we dock, go below to my cabin," Captain Enderby ordered. "Do not come out on deck again until I send you orders. There has been trouble in Cádiz again with the last ship from England. In spite of the harbor guards there was a fight. An

English sailor was killed, but he killed two Spaniards first," the captain added with satisfaction. "Señor Ortega says there must be no more difficulty or we will all be taken into custody."

The captain did not have to tell me twice. I felt I could even smell the hatred the crew bore toward the Spanish, but if the pilot caught this he gave no sign. Señor Ortega took the helm and I watched from the gunwale as we approached Cádiz, the "cup of silver," as the Spanish called it.

The city was hemmed in by the sea. A long peninsula walled the bay of Cádiz off from the ocean, just as the city, itself, was walled. We had been told the harbor was a perilous one. The entrance to the bay was filled with rocks, mud, and shifting sandbanks, but as Pastor Wrenn prayed loudly, Señor Ortega took us over. Amity and I gasped at the strange city made up of tall glistening white houses, many of them with bright blue-green and dark blue tile domes. For all that it was a Popish, Roman Catholic city of murderers, it was beautiful.

Hastily, we four went below as we docked. But I glanced over my shoulder at the hordes of small dark-skinned Gaditanos surging behind a file of soldiers who carried pikes and muskets. The guards, dressed in black and buff with silvered helmets, held the people of Cádiz in check. All the same they shouted, hissed, and waved their fists.

The soldiers turned to face the crowd over a barrier of raised muskets as our planks were put over the side and the Spaniards who were to unload the *Godspeed* were passed through. We heard the soft padding of the Gaditanos' bare feet and soon we heard the rumble of many barrels being rolled across the deck, barrels of Newfoundland fish being sent ashore to the wharf, barrels of Spanish wine disappearing into our hold.

I looked out of the high, many-paned window of the master's

cabin. By peering around to one side I could see a tiny piece of the wharf. The crowd was still there in the August heat hissing at us, and I shivered. They wanted us gone, remembering all too well how our sea raiders had met their silver ships not too many years before and stolen their New World treasures. I thought also how sixty-odd years ago the King of Spain had sent his multitudes of great warships, the Armada, to attack England, and how we English had been saved from invasion only by a miracle. A great storm had been sent to us by the Lord, my father had often told us, and the Armada had been broken by it. Many ships foundered. Some were wrecked upon the coasts of Scotland and Ireland while before the storm others had fallen prey to our great sea captains Drake and Hawkins.

At last the Gaditanos were finished. As the last Spaniard left the *Godspeed*, our planks were drawn up, our lines cast off by the soldiers, and we drifted away from the hostile city, but not before a shower of stones was thrown by the crowd. One fell with a crash of glass into the cabin where we waited. Yet I watched out of the window as we left the harbor, dropped the pilot, and set sail for England. Fleetingly I thought how odd it was that although we were of vastly different faiths and hated each other, they ate our salt fish and we drank their dark wines.

Obedient to Captain Enderby's orders, we waited in the stifling cabin. I wiped my face with my apron as did Amity and her mother. At last the little cabin boy came clattering down the stairs, grinning. He had a wicker basket over his arm, a basket filled with round yellow things nestling in shiny black-green leaves. They were beautiful.

"What are these?" I asked.

"Citrons," he announced. "They grow in Spain. The captain asked the pilot to buy them for us."

"But how do you eat them?" I asked.

Having been in Cádiz before and knowing all about citrons, the boy proudly showed us how to peel the thick-skinned fruit.

I watched carefully and did as he showed me. A citron was most peculiar. I was not quite sure if I liked its taste or not. "Do they have citrons in England?" I asked Mistress Wrenn.

It was Pastor Wrenn who answered my question, chuckling. "No, Penitence. They cannot be grown in England. They are worth their weight in gold there. You will not be seeing another citron—not unless you sup with Oliver Cromwell or with Charles Stuart, the 'would-be-king,' at some great nobleman's table. Now that is hardly likely for the like of you, a simple maid."

I had never heard Pastor Wrenn say such a ridiculous thing and I was surprised to learn that he could laugh. It must have been his relief at sailing out of Cádiz that made him giddy.

A Friend to Pastor Wrenn

THE WINDS were strong against the *Godspeed* as we struck out from the Spanish coast into the gray-blue Atlantic once more and it grew cooler as we sailed northward to England. Mists swirled around us those early August days. We could not see the coast of Devon, although the land-hungry sailors watched, straining their eyes for the first glimpse of their homeland.

It was a full week before we rounded England, Devon to Land's End, and beat up the ever blustery Bristol Channel to Bristol, home port for the *Godspeed*.

Now my heart began to beat faster each hour. Who would meet me? Laurel Killingtree? I knew from Captain Enderby that it would not be likely anyone would meet the *Godspeed* at the wharves. The lengths of voyages were too uncertain for that. Probably the Killingtrees knew someone who lived in Bristol, perhaps an agent of theirs, who would bring me a message telling me what to do.

I spoke further with the Wrenns. Supposing my grandmother Aylmer had died, Laurel Killingtree had changed her

33

mind, and I was left in Bristol. I was to send a letter to Swindon at once. Pastor Wrenn would come fetch me so I would sail for home with them. Penitence Hervey was not to be set loose in a sinful town like Bristol, no indeed! Pastor Wrenn had read his scriptures closely. He knew all the wickedness of the world. We Salem folk listened quietly to him in the great cabin while Captain Enderby, whom I had begun to suspect more and more of not being the best of Puritans, covered his mouth with his hand, smiling.

As it happened, no one at all came for me. I stood at the rail in the morning watching Pastor Wrenn, his wife, and Amity disembark. They had bidden me a careful farewell, but at the last moment Amity had burst into tears and hugged me as if I were about to fall into the clutches of the devil and she would never see me again.

The captain stood at my elbow as the Wrenns disappeared behind tall stacked bales of woolen goods. "If ye'd like, I would show ye the sights of Bristol, such as they be, when I have done with my accompts for the company, lass."

Of course I wished to see Bristol and waited impatiently. Captain Enderby gave me his arm on the wharf as gallantly as to a fine lady as we left the world of ships and masts to enter the city. Not that ships are ever truly left in Bristol, for they come into the very center of the city on three sides. "Their bowsprits have protruded into these narrow streets for six hundred years," Captain Enderby explained.

I had learned a bit about Bristol and had heard that it was large, but I must confess I gasped at its size and the number of its people. "Well over twenty thousand," the captain said.

Such fine tall brick and timbered houses and cobbled streets —I held my breath in awe when I was shown the centuries-old cathedral and St. Mary Redcliffe Church. The leaning tower of Temple Church was amusing but it could not compare truly with the surprising sight of dog teams transporting merchandise down to the wharves. I had never heard of such a thing. In Massachusetts Bay Colony we used carts and horses or oxen. Captain Enderby caught my astonished glance and explained. Bristol was honeycombed with cellars. The people were afraid that heavy draft horses would break through the streets.

The people of Bristol were much as Captain Enderby and I, I thought, as I looked out the corner of one eye as they passed. They were merchants for the most part, and their dress as sober and seemly as ours. My gown, or rather Elizabeth's second-best gray gown, was fit for England. I was muchly relieved, vanity that this was.

I listened closely as the captain talked to me. The daring Cavalier soldier, Prince Rupert, the cousin of Charles Stuart, had held Bristol for a time but the godly Oliver Cromwell had retaken the city and now it was wholly for Parliament. I approved. It was good to know that western England—that all England—was Parliamentarian in 1651. General Cromwell would keep us safe from the young King.

After a tankard of small beer at the fine Dutch House, Captain Enderby and I walked back to the *Godspeed*. The first mate had a message to show us. We both read it there on deck. It was from a "Master Quentin," the Bristol agent of the Killingtrees. He had received the news that the *Godspeed* had docked and had learned that I had sailed from Salem and was now in Bristol. Master Quentin, a man I was never to see, had sent a messenger to Campion Towers telling the Killingtrees of my arrival. His settlement with my mother's family, made months ago by Mistress Laurel Killingtree, was that I was to go to the

Turk's Head Inn to wait. A room had been set aside for me and within two days I would be on my way to Holt Heath and Campion Towers, for a coach and a companion would start for me the moment Master Quentin's messenger reached there. I looked questioningly at Captain Enderby, who folded the letter and returned it to me.

"Aye, the Turk's Head in Marsh Street. 'Tis a reputable inn, I know it well, and its owner, Mistress Whidby, a widow and a good woman. She will look after ye, Penitence."

It was settled then. That afternoon I left the *Godspeed* by hired cart, Captain Enderby riding beside me, to the Turk's Head. Uneasy, I looked back at the familiar ship. I would miss her. When we got down at the inn, an old white-plastered half-timbered building, the Turk's Head signboard, which bore the face of a ferocious-looking black man in a feathered yellow turban, did not make me feel very confident. The common room was crowded with men drinking wines from Cádiz and brown English beer. Here Captain Enderby took full charge at once, calling for the mistress of the inn to attend us.

The widow Whidby was a shriveled little woman in a rustling black gown. It was plain to see by the cut of her gown and her blue bead necklace that she was not of our faith, but her inn seemed clean and no more boisterous than Salem Town's Pine Tree. She knew Captain Enderby well and nodded when he spoke of Master Quentin's instructions. Yes, the best room in the house was prepared for me and Mistress Whidby herself would watch over me, seeing to it that I was safe and never permitted to wander about Bristol alone.

Not that I entertained any such ideas, for I heartily wished myself back in the tiny cabin on the *Godspeed*. The captain told the woman I was to leave with no one but a qualified person sent from the Killingtree family of Campion Towers, Holt Heath, in Worcestershire. The woman nodded and nodded but when he said "Worcestershire," her jaw dropped and she gazed in disbelief at me and at my clothing. But she immediately recovered herself and led the way up the stairs out of the common room, flinging open a heavy door at the end of the upper hall. Captain Enderby and the man with my trunk followed.

The captain looked about approvingly as did I. My room was large. The bed and red canopy were clean. There was a well-polished window seat, a chest and a clothespress, and, best of all, a great iron bolt across the door. The master of the *Godspeed* was well satisfied. We took our leave of each other, he promising to tell my father I had arrived safely, and I promising him that I would abide by the commands of the widow who owned the Turk's Head. He bowed and I curtsied and Captain Enderby, who was my last link with the New World and home, departed for his ship.

I was alone, the door bolted behind me. I went to the window seat and watched the little captain stride back down Marsh Street to the wharves. There was nothing for me to do but wait and wonder. I sat, wondering, alone, until dusk fell and a rap at my door and a serving woman's voice announced that my supper had been brought to me on a tray and would I unbar the door?

Dutiful to Captain Enderby's wishes I remained in my room that evening, my door bolted, and I kept to it the next morning, waiting, my gaze on Marsh Street below me. I had not slept well the night before, wondering about the things that sorely plagued me—the Killingtrees and Mistress Whidby's strange glance yesterday at Captain Enderby's mention of Worcestershire. My father had not been pleased to have me go to Worcestershire, I remembered all too well. My eyes grew heavy and I sighed and got up from the window seat. I would nap before supper. I had just set my foot on the little steps that led to the high bed when once more there was a rap at my door. This was odd. I had eaten my morning and midday meals. The last tray had been cleared away some time ago. Could it be someone from Campion Towers already? But that was hardly likely. It was a good fifty miles from Bristol to Worcester. I went to the door.

"Who is it?" I called out, my hand on the bar.

"Mistress Whidby," was the reply. "There is someone here who wishes to speak with you."

I shot the bolt and there stood Mistress Whidby, her lips pressed into a thin line, her brown eyes wary.

"Is it Captain Enderby or someone from Holt Heath?" I asked.

She shook her head. "None of those, mistress. The news is that the captain busies himself taking on cargo. It is a man, though, and my poor house must greet the like of him these days as though it were a fine honor." She sniffed. "Yet I warrant a Roundhead lass like yourself will be pleased enough."

I followed her down the steps, piqued at her calling me a "Roundhead," a name of contempt for Puritans. Whoever had come to see me was clearly no friend to Mistress Whidby.

A very tall man with long hair, so pale that I could not tell if it were gray or flaxen, stood at the foot of the stairs. He wore a high-crowned black hat, a broad white collar, and a long black gown, a scholar's or a pastor's gown, that fell to his shoes. His eyes were a frost-blue, his nose was a fragile bird's beak, and his lips in his thin, parchment-colored face were threads of violet.

I could not tell his age, but by his speech and his dress, he was godly—one of us, a Puritan.

"I am Dr. Amyas Moonjean of Gray's Inn, London," he announced in a deep musical voice, "and you must be Penitence Hervey, newly come from Salem Town in Massachusetts Bay Colony." At my nod he went on. "I am a friend to your Pastor Wrenn of Salem. We met once more yesterday at meeting in Swindon. He knew I journeyed to Bristol where I have business and asked me to find you and convey his affection."

Mistress Whidby interrupted shrewishly. "This is a busy time for me. I must see to the preparing of supper. Sit you both in the corner. The pot boy will bring you what you lack if you call." Then she was gone.

"It was kindly of you to come," I said, mindful of my courtesy to so distinguished a gentleman as Dr. Moonjean, a men who had come all the way from London and who was at the famous Gray's Inn, where lawyers were educated.

"Ah, Penitence," he said as he seated himself. "I was told your strange history by Mistress Wrenn. I wish you well at Campion Towers, a place that has long held my interest."

"You have been there?" I asked, hopeful for news, but the man shook his head, disappointing me.

"No, my child, not I, but I have heard of it and its folk ofttimes."

"Do you know the Killingtrees?" I asked.

"I know of them," he told me, lacing his long-fingered white hands together on top of the scrubbed wooden table. "They are not Puritans."

"I know that," I volunteered. "If you know of me, you must know that I have never met them. Can you tell me anything of them?"

I noticed that the man's knuckles whitened, but his voice was as melodious as ever. "How good a Puritan are you, Penitence Hervey? Pastor Wrenn assures me that you would do much for our faith. You know how we Puritans have suffered for our beliefs here in England?"

I drew back a bit. What did he mean? But, then, I told myself fiercely that I was as good a Puritan in my way, outside of my troublesome lack of humility and my fondness for color, as Amity Wrenn. Each of us had his own personal devil to wrestle. Had I not heard that often enough in meeting? Yet, I was almost angry with the question. I did not know Dr. Moonjean. He had no right to ask me such a question.

"I am in good standing in my church in Salem Town," I flared.

"Of course you are, child, of course. I put it badly and disturbed you. You have had a long and exhausting journey. Forgive me. What I meant to ask is this—what would you be willing to do for your faith? We all must sacrifice for godliness."

I had terrible visions of being burned at the stake. But, no, this was 1651 and General Cromwell and Parliament did not permit Puritans or anyone else, except perhaps witches, to be burned. I was not too sure about witches though, come to think upon it.

"As much as any other Puritan," I answered, "but I cannot take up a sword against the Cavalier armies or against the wicked new King. But if I were a man, I would fight in General Cromwell's New Model Army."

"Ah, so you think well of General Cromwell?"

"Oh, yes," I said "Oh, yes, I do."

Dr. Moonjean bent toward me. "Would you do something

for General Cromwell, who has done so much for England, and for the men and women of our religious belief?"

"Yes, I would," I promised. "But what can I do?"

Now the tall man from London was well pleased. He smiled. His was a pleasant smile, much less like winter than the rest of him. "Then, Penitence, I *shall* ask you. You travel to Campion Towers on the morrow. There are strange things occurring in and near Holt Heath and Worcester, which is only a few miles away. Keep your eyes and your ears open, child, and send to me what you learn."

I gasped. "A spy! You wish me to be a spy?"

Amyas Moonjean looked unhappy. "No, not a spy. Your people there at Campion Towers will come to no harm, I promise you that. It is not they who interest me or who interest General Cromwell. Cromwell looks to guard this isle. He has told me to send someone at once to Campion Towers. I prayed for help. It was delivered to me in your person, Penitence Hervey."

"You know General Cromwell?" I exploded.

"Very well, indeed, and he shall know of you ere long. You could do England a great service, Penitence."

I was dazzled by this. I nodded in agreement. My father would have approved. If I could help the great Oliver Cromwell, I would watch. But for what was I to watch? I asked Dr. Moonjean.

"For anything strange or out of the ordinary—particularly at night," he explained.

"Will you be in Holt Heath?" I asked.

"No," he said with a laugh. "I must return to London when all of my business in Bristol is finished. But someone will come to you at Campion Towers. You will know this person by a Bible text, a verse from *St. Matthew*. I take it you know your Scriptures?"

At my nod Dr. Amyas Moonjean arose from his bench in the empty common room. He had said what he had to say, and I had made a bond with him. He held up a thin hand. "You have my gratitude, Penitence Hervey, and the gratitude of the people of our faith in this land, be assured of this. Be true to what you have promised. Be a soldier, too, in our battle for Puritanism. Although you bear no arms, you are witness to the godly truth. You will fight against our deadly enemies as does General Cromwell. Do you swear to me to do what I ask?" Suddenly his voice turned cold and biting, making me shudder.

"I swear," I said.

Dr. Moonjean smiled his charming smile again and in a moment was gone. Whatever his other business in Bristol, it was urgent. Curious, I rushed to the windows to peer out. It was raining and murky, the air filled with the strange black smoke of sea coal, but when I rubbed the sooty pane clean I could see the high black coach and sleek black horses, a coach and six fit for a great noble. I watched Dr. Moonjean climb inside.

Slowly I returned to my room and threw myself onto the bed. I was dazed by this odd man and his even more odd request. But I had sworn an oath to him. I turned over and lay staring at the deep velvet of the canopy above me. I had not really noticed before how much the color of blood it was.

How strange it was. Each time I came to the point of learning something about the Killingtrees, a door shut in my face. I thought of the name "Killingtree," finally admitting to myself what I had felt when I had first heard it. It had made me think of a gallows or of a white poisonous tree in a sinister gloomy forest. It had frightened me as a child in Salem Town. It made me shiver now.

It rained hard all night but I slept through the torrent, a sleep of exhaustion studded with unremembered nightmares. I had no way of knowing when I awoke whether it was my encounter with Dr. Moonjean or Mistress Whidby's supper of Bristol elvers, tender young eels, that sat ill on my stomach.

The summer rain did not cease with the beginning of the day. It came down in great slanting sheets, dashing against my windows and flooding the gray cobbles of Bristol. I sat with my cheek against the cold glass, looking out, hoping to see a sign of life other than the dog teams and their drivers, but I saw nothing at all until a mud-spattered coach pulled by four plain brown nags came around the corner into Marsh Street, and halted at the door of the Turk's Head. I leaned forward, finally looking on with some interest, and watched as one of Mistress Whidby's thin little pot boys, his apron over his head, put down a wooden step and opened the coach door.

Out popped a very broad woman dressed in a purple cloak, her hood pulled up over her face and hair. She came into the inn with a rush, her coachman waiting patiently in the downpour which the rain beat on his dark cloak and wide-brimmed hat.

There had been no painted arms on the doors of the coach at all that I could see, but then mud could cover them. As I listened I heard footsteps on the stairs. At Mistress Whidby's call I got up. I drew a deep breath, unbolted the door, and caught my first sight of the astonishing Madame Marie Gawdy.

My companion from Campion Towers was a monstrously fat woman. In her purple traveling cloak she resembled a pavilion more than anything else. She had the fine rosy complexion that so many fat people have. Her eyes were round and brown and her mouth a baby's pout. She threw back her hood with a ringed hand and I saw her hair for the first time, chestnut brown streaked with white. A row of tiny curls lay on her forehead, while longer ones fell to her shoulders. Red eardrops glinted among the sausage ringlets.

She looked at me while I looked at her. She spoke first. "Mistress Hervey, are you not?" Her voice was hoarse, as I had guessed it would be, but was faintly accented.

I nodded. "Yes, I am Penitence Hervey."

"*Bien.* I am Madame Gawdy. I have come from Holt Heath to fetch you. Do you have a letter from Campion Towers? I must ask for it—to prove you are who you say."

I took Laurel Killingtree's letter from my apron pocket and gave it to the strange woman. She glanced at it and returned it to me. "Yes. 'Tis in Laurel's hand. You are surely the Hervey child." She looked me up and down and smiled in an odd fashion. "But so large a child! *Mon dieu,* they had not expected it."

"I am fifteen," I said, not liking this turn of conversation. "How is my grandmother Aylmer?"

"Failing more each day. She waits for you."

"The Lord be praised," I said.

Madame Gawdy eyed my gown and cap as I spoke. There was a glitter in her eye as if she measured me. She turned to Mistress Whidby. "Tell the coachman, Peter, to get himself up here and carry down the maid's trunk."

Mistress Whidby hastened to obey while the woman in the purple cloak gave her attention to me once more. "Take up your cloak, my child. We have a long hard journey ahead of us to Holt Heath. The road is bad, the weather worse. *Mon dieu,* I loathe such weather! Oh, your England and your English climate."

"A moment," I demanded. "Who are you? What do you do at Campion Towers? Who sent you?"

Madame Gawdy did not laugh. She boomed. "Spoken like a

true Killingtree—even if you are a little Roundhead. I am a widow, the widow of Hinchingbrooke Gawdy, dead these twenty years. I am companion to Mistress Laurel Killingtree. We were friends in France forty years past. I was born in Paris. I choose to be known as Madamè Gawdy, instead of Mistress Gawdy."

"Where is my great-aunt?" I asked, piqued. "She wrote the letter. I expected her. Why did she not come?"

"Because of your grandmother Aylmer, of course, and now because of your grandfather, Nicholas, who is ailing, too. Ask me no more questions, girl. We have two days' travel ahead. We must sleep at Gloucester tonight—or along the road."

I caught up my cloak. My trunk was ready, the straps buckled tight. So that was why this woman had an accent. She was French, probably a French Huguenot, one of the French Protestants who had suffered cruelly in their homeland. A generous England gave shelter to many of them.

Peter, a huge man, now came up the stairs of the Turk's Head, and put my trunk onto his back. He gave out a grunt of pleased surprise at its weight and in a moment was clattering down into the common room. Madame Gawdy and I followed him out, both of us nodding to little Mistress Whidby, who stood aside politely. She sank to the floor in a deep curtsy. I suspected she had been given a goodly sum of money to look after me and keep me safe.

As we wound our way northeast across the city on the road to Gloucester, Worcester, and Holt Heath, the summer storm worsened. Madame Gawdy and I hastily fastened the last leather window closing, leaving only a crack or two for air. The sky was as black as midnight outside and I could see my companion only dimly, for all her size. I could not speak with the Frenchwoman because of the rolling of the thunder. Sometimes between claps of thunder I could hear her cry out, either because the jolting of the coach had hurt her or because she feared storms. As for me, I sat enjoying the rare show of the English heavens. I giggled softly once when I heard Madame Gawdy gasp *"Mon dieu!"* at a particularly loud drum-roll of thunder.

In the next instant my giggle ended in a gasp. The storm was now directly overhead. A yellow-white flash, a solid sheet of lightning, showed me my traveling companion's face for a single second. Madame Gawdy had turned green with fright. She had shrunk back as far as possible, given her bulk, into a corner of the coach, and as the thunder pealed, her right hand passed swiftly over her breast and face in the sign of the cross.

Madame Gawdy was a Papist, a Roman Catholic!

The Peculiar Highwayman

THE WOMAN'S EYES had not been on my face. If she had been looking at me, she could not have missed my expressison of shock and surprise. I was relieved she had not seen me.

My thoughts ran wild. What was I to do? Should I run away when the coach stopped? Surely I could outrun the fat Frenchwoman but what of Peter, the coachman? And then I thought of Dr. Moonjean. Now I knew what he had meant. I knew of the heavy fines the Puritan Parliament imposed on Roman Catholics in England. Many Papists kept their faith as secret as possible. Most of them had gone to France to be safe during the Civil War, but here was a Frenchwoman and a Papist to boot, bold as brass in England. Now, I asked myself, were the Killingtrees Papist? Is that what my father had meant?

As another bolt of lightning shot across the dark sky, I made a hasty vow. I would not run away. No, I would see my grandmother before she died, and I would keep my eyes and ears open for Dr. Moonjean.

The torrent ended as quickly as it had begun, although a fine

47

needle-sharp rain still beat down on us. I pushed the leather window covering aside and looked out. We were in green country now. Gloucester lay ahead. The coach groaned and creaked in the mire. More mud spattered the old coach as I looked out to neat green fields, many of them planted with trees in full summer leaf, their branches sodden with rain, bending almost to the ground.

I glanced at Madame Gawdy whose face was again its usual rosy hue. I asked innocently, "What are the trees?"

"Apple and pear," she replied. "Gloucester is famous for its cider." Her eyes lit up in anticipation.

"Tell me about Gloucester," I said. "Did they fight here during the Civil War?"

The enormous woman took out a scented lace-trimmed handkerchief and sniffed at it. "Ah, yes. Edgehill is not far, mistress. Edgehill was one of the first of the great battles. The west of England has seen very hard times. Gloucester knows trouble well. Its foolish people stood for Parliament in the war. Yet, your Roundhead soldiers burned all but five of Gloucester's fine old churches. I often wonder why they did not destroy the cathedral where the martyr King, Edward II, lies enshrined. You Roundheads have no respect for kings!" she snorted.

I kept my temper. I wanted Madame Gawdy to chatter. Perhaps I could learn something about the Killingtrees, but no matter how I attempted to lead her into talking, she would tell me nothing. By the time we had stopped at a little tavern in Nailsworth, I had learned only that Gloucester was a seaport and that Roundheads for some unknown reason had not torn down its ancient market cross either. Of the Killingtrees I knew nothing more. After a huge Nailsworth collation of bread, cheese, Cotswold lamb, and Spanish wine, Madame Gawdy fell asleep, snoring away for hours while I looked out the coach window. At last the sun came out. I stared across fields of wild flowers, all strange to me except for the trailing woodbine and yellow primroses I had known at home. Finally, I too slept, awakening only when we jolted into Gloucester just past sunset. The soft damp air of England made me yawn despite myself.

We spent the night at the Bull and the Raven. It was too late to visit the cathedral but I spied the ornate stone market cross as we entered the city. After a large supper Madame Gawdy climbed puffing to her own chamber. I was relieved to learn that I had my own room, although hers and mine adjoined. Before I climbed into my bed I put my ear to her door. I could hear her mumbling and beneath that sound I could hear the faint click, click of beads. I knew she told her Papist prayers and, chilled by the prospect of what lay ahead of me, I went to my knees and prayed for guidance and preservation, asking that I not be corrupted.

We glimpsed the far-off Cotswold Hills at daybreak and once more were on our way, our nags rested. The weather was fine. I examined the coach sent from Campion Towers. It was as I had thought—old. The horses were not fine, even I could tell that, and I was no judge of horses, for my father kept none in Salem Town. As I had suspected, there was no coat of arms painted on the doors. Perhaps the Killingtrees and the Aylmers were not as wealthy as Elizabeth had hoped.

To a great pealing of cathedral bells we left Gloucester. We broke our midday fast at Tewkesbury. How Madame Gawdy could eat and drink! She waved a spoon at me in high good humor. "Tonight, mistress, you will sleep at Campion Towers in a true bed, deep with feathers. These inn beds!" and she shook her head sadly and with her knife daintily speared the last piece of meat in her vast pork pie and then finished my half-eaten pie without asking my permission.

After Tewkesbury we traveled through the Vale of Evesham, a beautiful green country where tall golden flowers stood in the fields under fruit-laden plum trees. Madame Gawdy now became more talkative, but she spoke mostly of the countryside and of her chief interest in life—food.

"We shall sup at Worcester," she confided. " 'Tis a fine city— not the likes of your Bristol," and she laughed. "Four times Worcester has beat back your Roundhead armies. It stands for King Charles, I can tell you, though there is a knavish Roundhead garrison there."

I was angry, but once more I kept silent. So, Worcester was not for Parliament? I guessed now why Mistress Whidby of the Turk's Head had looked at me in such an odd fashion when Captain Enderby had said I went to Worcestershire.

The woman in the purple cloak caught my thoughts. "You need not huff up your courage, mistress. The Cavaliers do not make war on maids. They are gentlefolk, not like some I could put name to, who are apes in velvet now. You will be safe in Worcestershire if you do no preaching or sing through your nose."

This was too much. I cried, "I do not sing at all!"

"All to the good," she said. "I have heard your tuneless Roundhead hymns but once. 'Twas enough."

I was tempted to say something about idol-adoring Papists, their love of scarlet trappings, stinking incenses and silly Latin music, but once more I held my tongue. I did not wish Madame Gawdy to learn I knew of her forbidden faith. I tried to change the subject as we entered the walled city of Worcester, once more at dusk, permitting me to see little but the dark line of the

Malvern Hills to the east. The ruddy sunset-lit River Severn reflected the black bulk of Worcester Cathedral, where the wicked tyrant King John lay. Madame Gawdy had told me that Worcester had enjoyed a long and lively history. It had been attacked in centuries past by Irish pirates and the wild Welsh, for the city was the gate to Wales. Still Worcester remained Worcester, a King's city, fighting off the Roundheads time after time.

"Someday they will nail Cromwell's ears to the wall," she boasted.

I did not intend to listen to any more of this treasonous talk. "Is Campion Towers large?" I asked. "How many people live there?"

To my surprise Madame Gawdy did not evade my questions again. "Not too large and not too small. The satisfactory size, I would say, mistress." She counted on her plump white fingers. "These days we have Master Nicholas and his lady, your grandmother Aylmer; Mistress Laurel Killingtree; myself; a kinswoman of yours, Mistress Amabel Sutton, an Aylmer, too; and your cousin, Douglas Sutton, who is, I believe, near your age. And, of course, there are the servants."

I settled back, satisfied. At last I knew something! So I had a young cousin. I had been afraid that everyone at Campion Towers would be very old. Perhaps Douglas Sutton would make up a little for my missing Amity Wrenn so much—even if Douglas was a boy. I had always found it easy to get along with boys.

Madame Gawdy stuffed herself with trout from the River Teme that night at the Star Inn, explaining to me between mouthfuls that Worcester had the best food in England and that I must taste jerkum, Worcester's famous plum wine. I took only a very small glass. It was sweet and very strong and when

I re-entered the coach to travel the few miles ahead to Campion Towers, my head swam like a fish in the Teme.

It was full dark when Peter whistled to the horses and we left Worcester, rattling over the stones of the street and onto the narrower road that led to Campion Towers. A full moon rose in the night sky as I lay with my head back against the hard leather seat. I should not have drunk any jerkum, I thought. It had been sinful and greedy of me to give in to Madame Gawdy's urging.

I wanted to sleep but I sat upright as I heard Peter call out hoarsely, "Madame Gawdy, there be summat ahead," only minutes after he had turned the coach onto another road.

Then suddenly I heard the drumming of horses' hooves. A rider was coming swiftly toward us.

"Who is it, Peter?" Madame Gawdy bellowed, fright in her voice. "Is it someone from the Towers?"

There was silence except for the sound of hooves and then one of our coach horses began to neigh, to be answered by another horse, farther away. The neighing kept up until the second horse was very close and then a man's voice rang out in the stark quiet.

"Your valuables or your lives! What do ye choose?"

"*Mon dieu!* A highwayman!" said Madame Gawdy. "We must get down at once."

I was terrified. What of the money my father had given me? I kept it in a leather bag on a string around my neck. Swiftly I jerked the string off and put the bag into a torn place in the coach's wall, a mouse-gnawed hole, I suspected. My companion looked at me in the moonlight, then nodded.

"My jewels are glass," she said in a whisper. "I have no money left. There will be nothing for his work this night."

We got down, Peter hauling Madame Gawdy's great bulk out onto the muddy ground.

The highwayman had chosen a good place, a deserted little vale nestled among low hills. Only the moon and a sprinkling of stars looked down upon the four people, the coach and the weary horses.

Our road agent sat bestride a fine sidewise-dancing horse. In the moonlight I could not be sure of its color, but I thought it might be a red-brown. As for the man, who kept a pistol trained on us, he wore a black cloak, a black Cavalier hat with a plume which could have been either black or red, and a black cloth over his face. Between the brim of his hat and his mask there was only room for his eyes. His hair was completely covered.

He was not gallant. He did not sweep off his hat to Madame Gawdy and me nor did he put away his pistol although he knew that women did not carry arms. "You," he singled Madame Gawdy out, "throw your jewels and your money onto the ground and ye'll not be harmed." His voice sounded muffled.

"I have no jewels—nought but glass," she spoke up bravely. "Who has jewels when there have been Roundhead soldiers about?"

I stared at her, admiring her coolness. Were highwaymen so common in England that she did not fear them? I could catch no trace of terror in her manner.

Now the pistol swerved to point at me. "Your valuables!" he demanded.

I took a leaf from Madame Gawdy's book and went her a page further. "I have neither jewels nor money. I am a Puritan. If you know anything of Puritans, sir, you would know we believe jewels are a vanity."

The highwayman laughed. "Not on a pretty neck," he said

softly. "Come here, Roundhead wench," he ordered. "Let me see your face."

Now I was truly afraid. What did he want? My knees a jelly, I went over to him. His horse snorted and moved away but the man urged him forward. The horse was a fine one, a solid color. Yes, it was a dark red as I had thought and so was the robber's plume. As I stood beside the highwayman, I noticed how strangely and stiffly his left boot lay in its stirrup. Was the highwayman lame?

I lifted my face to him in the moonlight as he had demanded. He whistled softly. "Aye, she is *very* like! But a true Roundhead. 'Tis a pity. Had ye been a king's lass, I would have kissed ye. 'Tis the thing to do in my trade."

"Well, then, Oliver Cromwell be blessed!" I cried.

"Get into the coach." He sounded amused by my words as he waved the pistol at me.

I got into the coach, trembling with anger at the highwayman's impudence. Kiss me, indeed! No former Cavalier, fit only for the hangman's rope, was going to kiss me, I swore. I would have bitten him. I congratulated myself on my cleverness at saving my money. But, then, a new thought struck me. Madame Gawdy was outside still. Would she tell the highwayman that I had hidden a purse?

I peered anxiously out of the window. Madame Gawdy, Peter, and the robber had moved down by the coach horses. Once more there came a soft neighing. The highwayman's red horse was nuzzling one of the coach horses. I could catch the faint sounds of speech, quiet talk—not the talk of anger or fear at all, quite as if they knew each other. I sat wondering—wondering, too, what the robber had meant when he said I was "*very* like."

At last Madame Gawdy returned, stepping over the puddles in the road as delicately as she could. She had kept my secret, it seemed.

The Frenchwoman fell back with a great creaking of leather. "*Mon dieu.* What a condition this country has come to! The roads are infested with poor men who must rob to live. It is this terrible war, I tell you."

I looked at her, open-mouthed. What an odd thing to say. We could all have been murdered! Madame Gawdy took our encounter with a desperate robber with wonderful grace and ease. I heard the quick beat of hooves as the highwayman galloped away, and an instant later Peter whipped up our horses. What a very peculiar highwayman that had been!

I started to retrieve the money I had hidden in the coach wall, but decided against it. No, I would take it out only when I got to Campion Towers and I would guard it well there.

The coach plunged through the night until at last we came to the rise of a hill. Here Peter stopped. Madame Gawdy sighed and shifted her body. "Campion Towers, mistress. It lies atop the next hill. Holt Heath lies on another road nearby."

I put my head out the window. A tall house lay in the moon-washed landscape ahead of us. Except for a yellow gleam in some windows at its top, it was dark. I did not find my first sighting of Campion Towers cheerful.

Now the nags knew that they came home at last and they left the hilltop at a steady hand gallop, needing no whip or urging from Peter. We swept along the road but just as our horses' hooves hit hard earth, past the black gates before the looming great house, we heard a ringing call, a woman's voice.

The coachman pulled his four to a sudden stop. Surprised, I

fell against the Frenchwoman, who shoved me back without courtesy.

"Get out at once," she snapped, "that was Mistress Killingtree!"

I hastened out of the coach once more and stood waiting while Madame Gawdy got herself free to join me.

A yellow lantern came bobbing across the courtyard of Campion Towers just as the moon fled behind a scudding cloud. I was aware only that the person who carried the lantern was tall and by the rustle of skirts a woman.

"Penitence Hervey?" a sharp voice demanded.

"Yes," I said, curtsying.

"No time for greeting now. That must wait. I am your great-aunt Laurel. Come with me. Your grandmother Aylmer may be dying. Come!" Then the woman, whose face I had never seen, did a strange thing. She raised her darkle lantern, pushed my hood back with her free hand and her laugh rang out. "The devil's image. You never saw *her* but for the portrait, but, Marie, this is the devil's very image."

The Killingtrees of Campion Towers

THE MOON still lay behind its cloud. I could see nothing and anger caught at me. My arrivals in England always occurred at night—first Bristol, then Gloucester and Worcester, and finally my mother's home. Each night I must wait for the morning. It seemed almost a conspiracy against me. Only Cádiz, the city I was not permitted to enter, had revealed itself openly. And Dr. Moonjean had asked that I would watch by night for strangers!

The heavy, iron-ornamented door of the great house stood ajar. We hastened inside and Laurel Killingtree called to someone for a candlestick. I could not even see much of the high-ceilinged room in which we stood. It was too dim for that while the candles fluttered in the wind. In any event my chief interest was Laurel Killingtree, the woman whose letter had brought me thousands of miles to England.

My kinswoman was tall, taller than many men. Her hair was silvery gray and dressed in the same manner as Madame Gawdy's, an unbecoming manner to my way of thinking for

57

such old ladies. Her face was cast in a hard mold, the lines about her mouth deeply drawn. Her hooded eyes under fine arched brows glittered as she looked at me. Whatever it was she saw, she seemed to approve, I felt. She caught at her black brocade skirts. "Come along now, child, I have no time to spare."

We began to climb the curving steps that led out of the hall, my great-aunt ahead of me, her yellow-tipped candle held aloft. We went up higher and higher, climbing ever-narrowing stairs and along dark passages. How many I could not say. Somehow I felt I traveled to the lights we had seen from the hill. But at last we stopped at a paneled door where Laurel Killingtree rapped. The knock was little more than a warning for, without answer or summons, she flung the door open and beckoned me inside the room.

It was made of stone and was well lit by candles in floor sconces. First of all, I saw a great bed of green velvet, the hangings drawn close. A dark rug of many colors lay on the floor, a luxury I had never seen.

A man in a long black gown, who had been measuring a cloudy liquid from a flask into a glass, came toward me. He was not at all pleased. "There is a woman dying here, mistress," he said severely to me. "Who are you? What do you want?"

I was about to answer but my great-aunt spoke first. There was triumph in her words. "She has a right here. She is a Killingtree —Nicola's child!"

I could not see beyond the closed bed but I could hear the sound of wood against wood and I could not mistake the loud deep-throated words, "What the devil do ye say?"

A tall, thick-bodied man in black velvet, his foot covered with bandages, came hobbling into view. He gaped at me as I did at him. His face was strong, his nose prominent, his gray eyebrows bushy, and his trimmed Cavalier beard was still fair but streaked with gray. He bore a resemblance of sorts to Laurel Killingtree but where she appeared cold, he was fiery. Everything about him bristled as he looked at me. He held a cane which he struck on the floor in a rage. "Damme, woman. What was that you said?"

My great-aunt was calm. "What I said, Nicholas, is that this is your granddaughter. This is Nicola's child, newly come from Massachusetts Bay Colony."

"I know of no child. There was an infant but it died."

"No, the child did not die. I found out about Nicola's daughter months past. I wrote and asked her to come."

"What?" my grandfather thundered. "You invited a Roundhead here—at this time? You fool. I want no Roundheads at Campion Towers."

Although great-aunt Laurel stood firm, I shivered. Then I thought of the Wrenns at Swindon. I would go to them at once. My grandfather hated me.

"Penitence is a Killingtree and an Aylmer as well. Philippa desired me to send for her," Laurel nodded toward the green bed.

"Philippa wanted her?" he asked.

"Yes."

Nicholas Killingtree looked at the floor in silence for a time. We all waited, and then the other man, the physician, came forward and spoke to my grandfather. "Let it be, sir, if it is to be. If your lady desired to see the maid, humor her wish. I advise it."

"Very well," Nicholas Killingtree agreed. Glaring at me, he limped back behind the bed.

The physician's next words were meant for me. "Take only a

moment, mistress. Your grandmother is very weak. Do not tax her strength."

I walked slowly toward the bed, went around its foot, and found my way blocked by my grandfather, who bit his mustaches but who gave way and seated himself in a chair next to the bed as I came toward the curtains. The physician followed, standing behind me, my great-aunt at his side. Now he came forward and drew back the curtains for me.

"Mistress Killingtree, there is someone to see you," the physician said loudly.

A very little woman, a white lace bedcap over her blonde-gray hair, lay back on the pillows, her hands crossed on the coverlet. Her face was wax-white as a candle and her lips were lavender.

Her eyelids opened and shut as he spoke again. This time the physician's words were for me. "Bend nearer, child." He raised his voice. "Mistress Killingtree, there is someone here you have wished to see!"

I leaned down. A faint breath of sweet herbs drifted up to me from the bed as the woman, my grandmother, opened her eyes to look at me. After a moment she smiled. Her tiny hand fluttered over to pat mine softly. "Nicola," she whispered. "You have come home. They are yours, dear—the land and the jewels. I give them to you. I kept them safe only for you, love." Her eyes closed once more and I heard her draw a deep slow breath of satisfaction.

The physician pushed me aside to put his head against my grandmother's chest. He straightened in a moment to draw the curtains tight against drafts.

"Aye, she will sleep now. You may have done her good, young mistress. Do not leave us now."

I nodded, pleased, of course, that I had helped my grandmother, but still I had no desire to stay at Campion Towers.

Laurel turned from the bed now too. "The girl will not leave." She looked at my grandfather, who sat glowering in his chair, rapping his cane on the floor. There was even more triumph in her tone. "She will not be going, will she, Nicholas?"

"This is your work, Laurel, done behind my back. It is your work and the devil's. You shall pay for it, too. How dare you try to blame Philippa, who cannot now call you liar? How dare you bring this wench here now? I pray that we do not pay dearly for it. Penitence, did you say her name was? A miserable name! A true Roundhead name!" He swung his head to face me. "How long do you intend to stay, mistress, now that you have come to collect the Aylmer inheritance? How long will you be here imposing upon me?"

I gasped. And I had thought I knew the measure of dislike from Elizabeth. How cruel old people often were. They used age and authority as a club.

Once more Laurel Killingtree spoke for me. "Until Philippa no longer requires her."

"You cheat Philippa. The girl is a fraud," he stormed. "My Philippa thinks this Roundhead wench is Nicola. When she learns the truth, I cannot vouch for what it will do to her."

"Penitence has brought Philippa happiness, Nicholas."

My name enraged my grandfather. He fastened onto it again. "Who dared name you that, girl?"

Well, let him know the truth. I was angry, too. "My mother. She did penance for her vanities."

"Be silent. That is enough!" he raged. "So they made a Roundhead of my girl, did they? So be it! For Philippa's sake and for the sake of my daughter's memory, you may remain in my house—but not as anyone named Penitence."

"What would you call me, then?" I flared.

He took my dare, thought for a moment, and then announced,

"Penelope." He rapped his cane hard on the floor as he repeated the name. "By Gad, Penelope! Penelope—as long as you are at Campion Towers—and scant welcome to you, too. A Roundhead, damme! A Roundhead is no kin of mine. Laurel, take her away and lose her if ye can. Then you fetch me that idiot Frenchwoman. I intend to have words with both of you. So that is what happened to Peter and the old coach? You said you did not know. They fetched the wench here!"

Laurel sniffed. "As you wish, Nicholas. I shall fetch Marie." She touched my shoulder. "Come. I will take you to your bedchamber!"

She led me through the large room, past gilded leather hangings, carved chests, and a huge oak wardrobe. We paused before the hearth, where a fire blazed against the chill. Laurel held her candlestick high. "Look up there," she ordered.

I did as she demanded. The tall woman was pleased with herself. "It was painted in 1634 by a pupil of Anthony Van Dyck," she announced with pride.

I did not speak again as she led me down another long black passage in this strange, old, musty-smelling house. I had no wish to speak to her about the painting of my mother, Nicola Killingtree. By now I guessed how much I resembled her, but I had not known that my mother had been painted in that same autumn-leaf-red silk dress I had found my favorite in Salem Town. Perhaps my mother and I were more like to each other than people knew.

Great-aunt Killingtree opened a door, showing me in. I waited while she lit two stubs of candles in the wood-paneled chamber. "Good night, Penelope. Sleep well," she said to me. In a moment she had left my room, but an instant later I heard the click of a key.

My door was locked from the outside!

I was angry, more furious than I had ever been before. I was among the Killingtrees, my mother's kinsmen, but as far as I was concerned, I was among enemies. My grandfather mocked my name and dared to give me one he found more suitable. My great-aunt locked me in.

I picked up a small stool and threw it at the door. The crash was so satisfying that I looked about for other things to throw or break. The candlesticks were pewter, which would not break. The two chairs were too heavy for me to lift. Enraged as I was, I was not about to set fire to my bed hangings with myself locked inside. But if I had been able to get out, I would have happily burned Campion Towers to the ground and everyone in it except for my grandmother. There was but one thing to do. I fell to my knees and prayed for guidance as I had never prayed before. This calmed me somewhat although I still seethed with fury when I thought of my harsh grandfather and his proud sister, Laurel Killingtree, and of the gluttonous Madame Gawdy. I kept thinking, too, of my grandmother Aylmer even as I relished my anger. It was not her fault that she mistook me for my mother. She was ill and old. She had given me the Aylmer inheritance. My grandfather had confirmed that himself. I was to inherit, it seemed, but what jewels and what land? I had to laugh despite my rage. What would Elizabeth say to this? Would her eyes still sparkle with greed over jewels she could not wear because she was a Puritan? How could she enjoy English land thousands of miles from Salem? I laughed again.

I jumped up onto the bed, hoping it would fall apart. It was not half so fine as the inn beds I had found in Bristol and Gloucester. The hangings had once been blue. They were now tattered and a faded violet. It seemed to me that the coverlet had been stuffed with husks of New World Indian corn. The bed linen was old but soft—so soft it would not bear another wash. Clearly I had not been given the finest chamber. The tapestries were as faded as the canopy. In the dim light of the stub candles their faded figures could have been anything at all —from battling warriors to dancing nymphs.

I kicked off my shoes and threw them one by one at the door and sent my cap flying after them. To the devil with the Killingtrees, then! I would play their game whatever it was and I would do Amyas Moonjean his service, too, if I could. But I would not stay in this house any longer than need be. I could not watch very well, locked in. I would go to Swindon as soon as the Aylmer inheritance was mine by law—not that I would know what to do with it—jewels and land, indeed. Could I sell such things? I leaped under a coverlet, pulling off only my cloak. I knew what the Killingtrees expected from Roundheads. If they disapproved of my sober clothing, then let them look in disgust at my wrinkled skirts. The Killingtrees were nothing to me. My mother had disowned them as they disowned her. They disowned me. I would disown them. The only person who mattered at Campion Towers was my grandmother who was dying. Let her think me "Nicola" if it made her happy.

I fell to sleep the moment my head touched the rough pillow, and I awoke only when full sunlight streamed across the room and I heard the key turned in my door.

It was Mistress Killingtree, dressed as she had been dressed the night before. She looked at the footstool, my shoes and my cap at her feet, and for a fleeting second I thought she might smile. "If you would choose to comb your hair and wash, you will find water, soap, a comb, and cloths fetched for you in the next chamber, which is to be yours," she told me. "Peter will fetch your trunk this morning."

I was tousle-headed and sleepy-eyed. Yes, I would like to wash so I followed her out, catching up my shoes and cap. "Do not concern yourself about my trunk, mistress," I told her. "What you asked in your letter, I have done. Give me a paper from my grandmother's hand about my inheritance. You and that old man and the physician were witnesses to what she said to me. I would be greatly obliged if you would permit me to have that old coach again today. I shall go back to Bristol. Perhaps I can find the *Godspeed* still in port but, if not, I have friends in England, I will go to them."

She was surprised at this. "You have friends? Where?"

This pleased me. "I have friends, Mistress Killingtree. Who they are and where they are does not concern you."

Laurel Killingtree's dark eyes grew more narrow. "Do not speak so to me."

I caught up a cloth, my face wet. I was getting angry again. "What do I owe you for insults, mistress? What do I owe to my grandfather? I came, as you asked, to see my grandmother Aylmer—not to see you or anyone else. I find you all ungodly. My grandmother thinks me 'Nicola.' I have made her happy; the inheritance was given to me. Give me a paper that says this. Then I shall go and happily."

"What a vast affection you have for your mother's family!" the tall woman snapped.

"What a foul welcome you give an invited stranger! Think as you choose, but I came here to see my grandmother. The inheritance is important, yes; but I do not care so much for it as you think. I have made a long and dangerous journey, mistress. I ask you to consider that."

Laurel Killingtree sat down heavily in one of the chairs in this still poor second room. Her manner was different. "Yes, I owe you something, I suppose. I should not have asked you here. It was your grandmother who insisted, despite what Nicholas chooses to believe. Family means much to her—too much. She asked me to find what had happened to Nicola's babe. She did not wish Nicholas to know. She cared enough to ask." My great-aunt turned to look at me. "Philippa has kept to that tower room for ten years. It has the finest prospect of the countryside and roads. It was her only pleasure to sit by the windows to see who passed or who came to Campion Towers. She wished to see you, so I asked a favor of you. I should not have done it, not even for Philippa. I should have learned long ago, old as I am, to ask favors of no man. Yet, I must ask another favor of you now."

I drew the bone comb through my hair and fixed a firm knot before putting on my cap. Let her ask her favor. Perhaps I would grant it—perhaps not.

"Your grandmother is improved this morning," she went on. "The physician asks you to stay here at Campion Towers until she dies. It will not be long and will take up little of your time— a few weeks at most."

"What of Master Killingtree?" I demanded, unwilling to call him "grandfather."

"He asks that you remain, too. He loves your grandmother as he has loved but four people in his life. One was your mother. He wants Philippa to take you as a granddaughter and for her to give up the false notion that you are Nicola. It is not decent for you to receive the Aylmer inheritance when Philippa believes you are another person. Would you find that just?"

"He did not love my mother," I said, paying no heed to her other comments.

"Yes, he did."

"He had a very strange way of showing it."

"Your grandfather is a strange man. He loved her always and he does still. He never took her portrait down from the tower room."

"Only because my grandmother wanted it to hang there. And what other people did he love?"

"His younger brother who was killed at Marston Moor seven years past," her harsh voice faltered, "and his brother's son."

"And what of him?" I asked.

She hesitated for a long moment. "Dead, too, mistress, or at least so sorely wounded that it does not matter."

"A pity," said I.

"We have had a Civil War," Laurel Killingtree said bitterly.

I made up my mind suddenly. I would grant Mistress Killingtree her favor and for three very good reasons. One, for my grandmother's sake; two, for the inheritance and a paper to show that the inheritance was truly mine; and three, for Dr. Moonjean. "I shall stay until the physician tells me to go or until my grandfather becomes so unbearable that I must leave."

"Thank you, Penelope," my great-aunt said.

"Call me whatever name you choose if it saves more quarreling with the old man." I looked about me. This room was larger than last night's cupboard. The bed and hangings were of gray-blue velvet, heavily fringed, but decaying, too. The tapestries were a bit less faded. I could even make out knights in armor hacking at each other. "I am to lie here, you said?" I asked.

Laurel shook her head in agreement.

I held out my hand. "It is more to my taste but I have seen finer in inns. Give me the key. Without it, I shall go at once. I am a guest. I will not be locked in! I will not steal your plate. Madame Gawdy told me there is a Puritan garrison in Worcester.

They would not relish knowing I was kept under lock and key in my mother's house."

The woman stood up and threw a key from her hand onto a table top. Then she said, "Madame Gawdy has been sent away. Does that please you?"

"Yes, she keeps strange company, I think," I said, meaning the highwayman. Well, thought I, that was one less Papist to deal with.

"What would you, a mere child from the colonies, know about Marie Gawdy?" my great-aunt asked loftily. "She is old enough to be your grandmother."

"I trust my grandmother never did have friendly words for lame highwaymen on red horses or talk so freely about the Cavaliers. I think Madame Gawdy truly believes that devil Charles Stuart will dare come again to England."

My great-aunt paused at the door. Her eyes were bright and fierce like those of a bird of prey. "You are as foolish as you are misguided in your faith. There is no Killingtree in you but your temper. You call us 'ungodly'! I return the word to you. The young serpent is no less venomous than the old. I would wish you a very short visit at Campion Towers if it did not concern Philippa. You will join us at supper. For some odd reason, your grandfather wishes it. In the meantime keep to this floor of the house. You will be taken to see your grandmother again tonight. Do not try to visit her without the physician's permission. I will send someone to you this morning to see you settled."

I waited until my unpleasant kinswoman had left and then I hurried to the tall window of my room and drew aside the dusty gray-blue hangings. The window was dirty so I rubbed at it with the hem of my skirt. Then I put my eye to the small space I had made but drew back with a sigh of disappointment. The window faced onto a court and I could see nothing but the gray stones of Campion Towers across the court and to my right. A high stone wall lay to the left. The floor of the court was grass, a sad-looking yellowish grass, long untended.

How could Dr. Moonjean reach me here, a semi-prisoner? I frowned at the thought. A verse from *St. Matthew*, indeed. That would be an alien text in this house. Papists did not read the Bible. Their priests told them what to believe and how to think. It was strange though, there had been no priest at my grandmother's bedside. But, then, would the Killingtrees dare show a priest to me?

Later an old manservant came shuffling into my room with a tray of food, plain porridge and cream. I was not to be entertained royally. I was in a great house but where were the bittersweet citrons? I remembered Cádiz and the conversation with Pastor Wrenn as I looked at the simple fare.

"How old is Campion Towers?" I asked the manservant, who stood waiting while I ate.

He replied in speech so odd I could scarcely understand him. The sense seemed to be that the house was old. An abbey had stood here in the Middle Ages.

I half-guessed what else he said. When King Henry VIII became a Protestant, he outlawed all of the Papist religious houses. The nuns and the monks were scattered. Some of the abbeys and monasteries had been torn down, while church lands were sold. The stones of the religious houses were often used to build country houses. I found it so difficult to understand the servant that I decided to ask questions that could be answered by "yes" or "no" inasmuch as he seemed to understand me well enough. I wondered if many people in Worcestershire spoke as he did? I hoped not.

"Was this house built on abbey land?" I asked.

He nodded.

"And they built it of abbey stone?"

He nodded again.

I was about to go on when I heard soft footsteps. Had Mistress Killingtree returned so soon? Certainly the footsteps were not made by the coachman's heavy boots although Laurel had said Peter would fetch my trunk.

"Jonas," a sharp piercing voice rang out. "If you have done with that, take the tray back to the kitchens."

The servant snatched up my tray and went out into the passage. There the same person spoke briefly with him, the tone one of petulant chiding although I could not make out the words. I got up, but as I was about to step out into the passage, my visitor entered.

Whoever she was, she was the prettiest girl I had ever seen. Her eyes were deep blue, her skin rose and white, and her hair, which fell in long ringlets, was the color of a crow's wing, blue-black. Her dress was made of bright blue silk with fine wide Flemish lace at the bodice and sleeves, while her blue shoes had tiny silver bows at the instep. She smiled. Her teeth were small, white, and even.

"So you have the land and the emeralds?" she exclaimed in a high voice. "Yes, with your greenish eyes, they could suit you well enough. But what will a Roundhead do with emeralds and with diamonds?"

I now knew what the Aylmer jewels were, but I was so surprised at this apparition that I was near to speechless. I managed to blurt out, "Are you Mistress Sutton—Amabel Sutton?" I remembered the other woman's name Madame Gawdy had spoken.

Her laugh rang out. "La, no, I am Douglas. You know—your cousin Douglas? Amabel Sutton is my mother."

Douglas Sutton

DOUGLAS was a maiden. Surprised, I sat down with a thump while my kinswoman leaned against the jamb of the door, her hands behind her, looking at me. "I heard you asking questions of old Jonas. His wits are dim. I will tell you what you wish to know about this house. It is to be mine when Sir Nicholas dies. He promised it to me. That is why I do not fret myself that Philippa gave you the Aylmer inheritance. Campion Towers is quite enough for me—although I doubt my mother thinks so too. Half of Worcestershire will wish to marry me with such a holding. Do you want to hear about the house? I find it interesting."

Douglas seemed merry and willing to talk. The house could wait until I could see it, I decided. "No, please tell me about the Killingtrees. I know little of them."

She nodded thoughtfully. "Yes, of course, Penelope. You know about the quarrel between your grandfather and your mother. I have seen her portrait in the tower room. It is true. You are somewhat like her. It was never your grandmother who

71

wanted your mother forgotten. It was Sir Nicholas. He could never forgive her for marrying a Roundhead."

"I guessed that," I said. "But who are you and your mother?"

Douglas laughed once more. She laughed a great deal. Even if her fine clothing had not marked her as frivolous, her constant laughter would have. The world was no grim place for her. For a moment I almost envied Douglas, but then I thought of my purpose at Campion Towers—of Dr. Amyas Moonjean, and of the fact that I was a soldier in the cause.

"We are all cousins here," she told me. "My mother's mother was an Aylmer. She was a cousin of your grandmother. It gets very muddled and quite makes my head ache to think of it. We came here to live when I was very young. My father died of tertian fever in Barbados. He went to the West Indies to help colonize the Caribbee Islands. That was in 1638. I do not remember him, but he was a gallant gentleman. There was another cousin here, too, for a time, but he was older than I—at least I called him 'cousin' even though he was a Killingtree and not an Aylmer at all. But he was kin to you."

"What happened to him?"

Douglas looked away, not meeting my eyes. "Julian died of wounds. If he had lived, Campion Towers should have gone to him, but even if he had lived, he could never inherit. The Roundhead Parliament had outlawed him. Sir Nicholas traveled to London to see if he could help Julian, but it was of no use. Julian was a fine soldier for King Charles I, one of the very finest, they say. La, how proud Nicholas was of his nephew— almost as if Julian were his son! Julian served in Prince Rupert's horse."

I turned this piece of information over in my mind. It was strange. My great-aunt Laurel spoke of someone dead or good as dead, my grandfather's nephew. Now Douglas Sutton spoke of another young person from this house of old folk and said that he was dead. How many people had lived here? How many lived here now? Dr. Moonjean would surely like to know that.

"Was Julian the son of my grandfather's brother?" I asked Douglas.

She glanced at me sharply. "Did Mistress Laurel tell you then?" She sighed. " 'Tis very sad. I mislike sad things. We will not talk about it any more."

I nodded. There was a glint in my cousin's eye that told me not to pursue the subject. "What happened to Madame Gawdy? She fetched me here from Bristol. They say she is gone away."

"Been sent away is more like it. Marie is the greatest chatterbox in all Worcestershire, Sir Nicholas vows. He wanted to get rid of her long ago. Bringing you here was the last straw. He would have sent her packing before long anyhow. I think she has gone for good, probably to Worcester. Laurel will see she does not starve and will see her often. Laurel likes Madame Gawdy and feels sorry for her. Madame Gawdy is dreadfully poor, Penelope. Her husband did not leave her one farthing. She lived here on Laurel's bounty. Sir Nicholas often got so angry with her that he made Laurel lock her in her room sometimes to get away from her tongue at supper."

I was surprised at this. The Frenchwoman had not chattered overmuch to me in the coach. But perhaps that was because I was a Roundhead.

"Are there many servants?" I asked. "This is such a large house."

"No," Douglas shook her pretty head. "There used to be hordes of them. But some of them went to fight. Some of the others went to Worcester. Sir Nicholas let the steward and the footmen go. He had to pay a heavy fine to the Parliament—nearly five hundred pounds—because he was a Royalist during the war although he did not fight, himself. He was forced to sell land to pay it and Sir Nicholas hates to sell land."

I knew about the fines the Parliament had placed on Cavaliers but I also had heard of fines levied on Papists.

Douglas went on blithely. "We have few servants now, only the cook, a few maids, a kitchen boy from the village, the stableboy, Garth, and Peter, the coachman, and, of course, old Jonas. The greater part of the house is closed. But it will be a great house soon again—very soon. How wonderful it once was! We had fine assemblies and companies and folk came from all over the county. I was too young for dancing, of course, but I watched them always." She looked dreamy for a moment. "Even some of the great folk from the King's court came here. I saw the Somersets here once. That is the family of the Earl of Worcester, you know. I have curtsied to the earl, himself. He said I was a pretty poppet."

I knew little of such gallant frumperies. Lords and ladies meant nothing to me, but still I asked, "Is my grandfather a knight or a baronet?"

Douglas was crestfallen. "Only a knight, but I know he will be a baronet someday—perhaps even a baron."

I was puzzled. Parliament did not bestow titles. These people knew Charles I was dead. Evidently they expected Charles II to regain his throne. I hid a smile with my hand. They lived in a fool's world. Of course, they would wish the King back—all Roman Catholics hoped he would return. But then they were reckoning without Oliver Cromwell. The Stuart kings would never come back to England.

My Aylmer cousin caught my smile and became angry. "I

should have known a Roundhead would not take interest in anything much I have to say, although you do ask many questions. I was sent to keep you company today and to do somewhat about your gown, Penelope. Sir Nicholas told me if you were to come to supper you must wear a gown that made you look less like a cook maid."

I felt my stomach tighten with anger. "This is my best gown, I will have you know."

Douglas sniffed. "You seem my size, I think. I have a gown you may have. It is my worst gown."

"I will not do it. No."

"It is for your grandmother. Sir Nicholas asks you to wear her jewels tonight. It would please her, he thinks. You will not have to wear the jewels again." My cousin was scornful. "But you cannot wear emeralds and diamonds with that gray gown and that large collar, can you?" She came toward me to push my hair back from my ears where it had as usual, fled the knot I had made. "I must dress your hair, too, I guess. Come along," Douglas ordered. "I shall take you to my chamber. 'Tis more gay than yours. I hate the bedchambers on this side."

It was becoming clear to me as I followed Douglas' blue skirts down the passage to the very end, that I was not to be left alone today. She pushed open a door and we were inside a pretty room with a fine blue and silver canopy bed, blue and silver fringed armed-chairs, paintings, and ornate wood paneling. I must have gasped because Douglas turned to me, clapping her hands in pleasure.

"Oh, you like it? So do I. Sir Nicholas fitted it out for me after the Roundheads were here. He let me choose the furniture in Worcester."

"The Parliamentarian soldiers were here?"

"Yes, five years past. They threatened to burn the house, of course, but Sir Nicholas was too clever for them. They took everything away they could carry—all of the good furniture except for Philippa's bed. Their captain made them spare that when Mistress Laurel gave him a scolding before his dragoons. Fortunately for us, we had some warning they were coming. We had time to hide many of the best things, the good paintings, some of the furniture, and some of the animals. We saved the red horses and a few of the cows and sheep. We had to buy many new things, though. My furnishings are new, of course. I am sorry about your room but there simply was not money enough. This is the finest room on this floor. Your furnishings had been in servants' rooms or kept in the cellars. They are quite old. I told you that Sir Nicholas is not so very rich now."

I scarcely caught her last words. "Parliament's soldiers never plunder or rob!" I cried in a hot rage.

"Oh, no?" scoffed Douglas. "Ask anyone in Holt Heath. The only reason they did not burn the house, too, was because Sir Nicholas bought the captain off for fifty pounds and had Jonas roll out a keg of brandy—one that had been hidden away. The Roundheads rode off singing, all drunk, with carts full of our fine things from Campion Towers following them to Gloucester."

Dismayed, I shook my head. I did not wish to believe her, but somehow I knew that Douglas did not lie to me.

"But why did they come here?" I asked. "You said Sir Nicholas never fought in the Civil War."

"He could not. In bad weather he has such pain in his arms and legs. It was all because of cousin Julian. They knew he once lived here at Campion Towers. The Roundheads came just before the battle of Naseby. Sir Nicholas thinks they believed Julian was hiding here."

"Was he?"

Douglas smiled sweetly. "Who would tell me that? I was but a babe then. Who ever told you news when you were a child? "Now," Douglas continued, "we must see what you can wear tonight. You must look more comely at supper, so I shall fix your hair, too. It would never suit at all well with the jewels as it is now. Please you, do what Sir Nicholas asks. He gets so angry it is frightening. I have even had him shout at me. It frightens me terribly. Pen, I think I know something you may not know."

"Pen?" I said, catching at the name she'd used.

"Yes, Penitence is a dreadful name. I shall call you 'Pen.' I like it so much better than Penelope. Penelope is a fine name for an old woman. I have been thinking upon it. I could call you 'Penny,' but I mislike how 'Penny Hervey' sounds. So what do you think of 'Pen'? It is rather like a boy's name, and so is mine, they tell me, although it is sometimes a maid's name, too."

For a long moment I pondered it. Yes, I liked "Pen" well enough, better than "Penelope." "Very well," I agreed, "but what will that old man have to say?"

"Sir Nicholas? He will go on calling you 'Penelope.' But surely you wish to know what I know that you do not know?"

The vivacious Douglas Sutton, whose moods changed like the spring winds, confused me. "What is it? Some great secret?"

"Pen, all Puritans certainly do not dress as you do," Douglas announced. "I have seen Puritan ladies in Worcester and in Gloucester. Many Puritans in Bristol wear gowns like yours but they are seldom ladies of quality. The Puritan folk of quality wear silks and satins and sometimes even jewels."

"I did not know that," I exclaimed, astonished.

"It is true enough. I heard not long past that General Cromwell's wife wears purple and green gowns. She has jewels as do her daughters. The person who told me had come from London and had seen Mistress Cromwell."

Douglas opened wide the doors of her clothes press. I saw her gowns, shining like the rainbow I had always loved almost as much as the autumn leaves. She reached among them, taking down a white satin gown with only the faintest tinge of gray to its shimmer. It had no lace at its low cut square neckline—only a band of dark green velvet.

"This is what I shall give you. It never did become me. Put it on."

I disrobed and put the satin gown on over my petticoats. The cloth was smooth and cool against my skin as I buttoned the bodice with trembling fingers. The gown was not of a particularly sinful color, I told myself. It fit me well enough as did the green satin shoes Douglas found for me.

Douglas had a fine table mirror with a gold-leaf frame. Knowing full well what I did was ungodly, I twisted and turned until I had seen all of the gown.

"I thank you, Douglas," I told her.

My cousin was pleased. "It is fine," she said. "The color is named oyster, if you did not know. It rather suits you. You must wear it often while you are here. Now, sit down and let me fix your hair. It is quite a pretty color, too, Pen."

I had not thought so and I did not look forward to having my hair dressed. But if it would make things easier for me at Campion Towers I would be foolish to care.

While my cousin combed my hair and wound it in thin bits of leather to make the long ringlets for each side of my face and then twisted it to set it in the forehead ringlets everyone seemed to wear, I thought of what I had gleaned. I thought of the heavy fine Sir Nicholas had paid and I wondered at Douglas' strange comments about a future change in the fortunes of the Killingtree family. How could the fortunes of Papists change in a land where the Puritan Parliament ruled, I asked myself? I looked about my cousin's room, expecting to find a crucifix or an idolatrous statue of some saint, but there was nothing. The Killingtrees were clever. I found nothing that would give away what they were—except for Madame Gawdy's crossing herself in the coach during the storm.

Somehow I had to gain the confidence of these people so I could be permitted more freedom. "Why do Sir Nicholas and Mistress Killingtree wear black when Madame Gawdy did not?" I asked Douglas, who was still busy with my hair.

"They wear mourning for poor martyred King Charles I," she told me. "They have worn black ever since the King was murdered by the Roundhead Parliament over two years past. I doubt that they will ever put it off now though. Old people fancy black."

I bit my lip at her comment that Parliament had murdered the King. That was not true. They had brought him to trial and found him guilty of treason. The penalty for that was death.

"But you do not wear black."

"La, no, Sir Nicholas hates seeing young people parading about like ravens. My mother wore black for the King for a year, so did Madame Gawdy, but they put it off as soon as Sir Nicholas permitted it. Marie Gawdy is gaudy by nature." Douglas giggled at her jest.

I changed the subject. "What ails my grandmother?"

As she finished with my last curl, Douglas explained. "No one seems to know, Pen. Even if the physician says there is no such thing, I reckon she has a broken heart. She was very ill, I heard, when your mother ran off to the New World and ill again when cousin Julian went to war. She closed herself up in the tower room then. That is where she has been ever since." Douglas held up a hand mirror with a back fashioned of silver roses and cupids. I was hardly a pretty sight with my head covered with leather curl strips. I said as much.

"No, you are not really at all comely in those," Douglas agreed. "My mother warns me you must never let a man see you in them."

"I never think I would."

"Have you ever been in love, Pen?" My cousin asked suddenly.

"No," I said, quite truthfully.

"I have, many times. I think I am always in love." Her face fell as she took the mirror from me. "But most of the young men are away now. There are others, merchants and folk like that, from Worcester and men who are old. That is the miserable half of the county that wishes to marry me." Douglas made a face into her mirror. "It is the other half who are gone away that I look to."

I guessed what she meant—the men from the county who had gone into exile, the young Cavaliers she had not seen since the war ended.

"Have you been kissed?" Douglas asked slyly.

I shook my head, the leather strips rustling against each other. "No, but if I had not had the luck to be a Puritan, I would have been kissed last night."

"Last night? But you were on your way then from Worcester in our old coach! La, do not tell me that Peter tried to kiss you. He is a bold creature. He has a wife and six babies in Holt

Heath. Sir Nicholas permits him to live there. Whoever in the world was it?"

"No one very high in the world, I imagine," I replied. "It was a highwayman who stopped us—a lame highwayman on a big red horse."

Douglas' blue eyes widened, becoming round as full moons while her mouth opened into an "O." The hand mirror fell to the parquet floor with a crash of broken glass.

Whatever I had said had disturbed Douglas mightily. She went to her knees, hiding her face, to pick up the pieces of the mirror. "Oh dear, my mother will be angry with me now. The mirror was a gift from Sir Nicholas. Things slip out of my hands so."

Douglas took up her place in the window seat, asking me, first, if I liked music. I liked it tolerably well, if the truth be told, but I said that I loved it, although I did not sing. So Douglas took up a cittern, beribboned with scarlet; she sang me songs I had never heard, frivolous Cavalier songs, but I expected nothing else. She sang well in a high sweet voice and put the cittern down only when Jonas appeared once more, this time with a larger tray. It was our midday meal, white bread, cheese, sweet red wine, and a beef pie.

When he had gone, Douglas spoke of him. "He waited because he is old and cannot climb the stairs twice. I trust you were not concerned because of your hair, Pen. Jonas is but a servant. Do you have servants in the colonies?"

"Some colonists do. Some have bondservants, but not my father. He does not approve of bondservants. 'Tis akin to slavery, he says."

Douglas wanted to make conversation, too. "Tell me about the New World—especially about the red Indians."

So I told her about Salem Town, describing the few painted savages I had seen in their bearskin robes. I told of our house, my father's cooperage, the terrible winters, the sufferings of the first colonists, and finally of Elizabeth, my stepmother, and my half brothers and sisters. I did not tell her, however, of Amity Wrenn or of Pastor Wrenn now in England, recalling how my great-aunt had reacted to the unexpected news that I had friends in England.

My cousin wrinkled her nose in distaste when she heard of my stepmother. "How fortunate I am to have a pleasant mother. We seem opposites, you and I, Pen. I had no father, but mother never married someone who might be cruel to me. 'Tis unfortunate your father is but a cooper."

I rather agreed with her but I spoke up for my father. He should have been a scholar or a pastor, I thought. "Oh, he is a great deal more than a barrelmaker. *His* father was a gentleman here in England. We are not so concerned with such matters in the New World, though. Many folk there work with their hands. My father is an elder of our church and much respected in Salem Town."

My cousin was pretty and merry, I thought privately, but somehow I felt she and I dueled. Certainly we were careful with each other, especially so since she had dropped her silver mirror. What was it about the peculiar highwayman? Whoever he was, he must have seen Nicola's portrait? That must have been what he meant by saying I was "*very* like."

"Would you like me to read to you, Pen?" Douglas asked.

"Yes," I agreed, without any great joy. Douglas showed no sign of leaving me and had said that she seldom took a nap during the day. I had hoped to use this as an excuse to get away to my own chamber. It was almost as if she watched me.

"We shall read to each other," Douglas said delightedly.

I thought this childish; but I gave in to her. My cousin's full twenty books surprised me greatly. I had never owned a book myself. We had only the Bible and *The Sincere Convert* in our house. Douglas had a Bible in Latin, a language I did not read, and two tiny books of French poetry, another language I did not know, and one which she confessed she knew little of herself. I was never permitted to see all of her books—only those she showed me—for they were kept in a wooden cupboard behind a locked door. Books were very precious. I suspected Douglas had a Latin psalter, too, a forbidden book, read only by Catholics.

"You have no sermons?" I asked, "or writings of Master Milton?" I had heard of John Milton in Salem Town but I had never read his works. All of us knew he was a godly man and of our faith.

Douglas was put out. "No, indeed! I have no ranting Roundhead preachings. I will have none of your Master Milton, although Sir Nicholas swears he does not mislike some of his poems." She turned to face me. "I have it! I shall read Sir Philip Sidney to you. I have his poems. I know many of them by heart. And you shall read Sir Walter Raleigh's *History of the World* to me."

And that is what we did. Douglas read love poems that sometimes brought a blush to my cheeks and then I read of stern-principled ancient Rome to her. We exchanged places as we read, each sitting in the window seat to enjoy the best light. I snatched only a few glimpses from her windows. Her room was at the very end of that long passage of Campion Towers, while mine was at the middle. My cousin's chamber looked outward onto a green countryside, which stretched away to a landscape of gentle hills. A few brown and white cows grazed in a pasture below a black stand of oaks, an almost sinister thicket of trees that could hide anything. Yet this was a happier prospect by far than my desolate stone-walled court. I wished that I could change with Douglas Sutton. What could *I* see as I watched by night?

I was not left to my own devices for a moment. Mistress Laurel Killingtree arrived after we lit the first candle. She carried a red velvet box. The woman eyed me in the oyster satin dress and nodded approvingly to Douglas. "It is seemly," she announced. Then she gave the box to me. "Here are the Aylmer jewels. You are to wear them as I am sure Douglas has told you. Philippa must see you wearing them."

I opened the jewel case carelessly. I had never seen real gems before and I was prepared to scorn them. But I caught my breath at the chill blaze of green and white stones, all tangled together —a necklace, bracelets, and earrings. The pieces were set in heavy gold. I picked up the necklace, which was bitterly cold.

"Do take her hair out of the leathers, first," Laurel ordered my cousin. "Philippa has awakened. She will see Penelope before supper."

Obediently my cousin removed the leathers and combed my hair out, winding it over her fingers until it fell in ringlets over my ears. It was strange but not unbecoming, I decided.

"She never had her ears pierced," Douglas said, as if I had committed a crime.

"No matter. The necklace and bracelets will suffice," and, as she spoke, my great-aunt put the Aylmer necklace about my neck. Then, she clasped the two heavy bracelets on my arms. The jewels made me shiver as I looked at them in Douglas' table mirror. They brought out the green of my eyes and diminished the gray. Somehow, wearing them I was no longer Penitence Hervey of Salem Town. I recalled my father's words as if they had been a warning bell. I must not be corrupted by these people.

Both Douglas and Laurel were satisfied with me and said so. I made no comment. I followed obediently as Laurel took me to the tower room, once more down the long passages of that house. But before I left, I caught up my little leather bag, unseen, because Douglas and my great-aunt were speaking together, and stuffed it into the bosom of the gown.

The physician was still in attendance. I had hoped that my grandfather would not be there but I was doomed to disappointment. He glanced at me briefly before he turned his head away. Then he nodded to his sister. He approved of my new costume it seemed. While I went up to the green-hung bed, Sir Nicholas stood leaning on his cane, gazing into the fire, while my mother's portrait looked down at us over his head.

My grandmother was propped up on pillows. Her eyes, once gray-green like mine but now faded, were open. She smiled a weak little smile while one finger went out to touch the necklace. "It does become you, Nicola. Green was ever your color," she said in her soft voice.

"I thank you," I replied, "but I am not Nicola. I am your granddaughter, your Nicola's daughter. I have come from across the sea to be with you, grandmother. You wanted me to come. You believed I was my mother last night, too."

"Not Nicola?" she said, and I saw quick tears in her eyes. "Nicola did not come home?"

Laurel Killingtree came up to the bed now. Her voice was meant to be heard. "No, Philippa. This is not Nicola. This is your granddaughter, Penelope Hervey. She is much like Nicola.

You were in error last night. You gave Penelope the Aylmer inheritance then. You had me write this girl asking her to come to Campion Towers. Do remember, Philippa! Are the farm and jewels to be *hers?*"

Philippa looked at Laurel. I saw something stir in her eyes. Then she spoke to me, "Give me your hand, child."

I put my hand in hers while she gazed at me for a long moment in silence. Then she sighed. "Yes, I remember now. So you are the Hervey child, Nicola's babe? You are greatly like my daughter. You are a true Aylmer. Yes, the Aylmer jewels and the farm are yours. I wish them to go to Nicola's daughter —to an Aylmer." She paused for a moment. Suddenly a strange stricken expression twisted her face. Her eyes widened. "But you are a Roundhead!" She tried to pull herself up. "Nicholas!" she cried. "Nicholas, the maid is a Roundhead! What have I done to you? What will 'The Twelve' say? I did not guess it would be so soon. Nicholas! Nicholas!"

Laurel Killingtree shoved me aside and the physician was with my grandmother in an instant, drawing the curtains closed. My great-aunt caught me by the arm. "Come along, your grandmother does not require you now."

Sir Nicholas gazed at his sister with a melancholy smile playing about his mouth. "Are you quite satisfied now, Laurel?" he asked. He pointed toward the bed with his cane. "There is your latest bit of work, mistress."

This time Laurel did not answer her brother. We left the room quietly as Sir Nicholas hobbled to his wife's bed. My grandmother was muttering but I head her last words clearly enough as her voice rose thinly over his. "No, Nicholas, she must not be sent away. Whatever else she is, she is Nicola's child. You must find a way! You must!"

Cranberry

I WENT with Mistress Laurel Killingtree, my eyes intent upon the candle she held. Only that faint light and the ghost-white of my cousin's gown marked our progress downward through the house to the great hall I had seen the night before. In the gloom my great-aunt was almost invisible in her mourning dress.

While I followed Laurel Killingtree, I thought of my grandmother's words. Dr. Moonjean had been right to be suspicious—something was going on at Campion Towers. But what was it? What had my grandmother meant when she said "it was so soon"? "So soon" for what?

We reached the hall, a room now well lit by tall wax candles in floor sconces. It was as I had remembered it, high-beamed and old. This, then, was probably part of the original abbey, for the tapestry-hung walls were of stone. A huge firehearth lay at one end of the hall and a great fire burned there.

Douglas was sitting at an embroidery frame, doing crewelwork. She sprang up when she saw me. A thin tall woman in a deep red gown, lavishly trimmed with cream-colored Venice

87

lace, rose slowly to her feet from her armed chair as she, too, saw us. This surely must be Douglas' mother, Mistress Amabel Sutton. My great-aunt crossed the stone floor and set her candle on a little table next to my cousin's crewelwork. She glanced at the embroidery and snorted, "You show precious little improvement, Douglas."

Douglas shrugged but said nothing. Mistress Laurel spoke to the woman. "Mistress Sutton, this is your kinswoman, Penelope Hervey."

I curtsied to Mistress Sutton as I had been taught, my eyes fixed decently on the floor. Then I raised them to her face.

With a shock as if I had been struck, I realized that Amabel Sutton, a woman I had never seen before, hated me. Her face was a white mask, her full lips drawn into a line that showed me she bit them, and her eyes, black and strangely seeming without pupils, were fixed not on my face but on my necklace. Her bitter gaze traveled to the bracelets and then up finally to my eyes. She looked hard at me for a moment while I gaped at her.

Her hair was as black as my cousin's but a broad streak of white, like a scar, lay over her right temple. Her eyebrows were thin and black in her long face. The complexion I had thought white was thick plaistered with paint. Red stones dangled from her ears while more red stones encircled her long neck. Somehow I felt that these, unlike Madame Gawdy's "jewels," were not glass.

She drew her breath almost in a hiss and suddenly turned her back on me. So this was Douglas' pleasant mother! Amabel Sutton was little like unto her daughter. Or was she, I asked myself?

Mistress Killingtree spoke dryly. "Yes, Amabel, the emeralds went to Penelope. Philippa is aware that she is not Nicola. Yet she gave them to her. You are not in luck. I should have thought Campion Towers would satisfy even you."

The Sutton woman did not reply. Clearly there was no affection between her and my great-aunt. I did not know what to do. Then my cousin looked at me in a sullen way and shifted over on her bench. It was an invitation to sit next to her and watch as she indifferently embroidered roses on a piece of linen. We seemed to wait for someone. Amabel Sutton stood with her back to me, looking toward the fireplace and the strangely placed black nails above it and to its side.

"Why are those nails there?" I asked Douglas.

The girl bit off a piece of yellow thread. "There were pikes, swords, and daggers there once. They made a fine show," she whispered. I nodded, shivering; I knew that Papists were not permitted to keep arms.

Now Laurel went to a virginal not far away, seated herself, and began to play. It was an air I had never heard before and was somehow melancholy. As she struck the last note I heard the hesitant footsteps of my grandfather. He came wordlessly across the great hall into a room that led off to one side. Laurel arose at once, shook out her black skirts, and followed him. Douglas put her needle happily into the linen and got up. She yawned.

"Come along, Pen," she said. "We are to go in to supper."

So I went with Douglas into the much smaller oak-paneled room, a room she told me had been added by Sir Nicholas' father for the family meals. Amabel Sutton brought up the rear, her eyes, I felt, stabbing my back.

Douglas slid into a high-backed chair. Sir Nicholas was already seated at the head of the long, polished table in an even taller chair. My great-aunt sat with Mistress Sutton across the way. There was but one seat remaining—next to Douglas, one seat away from my fearful grandfather. I stood until Sir Nicholas raised his cane and pointed to the empty seat.

Slowly I took my place and waited, all of us silent, while Jonas brought in the supper of fish, lamb, tender strange-looking green things (I later learned they were shoots of asparagus), bread, cheese, and nuts. We drank wine, a heavy white wine, out of amber-colored goblets. Our plate was pewter and by no means fine. I recalled what Douglas had said about the Roundheads plundering. The soldiers had probably taken the silver plate— or was it hidden away? In a house so large there must be many places to hide valuables, I thought.

It was an unpleasant supper. I would have gladly exchanged a meal of samp and small beer with Obedience and the younger children for all of this fine fare. No one spoke. No one looked at anyone else. Remembering what I hoped to do tonight—explore —I scarcely tasted my wine.

Finally Sir Nicholas threw down his knife with a clatter and said to me, "Well, Mistress Penelope, what do you think of this house?"

I was caught off guard. "I do not know," I said. "I have not seen it, sir."

"You shall see it tomorrow," he promised. "You shall be shown the Aylmer farm, too."

"Is it nearby?" I asked.

"It adjoins the Killingtree property," he told me, filling his wine glass from a bottle set beside him on the table. "It is still a rich farm—too rich for a whimpering Roundhead, I warrant."

"You have not heard me whimper," I flared.

"Aye, that is true," he admitted; "but what do ye think of the jewels?"

I touched the necklace. "They are a vanity, sir."

My grandfather nodded. "If you were not a Roundhead, I would say I agreed with you. They are silly baubles, but my lady liked them well enough." He leaned forward. "Those and the land would make you a good catch for any man—that is if any gentleman would look at a Roundhead. Maybe I can find you a Worcester lad who is willing to take such a rich maid to wife even if she is a Roundhead."

I stared at him. There was a strange gleam in his eye. So, he baited me, did he? I would let him have it back. "From what I have seen of men in England, I would rather not have one at all," I said coldly. Excluding Dr. Amyas Moonjean, I said, "I have met but two—one was a highwayman, the other an ill-tempered knight. There was little to choose between them. If I am to marry, I shall choose my own husband and I shall wed from the New World—an honest, godly man. It seems I have heard of gentlewomen who have loved Roundhead gentlemen."

Sir Nicholas threw back his head and roared. "Damme, well said, girl! Ye have the look of an Aylmer but the spirit of a Killingtree. Damme if ye do not give back as good as ye get."

I was astonished at myself. I had never spoken so rudely before. Elizabeth would never have permitted it nor would my father, who would have scolded me for my lack of humility. How different these Cavaliers were. Was I becoming corrupted so easily, with no one to give me spiritual advice and comfort?

My grandfather went on. "That is no fit color for such a one, Roundhead or no, that puling white. Douglas, girl, had you no other?"

Sly Douglas spoke out sweetly. "No, Sir Nicholas, it was the one color she would wear."

This was not quite true. I had not been given another choice, but I held my temper.

"Laurel," the old man shouted across the table, "hie yourself to Worcester tomorrow and fetch the seamstress here. Let her bring samples of the stuffs she has. I will choose what Penelope is to wear."

"I will not wear sinful gowns," I warned him.

"*I* say what is sinful or not sinful in this house, mistress! If you are to remain here, ye shall not creep about like a mouse in browns and grays. From what I see, you are no good Roundhead in any event. Too much spirit and fire in ye."

This was too much. Did he intend to make me look like some painted Jezebel, decked out in pride, paint, and wickedness? I opened my mouth to protest but suddenly I felt a sharp pressure on one of my borrowed shoes. My cousin Douglas was looking meekly at her plate but she surely kicked me. I was so shocked that I closed my mouth in a gasp as I caught her soft whisper.

"Do not be a booby, Pen. Take what he offers. Never anger him. If you do not want the gowns, give them to me."

Sir Nicholas felt he had won the day. He called over his shoulder to Jonas. "Bring the jerkum, lad. Then, I will bid ye all good night."

Five glasses of plum jerkum were brought on a tray, the last one carefully put at my place by Jonas.

"To our lady!" Sir Nicholas said, lifting his glass, his eyes on the ceiling.

There was a Papist health if ever I had heard one, but I touched my lips to the wine glass just the same. Sir Nicholas watched me. Then he shouted, "To Philippa, damme! Drink to your grandmother, girl."

I drank the famous wine of Worcester almost angrily, meaning no disrespect to my grandmother, but I remembered how it made my head swim. Almost at once the candle flames seemed to grow taller. My grandfather got up, and I left my place, then, and curtsied to him as the others did. I put my hand on the table to steady myself. Jerkum was a remarkably strong wine.

My great-aunt took me by the arm. "This way, Penelope. I shall take you to your room."

"No, Douglas can do it," I protested.

"Douglas is coming," and so she was, hurrying behind us as we swept out into the hall and up the stairs. I was so giddy I could hardly stand; once my candles were lit in the dusty, sorry chamber, I was ready to fall onto the bed. Mistress Killingtree unclasped the necklace and bracelets, saying, "I shall keep these safe for you, Penelope."

And then she was mercifully gone. My legs did not wish to obey me, but I forced myself to take the key Laurel had given me and lock the door, this time from the inside. I trusted no one at Campion Towers. I unfastened the bodice of the satin gown, stepped out of it and moved toward the bed, telling myself I would rest for a short time, and then let myself out so see what I could see.

That was all I remembered until the next morning when sunlight slanted across my bed. My cousin Douglas nearly broke my door beating upon it. I could not tell at first what was happening, my head ached so, but then I heard her voice calling, "Pen, Pen, let me in!"

I got to my feet and stumbled to the door. Somehow, moving about helped, although I felt my fingers and feet were molded of lead.

Douglas was dressed in black velvet. A long black coat with gold embroidery, much like a man's, topped her black skirt. She wore a black hat with a yellow plume and was as pretty in that manlike costume as in her blue gown of yesterday.

In her arms I saw a heap of black velvet and another black hat, this one with a green plume. Tucked under her arm was a whip.

"Come on, Pen. Wake up. Please you, hurry. You are to see the Aylmer farm today. My mother and Sir Nicholas are waiting. Wear this costume," she said as she tossed the riding attire onto my bed.

I had slept in my petticoats and Douglas giggled but at my glance kept her silence. I put on a white linen shirt with a broad lace collar and was about to pull on the skirt when Douglas protested. "La, no. It is plain to see you have never worn such things. You shall not need half so many petticoats."

I discarded petticoat after petticoat until she was satisfied and let me put on the skirt and draw its string tight at the waist. She had brought me boots, too, of soft black leather and they fit me well enough over my own white wool stockings. The plain coat without gold thread—which, no doubt, marked it as my cousin's second-best—fit me well enough. I brushed my hair which, to my surprise, still held yesterday's curl and scrubbed at my teeth with a cloth. Then I threw cold water from a basin onto my face. Finally I put on the low-crowned hat. I felt quite sinful in that Cavalier hat, but I did wish for a mirror as I went with Douglas down to the room where we had supped the night before.

Our morning meal was porridge and cream and a bowl of strawberries, too, which Douglas nibbled greedily. I had seen strawberries only rarely. Neither Elizabeth nor I had a green thumb.

"They come from Worcester; they grow them under glass. Philippa is partial to them," Douglas explained.

Neither Mistress Sutton, great-aunt Laurel, nor my grandfather appeared, which pleased me. Their absence was soon explained by questioning Jonas. Mistress Killingtree had gone to Worcester to the seamstress, while Mistress Sutton and the master were waiting at the stables.

As we hurried out, Douglas urging me along, I got my first real viewing of Campion Towers. The house was entirely of gray stone, and strange-looking from the front, flat except for the two unmatched towers, one considerably larger than the other.

Douglas took a moment to identify the towers for me. "The large one is where your grandmother lies, Pen. The other is the abbey bell tower. It is very old. The Killingtree chapel is under it. There are no bells there now. They were taken down the first of the war, nine years ago, melted, and cast into cannon for the King."

I nodded grimly. These Papist bells had killed brave Puritan soldiers, then.

"Where is our wing, Douglas?" I asked, for I could not see the dreary little court I had looked on from my window.

"Behind the house, which is shaped like a U from the rear. We are in the left wing. Sir Nicholas and the others have their chambers in the right. The Killingtree who built the house kept as much of the abbey as he could. The large hall is the abbey refectory. That was where the monks dined, you know."

I did not know, of course, but I let Douglas talk on as we crossed the front of the house, going always to the right. I noticed that the grounds were untended, the grass high with wild flowers growing among the rose bushes. Douglas sighed and struck at an ugly weed with her whip. "I remember when we had twelve gardeners." Her manner brightened. "We shall have them again, too."

I glanced up at the right wing of Campion Towers, which had

three stories of windows. My first feeling about the house had not altered. It was sinister somehow. The windows were blind—but watchful. There were other smaller buildings behind the great house. Through an open door I spied the old coach I had traveled in from Bristol.

"Mistress Killingtree and Peter have gone in the fine coach," Douglas told me. "Laurel refuses to ride in the old coach and so do I."

A long, low stone and wooden building lay close by the coach house. As we approached it, Sir Nicholas came out of one of its several doors. "Ha, Douglas!" he shouted. "I will not see you off today. I have business. You and Mistress Sutton are to show your cousin the farm if ye choose." He gestured toward me. "Come see the horses, girl."

I followed him, not at all sorry that he was not to ride with us. I was no horsewoman. I had ridden a horse only twice, and each time it was a gentle animal, a broad-backed cart horse.

The air was thick with the smell of hay. To my left there was a little room filled with bridles hung on pegs and with saddles of several shapes set on blocks. Sir Nicholas led the way down a line of stalls to Mistress Sutton, who was drawing on a pair of leather riding gloves, her eyes intent upon her task. Like her daughter and myself, she was dressed in black velvet, but the plume on her hat was scarlet.

My grandfather tapped on a closed stall door with his cane. A boy with a shock of dark brown hair, a rosy face, and round brown eyes popped out, a curry comb in his hand. He bobbed to us and stared at me in open wonder.

"That is Garth, the stable boy," Douglas said. "He sees to the horses."

"How is the mare Berry today?" Sir Nicholas asked him.

"Well, sir."

"Can she be saddled for my granddaughter?"

"Aye, that she can, sir."

"Well, do it, lad," and leather-clad Garth was away, hurrying down the line of stalls.

"What do ye know of horses?" Sir Nicholas asked me.

"Very little," I said

"You are to ride Berry. She is one of the red horses of Campion Towers."

Sir Nicholas spoke with great pride. The red horses, whatever they were, were dear to him.

"I have heard my cousin speak of the red horses, sir. Would you tell me about them?"

Sir Nicholas was pleased. "Come with me." Over his shoulder to the others he said, "Stay here. I will show Penelope."

We passed stalls where the four brown coach nags came to look over the doors and whinny, but Sir Nicholas had no time for them.

There were only six stalls remaining and Garth stood at the door of the fifth, fumbling with the latch, a rope halter in his hand. The boy grinned at me.

Sir Nicholas whistled loudly. Five heads popped out of five stalls, all at once. All five horses were red but each such a different hue of red. No two were alike. All had delicate faces, soft lustrous eyes, and long dark red manes. Even I knew these to be very special horses.

My grandfather spoke to the first horse as if it were a person. "Eh, Russet, lass, ye know who it is?" and he took a bit of loaf sugar from his cuff, put it onto his palm, and gave it to the horse. At each stall he did the same, calling each horse by name and talking to me about each animal. Pippin was a mare, Pimpernel a filly, Rufus a stallion, and finally in the next to last stall, the red horse called Berry.

"Which one does Douglas ride?" I asked.

"Pippin. Mistress Sutton prefers Russet."

"Which is yours, sir?"

"Rufus, the sire of the filly and the mares, Berry, Pimpernel, and Pippin."

Garth brought out Berry. She was not a small mare—to my way of thinking, she was very large. She came obediently to Sir Nicholas, put her head to his shoulder, butting him, and then snuffling at his arm.

"Reach into my cuff," he ordered me. "You give her another lump of sugar. That way, she will remember you."

I did as he demanded although I was frightened. I put the grayish sugar on my palm as he had done and held my hand under the mare's nose, praying that she would not bite. I learned later that a horse cannot bite if one's palm is kept open. Berry lifted her lips delicately and sniffed at the sugar. She looked at me with her liquid eyes; then an instant later I felt her soft lips on my palm, tickling me. The sugar was gone.

"Stroke her, Penelope," my grandfather told me. I patted the red horse. Her skin was like the satin gown I had worn yesterday, if not more soft. It seemed to me that her color was a deeper red than the others. There was a true purple to her shining hide.

"She is the color of a New World cranberry," I said.

"Well, then, she is a 'Berry,' indeed. Rowanberry is what we named her, but 'tis 'Berry' she has become to us."

"She is become the color of Will Scarlet," Garth volunteered.

Sir Nicholas glared at the stableboy. Garth backed away, the color draining from his face.

"Will Scarlet?" I asked, puzzled, knowing only that this was a name of one of the henchmen of Robin Hood, the famous outlaw.

"Aye, a horse I once had, the best of the red horses." He turned away to look toward the empty stall, the last one. "I bred the red horses, myself—the swiftest in Worcestershire. Not another horse in this county is a finer hunter than Rufus.

"I went to France when I was a young man. There I found Rougemont, the red stallion, and what a red mountain of a horse he was. Strawberry, the dam, the red mare, I bought for a king's ransom in London. The red horses came from those two, Rougemont and Strawberry—dead and gone now for years. I would not permit the red horses to go to war—not even for King Charles when he wrote me asking."

Then Sir Nicholas went off toward the great house, leaving me with my cousin and her mother. Douglas held Cranberry, the horse saddled and bridled now. The side saddle was padded with scarlet velvet and the reins were of scarlet leather.

Garth hurried to fetch Russet and Pippin to us, a horse on either side of him. As I watched, he deftly put the bit into each mare's mouth and then, with a grunt, heaved the heavy saddles, identical to mine, on each horse's back. He girthed each mare quickly; Mistress Sutton shook her head and struck Russet with her closed fist just in front of the girth. The horse groaned as a rush of air came out of her nostrils and mouth.

"Russet is a wind sucker," Douglas said. "You have to be wary of her for that."

Mistress Sutton led Russet, now that the mare's girth was tightened once more, over to a mounting block. Holding the reins in one hand, she mounted, putting her left foot into the one stirrup, her right knee over the saddle peg. Douglas mounted Pippin, the lightest hued of the red horses.

It was my turn now. I tried to copy Douglas, but somehow, with my horse's twisting and turning, I could not get my knee over the peg. Garth was kindly while Douglas giggled and Mistress Amabel watched me in contempt. Garth held my foot in his hands and helped me swing into the saddle. Finally I got my knee over the peg and, glancing at Douglas, I arranged my skirts to sweep gracefully over the saddle. At least I trusted they were graceful.

I did not feel at all secure, though we left the stable at a calm walk. Cranberry's neck twitched while one ear was pricked back toward me inquisitively. I felt that the horse caught my fear.

Douglas, Mistress Sutton, and I went in single file out of the stable, but just as Cranberry passed through the doors, held open by Garth, Russet lashed out with her back hooves at my horse. Cranberry neighed and reared and I slid off onto the hard-packed ground, inches from a drying puddle. It jolted me cruelly. For a moment I felt the sun whirl about me, and I heard my cousin's ringing little laugh. I looked around, half-dazed. Cranberry stood a few feet from me, her flanks shuddering now. There was an expectant look in her eye. Amabel Sutton had Russet well under control. The other red mare did not move a muscle, while the woman sat motionless, smiling at me, a smile of cruel pleasure if I ever had seen one.

"Have a care of Russet's hooves, mistress," she said coldly. "She does not favor Berry."

I got up and brushed off my skirts and coat. "And I do not favor your Russet," I told her. I felt that Cranberry had been unjustly treated. Hot anger rose in my throat. I wished Cranberry had tried to bite the other horse. I patted her and turned to Garth who was now at my side and looking worried. "Please you, help me mount again," I said.

"Aye." The stableboy made a cup of his hands for my foot and I was soon mounted. This time I seemed to have the knack of swinging my knee over the peg more easily.

"We shall be wary of you, mistress," I said half to Amabel Sutton and half to her treacherous Russet. I thought my fall had been no accident.

I had forgotten about my grandfather but as Cranberry and I stepped out at a goodly safe distance behind Russet, I heard his bellow, "Good girl, Penelope! Good girl!" and far away from us, a small figure in the distance, he raised his cane in salute. I was pleased at his praise.

We passed out through a ragged hedge opening. Another hedge, a taller one, lay ahead of us, across a green meadow pied with tall red wild flowers. I knew enough to tighten the reins for we were going to trot, I suspected. I would stay close to the more amiable Pippin. Perhaps Douglas would look after me.

What happened next took me by surprise. Amabel Sutton cried out and dug her heel into Russet's ribs. She shouted again and in a brief moment her mare went from her dancing skitterish walk to a hand gallop and then into a full gallop. The woman's scarlet plume bobbed gaily along the meadow. Douglas turned her head, flashed a smile at me, gave Pippin her head and a crack with her whip and she, too, was off in a soft thunder of hooves, clumps of green turf flying under Pippin's shoes.

Cranberry snorted and reared. There was no holding her. She gathered her legs beneath her as I had seen rabbits do and was off, tearing across the meadow toward the hedge. I pulled on her reins with all of my strength. It availed me nothing. I held my seat as we pounded behind Pippin and I gasped in fright as I saw

Russet take the hedge in one great soaring bound. Pippin went over, too, Douglas' black skirts sailing out to one side like a raven's wing. I closed my eyes, feeling Cranberry's muscles bunch, and I screamed as the red mare rose into the air and took the hedge at her own discretion, the reins slackening under my hands.

For a wonder I stayed on, even though we landed with a crashing jolt on the other side. Russet and Pippin were still ahead of me, still running. The Suttons had not waited to see what had happened to me. They cut toward the west around the copse of oaks I had seen from my cousin's window.

I had expected Cranberry to follow the other horses but she had notions of her own. The mare put her ears back and her stride lengthened as she cut across the second meadow, traveling due west. I pulled hard at the reins but the red horse would not obey me. It was as if she had no rider.

At a full gallop Cranberry, the runaway, took me toward the oakwood. There was nothing I could do. I leaned over, my head close to the mare's neck, praying that the horse's reckless headlong gallop would not take her under low-hanging branches, sweep me off, and kill me.

Something for Amyas Moonjean

THE RED MARE climbed the knoll at a gallop and in a moment plunged into the grove of trees. I looked ahead of me as much as I could, still keeping my cheek next to Cranberry's floating mane. The great dark trees stood farther apart than I had dared to hope. Shafts of sunlight entered the wood.

I peered down at the ground. We followed a path of sorts, but I was afraid to fall deliberately, for there were no soft mossy spots to cushion my fall. I felt anger through my fear, anger against both Douglas and her mother. No, I would not break my neck to please Mistress Amabel Sutton.

We came out of the wood at the top of a hill. A dirt path led down and Cranberry mercifully took it, pounding along. I raised my head now that the trees no longer threatened. Tall soft grass lay on each side of the path. I was tempted to fall but again I hesitated. The grass might contain sharp stones. Small boulders filled the path. I decided to stay on if possible and I snatched at the reins, hoping that Cranberry was tiring.

But the mare was not ready to come to a halt or to take to a more gentle gait. She swept down the hill and along a wider road at its foot. Then she swerved to the right, choosing another path, and once more we climbed. I glanced ahead in despair. How many hills lay between me and safeness? The mare was sure-footed as a cat, but how long would my fortunes hold?

And then, as I shouted in vain to the horse to halt, I caught a moving out of the corner of my eye. It was another horse and rider. They came over the crest of the hill and stood watching, dark motionless outlines.

"Help, runaway!" I yelled, but the rider did not come to rescue me.

Instead Cranberry went to him. She went dashing up the hill. In a second we would crash into the other horse. I closed my eyes and prayed—then an amazing thing happened. I heard a piercing whistle and Cranberry halted, almost in mid-stride, it seemed. One moment she was at a full gallop—in the next, she, too, was motionless.

I was so surprised and unnerved that I sat up and looked at the other rider open-mouthed. As I looked, Cranberry sighed deeply, twitched her withers and then her flanks. I slid gently from the saddle.

I fell to the grass, which was as soft as it had looked. The earth was wonderful but at once I sat up, angry at the explosion of laughter from my companion on the hilltop. I scrambled to my feet. First of all, I caught at Cranberry's scarlet bridle and hung on. I would go as I had come—with the red mare—but I would lead her back to Campion Towers.

I glared at the man who shared the hilltop with me. "I thank you for courtesy," I told him.

Whoever he was, he was not old. Gauging a rider's height is not easy but I guessed the stranger was tall. His hair was long and golden brown, his eyes a bright hazel, I thought, under the brim of a brown hat, a Cavalier hat with a red plume. His face was thin and brown and his mouth well-shaped but somehow sad. One sharp line marred its left corner; yet he had a good face with no weak look to it.

His clothing was not rich nor his linen fine. He wore a coat of buff leather and breeches of the same. His collar was plain, while no lace peeped from his cuffs. His high boots were of black leather. I stared at them for a long moment.

I had been so preoccupied in glowering at the ill-mannered rider that I had not given much attention to his horse, but now I examined it. It was large, far larger than my Cranberry, but they were remarkably similar—both the same purplish red. Will Scarlet, I asked myself in alarm? I guessed who this man was—the highwayman! So he skulked about Campion Towers by day, too?

He spoke now. His voice was gently bred and his words far more courteous than his manner. "I ask your pardon, mistress. I should not have found you amusing but I have rarely seen anyone take a fall from a horse that does not move. It was quite a remarkable performance."

I wanted to get away from him as quickly as possible without arousing his suspicions. "It is of small matter," I said as calmly as I could. "If you will but tell me the way to the Aylmer farm, I shall not concern you further."

"You stand upon it," he told me. "The farmhouse is in the vale below. This path will take you there. Do you need help in mounting, mistress?"

"No. I intend to walk. I am weary of riding."

I hauled at Cranberry's reins, feeling like an idiot when the horse refused to budge. The stranger grinned. "Come on, Cranberry," I urged, grinding my teeth, but still the red mare would not move.

The stranger laughed again. "Aye, she has got a will of her own. 'Cranberry,' do you call her? 'Tis a good name."

He touched his horse with his knee and bent down from the saddle. He took the reins from my hand before I was aware of what he had done and then to my surprise he whispered into Cranberry's ear. The mare seemed to listen, her intelligent eyes intent upon me. Finally he was finished. "She will give you no more trouble, mistress."

I sniffed. How silly! As if talking to a horse would change its ways. I took the reins from the man's brown hand.

He smiled at me again. His teeth were fine. Well, handsome is as handsome does, I thought. I gave a tug on the reins and Cranberry moved obediently forward. His trick had worked!

"What did you say to her?" I asked, astonished.

" 'Tis a black secret," he confided. "It was taught me by a gypsy tinker, but if you must know, you need only call her 'beauty' and she will obey you. She believes that is her true name."

I had to laugh. Gypsy tinker, indeed? Even in Salem Town I had heard that some people had a way with horses. The sinister stranger knew Cranberry. That was all. Perhaps he had been in the stables at Campion Towers or had come from Holt Heath before he took up his present desperate occupation.

"I thank you," I said and, greatly daring, I asked him, "Who may you be?"

Dr. Moonjean might very well be interested in this.

The man swept off his hat and bowed slightly, rather more gracefully than I had believed could be done on horseback.

"James Rowland, at your service, mistress, and who may you be?"

"Pen Hervey."

He clapped his hat back on his head, a puzzled look on his face. "Pen? What sort of name is that? It is a nickname for another?"

"I am not really sure any more," I replied and, catching up my skirts with one hand, I nodded to him and led Cranberry swiftly away over the brow of the hill. I wanted no more conversation with James Rowland, or whatever his real name was, for I would not believe one word he would ever say.

Tall red blossoms swayed in the breeze as I left the stranger on the red horse. I looked back only once and found that he had gone. My reaction rather surprised me—I felt half relieved, but I also wished he had stayed to watch me out of sight.

I gazed about me. So this is my land, I said to myself! As a cooper's daughter, I knew little of soil, but I knelt for a moment to crumble some earth between my fingers. It was brown and sun-warm. The grass was high and lush and everywhere clumps of wild flowers sparkled in the grass.

We toiled up yet another hill, following the dirt path. I paused to examine the ground several times, for I saw the prints of many hooves. Some were the prints of horseshoes; others, and there were far more of these, were tiny and sharp, deeply set into the drying mud of a day's past summer storm. Often the little tracks obliterated the larger. I wondered what they could be. Were they deer?

Yet, I had learned one thing. This path, now lonely, was well traveled.

Cranberry and I gained the low hilltop and I looked below. Then I laughed. The mystery of the tracks was no longer one.

A great flock of white sheep grazed the hollow below me, dots of white in the broad green meadow. The tinkling sound of their bells drifted up to me. Of course! We were not far from the Cotswolds. This was sheep pasture. Also, I wondered, were the sheep mine, too?

A copse of tall trees, not oaks, lay at one end of the vale and at the edge of these I saw a tumble of gray stone and wood. I believed I saw ruins.

I waited on the hill, trying to make up my mind. James Rowland had told me I would find the Aylmer farmhouse in the vale. If there had been no sheep, I would not have hesitated to go down. But I had never really been near a flock of sheep before. What if they attacked me? How could I protect myself afoot?

I looked at Cranberry and spoke aloud, "Do you suppose we could try it again?" I added a caress to her mane and used the word the stranger had told me, "Will you behave, beauty?"

Cranberry gazed at me. She rubbed her head on my sleeve. Very pleased, I led her over to a convenient boulder. The red mare stood quiet while I mounted, got my knee over the peg, arranged my skirts properly, and gathered up the reins. Silently repeating a little prayer, I clucked to her and she stepped forward briskly, a satin ear pricked back to hear what I would say next. She did not seem to wish to run away now. We walked down into the vale and along the path through the sheep.

There was no one in sight, but as we went around the grove of trees I saw another red horse, its reins trailing, cropping the grass at the side of the road. Cranberry neighed and broke into a trot, yet it was easy to rein her in when she reached the second horse. It was little Pippin.

By now I was close to the gray building, whatever it was. I realized that it was not particularly old even if it was a ruin.

It was a collection of buildings, a stone house with a fallen-in roof, and a conglomeration of wooden sheds adjoining—all in stages of decay. So this was the Aylmer farm? I had inherited little, it seemed to me.

"Douglas?" I called out, "Douglas Sutton?"

The answer was immediate. My cousin appeared at once in the doorway of the house. She waved to me. "Here I am, Pen!" Her eyes took in my horse and my carefully arranged skirts at a glance. She cried out, genuine surprise and pleasure in her voice, "I guessed you would stay with Berry. Come see your farm."

I had spied a stone block not far from the house and rode over to it. With Douglas' interested blue eyes upon me I got down as gracefully as I could. Then I paused, the reins still in my hand. What was I to do with Cranberry—take her into the farmhouse? Not that this would be amiss, judging from its sad appearance. It would not make an adequate stable.

Douglas gestured toward Pippin. "Oh, let her free, Pen. You have only to whistle to call her back. She will not run away. The red horses never do."

Douglas was hopeless. She had never grown up. My cousin had only followed her mother as a careless nestling follows a parent swallow. My quarrel lay with Amabel Sutton.

Cranberry ambled off to join Pippin. "Where is Mistress Sutton?"

Douglas shrugged. "Gone off to Holt Heath. She had business there, she said. She asked me to come here to show you your land."

"How did you guess I would come here?" I asked, puzzled.

"I knew that Berry would fetch you. She headed this way. There is really no other place to go." Douglas was curious. "Did you have trouble with Berry, Pen?"

I could not help being sour. "Not a bit. I have not had such a pleasant time in months, Douglas. My headache is gone." And for a wonder it was.

Wit was lost on Douglas. "Yes, the mare does have nice gaits," she agreed. "I am glad the Berry likes you."

"So am I," I said dryly.

"Well, come in, silly. Come see what your grandmother Philippa wants you to have." Douglas pulled at my sleeve.

It was chill and damp inside the house. Privately I had decided I did not like stone houses. Campion Towers for all that it was a great house seemed dank to my way of thinking and its many passages were drafty. Here, pale yellow grass grew on the floor in long hairlike tufts. The windows were empty, while the shattered wooden door hung on broken, heavily rusted metal hinges. I saw a firehearth, a three-legged stool, and a battered trestle table—nothing more in the largest room. I peered quickly into the other two. Both were bare.

Douglas had seated herself on the table. As I returned she said, " 'Tis a good thing no Aylmer wishes to live here now. I would never want to. Would you, Pen?" She sniffed in pretty disgust. "Of course no Aylmer has lived here for thirty-five years—not since Philippa's parents died and she wed your grandfather. She married above herself, they still say it in Worcester. They were sweethearts when they were children. When she came to Campion Towers, Sir Nicholas put a steward on her farm. He lived in this house. The Roundheads came here, too, Pen. They drove off most of the sheep to feed their army." She gestured. "You can see what the soldiers did to the house."

I did not reply to this. I had had enough of insults to my faith. I walked toward the great firehearth. It covered one entire end of the hall. The jack for turning the meat was also rusted and broken. Oddly though, a stub of candle sat fixed in its own grease on the hearth. The tallow was fresh and yellow, not gray as an old candle would be. I wondered at this. I knelt to examine the candle and as I did the bitter odor of the ash-choked chimney filled my nose. I sneezed twice. This was strange. Long-dead ashes would not be powdery. They became caked hard when they picked up moisture from the air. I skimmed my hand over them. The ashes were warm.

"Who lives here now?" I asked.

"The shepherd," Douglas replied.

"I saw no shepherd."

"Old Owen is always about somewhere. I heard his dog barking just before you came. They say he is a Welshman. Perhaps he does not speak English. He will come out when we have gone away."

"Who owns the sheep?"

"Sir Nicholas. They are not yours."

I caught her little rebuke. "I thought this was farm land, Douglas."

"It was once but the grain was burned in the fields by the Roundheads. It was too late to plant again—besides the soldiers drove the workers off. The farm folk never came back. Sir Nicholas then took the land for his sheep. He gets a good price for his lambs and his mutton in Worcester, and his wool sells well enough there, too. When it is time, the shearers come here from all over the county."

My cousin jumped from the table. "Let us go now, Pen. I hate it here. It makes me shiver. I think the house is haunted. In Holt Heath they say it is. Sometimes they say there are lights here by night. Your grandmother's steward was murdered by the Roundheads. Peter swears the steward comes back and walks about by night."

I glanced at the candle. Ghosts would not require a light nor did they need to warm themselves by a fire.

Douglas went on. "Pen, there are many vagabonds about. Sir Nicholas warned me that strangers have been seen even in Holt Heath. Summer brings them out of their holes. They can be like wild beasts."

This made sense. I brushed ashes from my skirts. There might be dangerous folk about easily enough. Who knew that better than I? My thoughts went to Dr. Moonjean's words. I was truly a soldier in the cause and there could be danger in Cromwell's cause—more danger than I had guessed.

It was pleasant to go out into the warm sunshine again. Douglas whistled and both Cranberry and Pippin came at a trot, their scarlet reins swinging. Each of us mounted from the stone block. Then Douglas swung Pippin to face me.

"It is not far to the village," she announced. "We shall go there. I shall lead the way." Douglas urged Pippin into a gentle trot and I did the same with Cranberry. We jogged along amiably side by side. Cranberry had no quarrel with Pippin.

Douglas pointed with her whip. "See, Pen. What did I tell you about the shepherd?"

In the distance across the meadow a dark figure stood at the edge of the flock of sheep, watching us as we rode toward the village. I was much too far away to make out his face but I could see the tall shepherd's crook in his hand and at his feet I spied a smaller dark object. As I watched, the small black figure leaped up and came running toward us. I could hear its sharp bark.

I could not help but think how pretty my vale was. I liked its rich colors—the lively green of the grass, the white sheep, the brown road, and particularly the red flowers that lined its length like soldiers. In our black costumes, gaudy plumes, and riding our red horses, we suited its gaiety.

"What are the flowers—the tall red ones?" I asked Douglas.

"Red campion. There is white campion about, too," she replied. "Surely you have campion in the New World? It is a common flower."

I shook my head. "Not that I know of, but I have seen these red flowers all morning everywhere. I see how my grandfather's house got its name."

My cousin reined Pippin in so hard that the horse almost reared from fright, while Cranberry danced sideways at Pippin's sudden motion. Douglas stared at me in astonishment and then began to laugh. There was little merriment in her laughter—chiefly scorn.

"The name has nothing to do with flowers. The house was named because of Edmund Campion."

"Who was he?" I asked.

"Edmund Campion was a priest—a Roman Catholic priest—a Jesuit, executed in London a long time past."

I felt a chill strike through me. "What did a priest have to do with the house?" I asked slowly.

"Edmund Campion was here—or so they say," Douglas explained, putting Pippin back into a walk. Our horses' hooves made soft sounds as my cousin talked. "The legend is that Campion was hidden there. It was called the 'great house' or 'The Old Abbey' before 1580. Queen Elizabeth's men hunted for Campion but they never did find him in Worcestershire. They caught him though in Berkshire later and took him to London and kept him in the Tower of London. The old Queen had him tortured to make him tell what he knew about the English Papists and to give their names. Finally Queen Elizabeth had him executed. Elizabeth hated Papists and persecuted them. Oh, the tales the old women can tell about Henry VIII and Elizabeth and how their soldiers hunted down the people who belonged to the Roman Catholic religion here in Worcestershire! It makes my hair stand right on end to listen to them."

I was silent, waiting for her to go on. Douglas took my silence for the invitation it was.

"Edmund Campion was preaching and saying mass here, of course. He belonged to the Church of England at first, Pen, but he went to France and became a Roman Catholic there. That is where he joined the Jesuit order. The Jesuits sent him back to England to bring people who had once been Papists back into the old church. Because it was against Henry VIII's and Elizabeth's laws to hear mass, many Papists were backsliding."

"Did Campion ever tell Queen Elizabeth's men about being at Campion Towers?"

Douglas shook her head, her sunshine-yellow plume fluttering in the soft winds. "No. Not even when they tortured him in the Tower of London. I was told when I was a little girl that he preached secretly in Holt Heath and Worcester and that he stayed one night with the Killingtree family. The soldiers of Queen Elizabeth must have thought so, too, for they searched every house in this part of the country for him. Sir Nicholas' grandfather got into a great deal of trouble over it. They even haled him up to London to face the Queen's terrible court, the Star Chamber. But they could never prove a single thing no matter how much the Queen's lawyers shouted at him. They threatened him with torture, too, but they must have known that nothing would ever make him speak. He gave back as good as he got. They kept him in the Tower for a time, but he had friends at the old Queen's court. His friends got him freed before long. When he came back to Worcestershire, he learned that the villagers spoke of his house as 'Campion Towers.' The Queen was always suspicious of him, mayhap because of the name. He was never welcome at her court; the name, Campion Towers, stuck. The house has been called that ever since. When the Roundhead soldiers came, they named it 'Papist Towers.' That made Sir Nicholas very angry. It is a strange thing. In the last century the Aylmers were very rich, Pen, far richer than the Killingtrees. Queen Mary, Elizabeth's Papist older sister, favored them. She gave the Aylmer jewels to your grandmother's great-great-grandfather because he served her well in Spain. They say in the village that if Queen Mary had lived longer, she would have given a barony or an earldom to the Aylmers. But when Elizabeth took the throne, the Aylmers were fined so heavily because of their religion they had to become farmers once more, just as they had been at first."

I had wanted to ask if my great-great-grandfather Killingtree had been a Papist, but the words caught in my throat. Surely he must have been if he sheltered a priest. But now I had learned something even more fearful. My Aylmer ancestors were surely Roman Catholic if they had been favored by "Bloody Mary" Tudor, that terrible Queen, wife of a Spanish King who burned Protestants at the stake. No wonder the Aylmer emeralds and diamonds had weighed so heavily about my neck. I vowed I would not wear them again.

My cousin struck Pippin lightly with her whip and the horse broke into a trot. Cranberry followed suit. Douglas had spoken her piece—this was 1651; Edmund Campion had been dead for more than seventy years. Queen Elizabeth had been in her tomb for nearly half a century. Like a child, Douglas Sutton lived only for the present and hoped for baubles from the future.

Mistress Cardwell, Seamstress

I HAD NOT expected Holt Heath to be a Worcester, Bristol, or a Gloucester, certainly, and I had not truly expected it to be a Salem Town either, for I knew that Salem was reckoned a town even by English standards.

The hamlet lay in a tiny vale. It was little more than a collection of four or five buildings—a forge where the blacksmith's coal fire smoldered, a tavern, again half-timbered with a thatch roof, marked off as an inn only by its signboard which depicted a man dressed either in green leaves or green fur, which, I did not know, for the sign was dim and old.

"That's the Green Man Tavern," Douglas explained.

My eye fell on two other buildings. One was a little thatch-roofed house behind a brick wall and the other was surely the village church, for it was made of gray stone and had a cross at its top. I had not expected to see a Puritan chapel, of course, and I knew that Anglican churches had crucifixes atop their steeples —but so did Papist churches.

"That is All Hallows Church," my cousin volunteered. "The

117

rector lives in the little house. He is a very old man. He holds services in our chapel at Campion Towers after they are held here. His name is Master Meredith."

I nodded grimly while Douglas looked away. I could well imagine what sort of services Master Meredith read to the Killingtrees in their private chapel—services in Latin, no doubt —the Papist mass.

"All Hallows had fine stained-glass windows," Douglas told me, "but the Roundhead soldiers shattered them and tore down the altar rail as they did in our chapel. Sir Nicholas replaced the windows and the rail here at All Hallows out of his own pocket. He could not find stained glass."

Papist windows and a Papist rail. I nodded to myself once more. The Puritan soldiers had done well to purge Anglican houses of worship of Roman Catholic frippery—of costly glass windows depicting saints, of rails that kept the congregation from the altar, of ornate carved wooden pulpits, and of plaster statues of yet more saints. Nothing could be more plain than our meetinghouse in Salem Town. At that moment I gloried in it, although I had sometimes privately criticized it for its barrenness and simple pews. We Puritans did not kneel nor did we hold with choirs. Our own voices lifted in hymns pleased the Lord most.

I turned my eyes away. The other houses resembled the Green Man Tavern. "Who lives there?" I asked, pointing.

"One house is Peter's. His wife inherited it. The miller owns the other. His mill is on the stream nearby, behind the trees."

"Where is your mother?" I asked.

"With the miller's wife, I think," Douglas replied. She hauled on Pippin's reins, heading her mare toward the finest house of all, one with several many-paned glass windows. Then she reined in and called out her mother's name.

I was surprised. If I had only once dared stand outside a house and call for Elizabeth! Cavalier manners were certainly strange. But even Douglas, I noted, did not call a second time.

After a time Amabel Sutton came out, a stout woman following her, a woman who wore a fine lawn apron over her green gown. The miller was a rich man, judging from the many windows and his wife's attire.

With one irritated glance, Mistress Sutton took in her waiting daughter and myself. She turned back to the miller's wife. "It is settled, then? You understand what Sir Nicholas asks of your husband?"

The woman had a deep voice. "Aye, my lady. When he comes from the mill I will tell him at once."

"Fetch me my horse then," Amabel Sutton demanded.

The woman bawled loudly over her shoulder until a tousled-haired blond boy, probably the miller's son, came running from the house and darted around its side to the stables. In a few minutes he returned with Russet and helped Mistress Sutton mount.

At her first glimpse of Russet I felt Cranberry stiffen. Of her own accord my horse moved away out of range of Russet's vicious hooves and temper—a temper I thought quite matching her rider's.

Amabel Sutton glanced coldly at me and spoke only to Douglas. "So you found her, Douglas? Did she see the Aylmer farm?"

"Yes, mother," Douglas said meekly and then urged Pippin into a steady trot to keep pace with Russet.

I clucked warily to Cranberry, who kept a careful distance from Russet. I would trust to Cranberry's judgment where Russet was concerned. Clearly she and the older mare were confirmed enemies.

We followed a much-used road through a sun-dappled wood and soon we were before Campion Towers. Garth and Peter came running to lift us down and lead our horses off, but not before I patted Cranberry and called her "my beauty," whispering softly into her ear. I thought fleetingly of James Rowland.

Seeing Peter made me remember Laurel's trip to Worcester. She had returned quickly. Had she brought the seamstresses with her? I hoped not, for I was weary and in no mood to stand for hours being pricked with pins.

I was not in luck.

Laurel Killingtree sat at the virginal and when we came into the great hall, she got up swiftly. "Penelope," she called out, her somewhat harsh voice ringing in the large room, "Mistress Turtledove and Mistress Cardwell have come with me from Worcester."

She gestured toward two women who sat together on a bench, a great wrapped bundle at their feet. One was tall and thin, garishly dressed in scarlet velvet; the other was small and rather mouselike, her dress a dull pewter-colored silk, her hair the exact gray. Brown traveling cloaks lay folded on the bench beside them.

I fancied Mistress Turtledove to be the little woman in pewter gray, but I was wrong. This was Mistress Cardwell, the chief assistant to the "finest seamstress in Worcester," according to Mistress Killingtree, and the large bundle contained cloth from which we were to make our selections. Both seamstresses were in awe of my great-aunt and of us. They curtsied deeply to the Suttons and to me and I nearly returned the curtsy until Laurel hissed sharply at me when I caught up my skirts. Although the seamstresses were richly gowned, they were beneath my station. I blushed. I had not thought that a seamstress was below a cooper's daughter but here in Worcestershire I was first and foremost a Killingtree.

I was by no means pleased at what lay before me, but Douglas said, "It is exciting, Pen. Sir Nicholas asks to see the stuffs. He has no interest in what I choose when Mistress Turtledove comes."

"He only wishes to be certain that I do not get away with anything. He thinks I would choose drab, dull cloth and still be like a kitchen maid—even in silks and satins."

Douglas giggled. "Sink me! You have got a tongue, Pen."

"Yes, I seem to have found it." My eyes were on Amabel Sutton, who now drew off her riding gloves.

The woman had not spoken to me since we rode out of Holt Heath together. Now, she must have been aware that I stared at her. She looked up slowly and her eyes met mine. They were narrow and ice cold as they measured me. The contempt that I had seen the night before had vanished. I would not say that she looked at me with respect, yet somehow her behavior toward me had changed. I lifted my chin to return her glance and she smiled in a twisted fashion, then her eyes moved away to Mistress Turtledove, who was describing to a fascinated Douglas the latest neckline newly come from France.

Our midday meal was cheese, bread, wine, and cold roast meat. After a time Laurel joined us at the table with the announcement that Sir Nicholas was with Philippa, who also wished to see the velvets, satins, and brocades from Worcester. We were to go to the tower room.

"Did you have a pleasant morning, Mistress Penelope?" Laurel asked me. "Did you see the Aylmer farm?"

"Yes," was my reply. This seemed neither the time nor the place to tell her of Amabel Sutton's conduct. Yet, I was determined to tell Laurel when I found the satisfactory moment. I would not ride with that woman again. As Cranberry carefully avoided Russet, I hoped to avoid Mistress Sutton.

My great-aunt seemed to expect something more of me, so I added, "Douglas tells me people say the Aylmer farm is haunted."

Laurel turned on her. "Foolish superstitious nonsense. One should not believe everything one hears, Douglas. Nor should one tell everything one knows."

Douglas muttered, "Yes, Mistress Killingtree."

My great-aunt sighed, much as I had learned to sigh when dealing with Douglas, and that was the end of our conversation. When we rose, Amabel Sutton remained at the table.

The three of us, Laurel, Douglas, and myself, went out through the great hall and were joined at once by the two seamstresses, who had been fed in the kitchens.

Mistress Cardwell carried the heavy bundle of cloth through the house and up the many dim stairs. I felt sorry for her but could not help her. Laurel Killingtree would never permit it.

Campion Towers was not pleasant even by daylight. The wood-paneled passages were dark and musty. They seemed endless, branching off to the left or the right into the dim distance. No matter how long I lived here, I was certain I would never be able to find my way alone through the tangle of stairs and passages. Yet, I must try tonight, having failed twice before.

Mistress Cardwell, panting under the weight of the bundle, plodded behind me as we entered the tower room where my grandmother lay.

Mistress Turtledove and Mistress Cardwell curtsied nearly to the ground before Sir Nicholas who only grunted at them and motioned to them to open the bundle.

My grandmother sat up in bed, her cheeks flushed with

excitement or perhaps with fever. She crooked a finger at me. "Penelope, dear, come sit on the bed. I hear you went riding one of our red horses to see your farm."

She patted my hand. "Your farm is beautiful. I knew you would fancy it. I loved it when I was young."

I glanced at my grandfather quickly and his eyes met mine. He nodded. I understood him. Philippa, the invalid, had never been told what had been done to her house during the Civil War.

"Yes, it is beautiful," I said. I saw Sir Nicholas relax. For a moment I had thought he was going to smile at me.

Philippa cried out in pleasure when Mistress Turtledove unrolled a length of shimmering blue-green satin with a flourish.

"From the best draper's shop in London," the tall seamstress announced proudly. "I have stuffs here even finer—fit for a queen, I would say."

I heard Douglas catch her breath as cloth after cloth followed, to be thrown loosely over the chairs and the foot of the great bed—purple brocade with a gold thread, red satin, pearl-colored velvet, soft coral silk, a misty willow-green silk that made me yearn, pewter satin, a deep red velvet the very hue of Cranberry's hide, and finally a yellow as fresh as new churned butter.

"I do not need more than one gown," I protested to my grandmother.

Sir Nicholas heard me. "Nonsense!" he snapped. "She needs at least four, Philippa."

Philippa gave in with a smile. I guessed that she had spent her lifetime giving in to her blustering husband but I was amused to learn how easily she dealt with him. "Very well, Nicholas, if you say so," she granted in her soft breathless voice. "But do let Penelope choose what she wishes. She is to wear the gowns."

"No," he bellowed. "She shall not choose. What you say is

true. She shall wear them but *I* must see them. She would opt Roundhead linsey-woolsey if I gave her free rein."

"Let her choose *one* of them." My grandmother cajoled him. She winked at me. "I know what we shall do, Nicholas. I shall choose first, Laurel will choose second, and then you will make your choice. Penelope may pick the last one."

Sir Nicholas looked black but gave in. He settled himself in his chair by his wife's bed. "Let it be the red—damme, the red," he said roughly. "Well, what about you, Laurel?" He shot a savage glance at his sister who stood beside him.

My great-aunt was not to be intimidated by her brother. She fingered the coral silk and pursed her lips. "It is of good quality. I will have no trumpery goods. I fancy this for Penelope."

Philippa laughed. Her laughter was like a girl's. "You two chose out of turn. I was to be first, remember—but no matter. I still have my choice—the willow-green. It is what I would have worn when I was Penelope's age."

I was grateful. I fancied the green most, too. But how had my grandmother known? We must be much alike.

"Now, girl. It is your turn. Do your worst!" Sir Nicholas scolded.

I tore my eyes from the yellow and the blue-green satin. They were beautiful and shimmered enticingly, but they were not for me. I slid down from the great bed and went to where the cloth lay draped at its foot. All were mouth-watering. I touched the pearl-colored velvet and then the pewter satin. I pointed to the pewter. "This one," I said.

"An excellent choice," Mistress Turtledove agreed. She took meek little Mistress Cardwell by the arm and spun her briskly about, pulling rudely at her skirts. "The satin is of better quality than this silk, of course, but see how well it makes up and catches the light."

My grandfather was angered by my choice. He snorted. "Exactly what I guessed a Roundhead would choose. Laurel, this is your fault. Why did you let these women bring such drab colors?"

"They are fashionable, Nicholas," Laurel said, while I grinned at Douglas, who stuck out her tongue at me. Douglas did not want any pewter gown either.

This sober gown could go back to the colonies with me. Perhaps someday I would travel to Boston in Massachusetts Bay Colony and in that city even a Puritan could possibly wear a fine gown and not be considered wicked and vain. I thought of what Douglas had told me about General Cromwell's wife.

I paused for a long time before the cranberry-red velvet. It was as soft as it appeared. "It is just the color of Cranberry," I said aloud.

"What is that you say?" Sir Nicholas asked.

"The color of the red mare I rode today."

"You liked her?" he asked. He sounded pleased.

"Yes."

"And you want a gown to match my red horse, is that it?"

I did not reply but he had guessed my thoughts.

"Well, you shall have it!" he said with a bark of a laugh. "Ye'll make quite a show on the mare dressed in a costume of that stuff." Douglas sniffed loudly until he turned his head to look at her. "Pretty flirt-gill—little beggar," he muttered. "Very well, two riding costumes out of that dark red stuff."

With this, the choosing was at an end and we left, Mistress Cardwell folding and taking up the bundle.

I curtsied to my grandfather. "Thank you, sir," I said and

then because I felt she would like it, I kissed my grandmother on the cheek. "I am glad you are improved," I told her. "Will your physician come back?"

She made a little face. "He has only ridden to Worcester to the apothecary for more cordials. He shall be back by dusk to bleed me again. He thinks that powder with pearls or oil of St. John's wort could help me now." She held my hand briefly once more, her fingers frail in mine. "Come see me tomorrow. You are the best cordial I know."

"Thank you for the green gown," I whispered to her.

"I knew you wanted the green. It was in your eyes. Green is the color of sadness though. Goodbye, my dear. Don't permit your cousin to get all of your gowns away from you. She is a remarkable wheedler."

"I promise." Privately I made up my mind that the willow green would go back to the colonies with me, too. I cared nothing for the Aylmer jewels but the green silk was a true remembrance of my grandmother—so gentle and generous that I could scarcely bear to think of her as a Papist.

Next we trooped along to Mistress Laurel's chamber, a room in the right wing of the house, somewhat larger and with better light than my cousin's. My great-aunt's room was red and gold. Her bed and its hangings were of deep yellow linen worked with red wool. An embroidery frame stood next to her fireplace and on it was stretched a half-finished piece of fine crewelwork, ornate with birds and flowers. My kinswoman was a master of the art of embroidery.

Mistress Turtledove opened a smallish packet wrapped in brown cloth. She had carried this with her while her helper staggered under the weight of the bundle. Now she took out three little toy babies dressed in tiny silk gowns of gay colors.

These she set on Laurel's table. "Here are my poppets," she announced, pride evident in her voice. "They arrived not three days past from London. They are the latest mode from Paris."

Douglas took one up and looked at it critically. "I favor this one," she said.

"Penelope and I will choose, Douglas!" Laurel's tone was sharp. "You have gowns enough for three ladies of fashion. Remember, Douglas, that you live in Worcestershire—not in London. We hold no court for great folk here."

Douglas scowled and flounced over to sit on Laurel's high bed. Now I looked at the poppets, too. The laces and ribbons were garish. The bodices were cut much too low and showed overmuch of the shoulder.

"You choose for me, please," I asked Mistress Killingtree.

My great-aunt looked at each poppet in turn. She pointed to the second. "This will do well enough for the green and the pewter. The third doll will be suitable for the red and the coral. The other poppet will not do at all, mistress. We are not court folk here at Campion Towers. The gown is disgracefully revealing. Furthermore, no one could possible breathe in that bodice."

Mistress Turtledove compressed her lips. It was easy to see which was her favorite.

Laurel went on, paying no heed to her. "You will take the measures of my great-niece now. Then Peter will take you back to Worcester. We shall expect you to bring all the gowns for a fitting a week from today."

The tall seamstress nodded. She snapped her fingers at her assistant. "You will take the girl's measure, Mistress Cardwell, while I wrap the poppets away." She looked at me and shook her head. "We cannot measure you, Mistress Hervey, in a riding costume. Your petticoats are preferable."

"I have only two petticoats now," I said.

"They will be enough." Mistress Turtledove was satisfied.

I removed Douglas' hat, coat, skirt, and white shirt to stand in my smock and linen petticoats. The room was cold and I shivered.

Mistress Cardwell came to me with some lengths of string. The woman's face was quite hideous as the light fell upon it. Smallpox had struck heavily at her. Great pits marked her cheeks, chin, and forehead. I knew that no amount of white paint could cover pock marks. How I dreaded the smallpox! If it did not kill, it scarred. Few indeed escaped its ravages.

The little seamstress deftly wound strings about my chest and waist and snipped them off at the proper length with a pair of silver scissors hanging from a black ribbon at her waist. Then she measured across my shoulders and finally the woman faced me, winding the string about my upper arm to get the proper fit for the fashionable tight sleeves.

Her fingers were cold. She looked into my face, the string held in her hand. Her eyes were a flint gray and her voice a whisper as she spoke to me, her lips scarcely moving. "Penitence Hervey of Salem Town in Massachusetts Bay Colony?" she asked so low that only I could hear her.

I nodded, too surprised to speak.

"Where did you come to port, mistress?"

"Bristol," I said as softly as she.

"Aye, and your captain's name was Enderby?"

I nodded again.

"You were two days at the Turk's Head in that city?"

"Yes."

"A person came to you there? What was his name?"

I hesitated.

"His name was Moonjean, was it not?" she whispered.

Once more I nodded.

"I'm bidden to tell you that the text is *St. Matthew*, 21:38."

And with these words Mistress Cardwell gave me a long silent look and let the string fall. "It is done, Mistress Turtledove. We can begin now."

The Text

My heart pounded while Dr. Moonjean's agent carefully gave the measuring strings to Mistress Turtledove. I dressed, my face averted from the others so I would not betray my excitement. Now I was truly a soldier in the godly cause. I was to be of purpose.

Douglas and I went to our wing of Campion Towers. I said that I was tired and, given the events of the day, I was. I really wished the privacy of my room to think. Since it was impossible to think in Douglas' company, I was happy to close her door behind me.

I went slowly to my chamber. This was the first time I had been alone at Campion Towers and free to roam. There was nothing for me to see in the gloomy silent passage, which was lit by only a few tall thin windows. The walls were wood-paneled and the wooden floors were much stained, scarred, and neglected. I would not explore the great house now even if I had had the inclination. Surely there would be servants about and

I must not be suspected by anyone. Mistress Cardwell's very careful and secret manner had confirmed that.

I did not count the doors opening off each side of the passageway. I knew my cousin's room and I knew mine. I marked out my present chamber and the poor room I had been locked in the first night. The other chambers—and there must have been fully a dozen of them—were unoccupied. This Douglas had told me yesterday.

I went inside my own chamber and sat down. Mistress Cardwell had done nothing more than identify herself to me. Yet she, too, was surely a Puritan. She had not said that I would hear from her again. I was to wait, I supposed, until she returned with my gowns for a fitting. Or perhaps she would send a message by someone else. I would surely know Amyas Moonjean's agents by the text she had given me, *St. Matthew*, 21:38. There was nothing for me to do but wait, keep watch, and gather what information I could regarding what went on at Campion Towers.

I went to sleep and dreamed of red flowers, acre upon acre of red campion, stretching on all sides of Cranberry and me as we rode along a narrow white path that climbed steadily until the mare whistled for breath and I gasped as fleecy gray clouds, cold as death, floated past us.

I awoke slowly. It was dusk now. I tossed the old ragged coverlet from me, got up, and stretched. It would soon be time for me to go to supper with Sir Nicholas and the others. I struck a spark from flint and tinder and lit my two candles in their painted china holders. For a long moment I debated with myself. Should I wear Douglas' gown again or one of those I had brought with me? I decided to wear the oyster-colored silk at supper. Why argue with my grandfather? I smiled as I dressed my hair in long ringlets as I had seen Douglas do, winding them over my fingers. I had no mirror but I could tell by the touch that they were sleek enough to satisfy.

I hung Douglas' riding costume on a peg in my small clothespress. This I supposed I would wear the next day. I had the oyster gown halfway over my head, my face hidden in its soft folds, when suddenly I thought again of the number of the text Mistress Cardwell had whispered to me.

Pastor Wrenn had often spoken kindly to me about my knowledge of the New Testament, although like most Puritans, I knew the Old Testament better. I had many verses by heart and had often taken much comfort from them, but this particular verse from *St. Matthew* was strange to me. I wanted to know what it said—not that it mattered overmuch. The text, itself, was enough to let me know who else served Amyas Moonjean, Oliver Cromwell, the cause of Parliament, and my faith. But I was curious.

Tomorrow I would ride to Holt Heath. If I asked my grandfather to let me ride Cranberry again, he would not refuse me. There would be no Bible at Campion Towers—Latin missals and breviaries perhaps, but at All Hallows Church I should find a Bible. Even if it only pretended to be an Anglican church, All Hallows would possess a Bible to keep up the pretense.

That would give me something to occupy my time tomorrow. And tonight I would explore!

As I reached these decisions, my door opened and Douglas popped inside. "Are you ready, Pen?" she asked. "It is time to go to supper."

She came inside. Her gown tonight was rose-colored satin—

the exact shade of the outer petals of a newly opened briar rose. It gleamed in the light of her candles. My cousin's white skin shone and her eyes were now so dark that if I had not known they were blue I should have sworn they were black. She wore a brooch of deep red stones.

"Are they rubies, Douglas?" I asked.

"What, these?" my cousin's hand went to the brooch to finger it while she made a face of distaste. "La, no, Pen. They are only garnets. Garnets are not fine. I only wear the paltry things because they set off the whiteness of my face. There is nothing like garnets to do that, you know. Mother has my rubies. She fancies them and says they are too old for me yet."

"They are your rubies?" I asked, a little surprised.

"A gift from Sir Nicholas. He never minds if my mother wears them sometimes. I asked him."

I was silent while Douglas prattled on. "You will have some very fine gowns, Pen. Which will you take home with you when you return to Salem Town?"

I knew very well what my cousin was after. I was tempted to say that I would never return to Salem or that I would take all of them with me, but I had not been taught to lie easily.

"You shall fall heir to the red and the coral. This is my promise."

Douglas smiled. Her dimples were very pretty. She had never favored me with this smile before, but now that I had given her something I received dimples in place of gratitude.

"I did not fancy the willow green or the pewter. You must have guessed what I would want, Pen."

"I guessed," I said wearily, and got up to blow out my candles and follow her to supper. I was hungry.

This time we found Sir Nicholas waiting, too, in the great hall.

He sat beside the fire, his foot propped on a tapestry-covered stool. He lifted his cane in a pleasant manner when he saw us and called out, "Ah, here they are now—as pretty as two roses."

I had never been called pretty before and I blushed. It was vanity, I knew, but it warmed me.

Laurel, however, was not pleased with his words. She sat across from her brother and spoke coldly to him. Did they always quarrel? "Do not put foolish notions into Penelope's young head, too, Nicholas. Where Douglas is concerned, it does not matter. You ruined her nature beyond remedy long ago. You have shown the Suttons charity, but you have made the child pay a fearful price for it."

I gasped at my kinswoman's harshness but Douglas did not even flinch. She paid no attention to Laurel, but hurried over to my grandfather and kissed him on the cheek. He moved his foot for her to seat herself on his stool, her skirts a pink bell about her silvery shoes.

There was no chair for me so I stood, uncertain what to do. My great-aunt took notice of my hesitation. "We do not wait on Mistress Sutton tonight, Penelope. She will not be with us." She got up, eying Douglas sternly. "Enough of this foolishness, girl."

Laurel, I suspected, did not want Douglas to beguile away everything. No wonder she had written me at my grandmother's bidding.

We went into supper, a fine supper of roast pork with mint sauce, curd cheese cakes and seed loaf. To my pleasure we had asparagus again.

Sir Nicholas talked mostly to Douglas, who was more charming than I had ever seen her. I felt that Douglas was beginning to suspect me as a threat to her place at Campion Towers. When she made Sir Nicholas laugh, she glanced at me triumphantly. I thought as I ate. Sir Nicholas must be the key. He had praised me too. But Douglas had never become accustomed to sharing. I had no true friends at Campion Towers.

I put down my knife and sighed. I must have sighed loudly for my grandfather suddenly turned his attention to me. "What ails ye, girl?"

"Nothing, sir," I replied.

"Are you ill? Do you need a physick or a cordial? The doctor is returned."

"No, I am not ill."

"Do you yearn for your home, then?" he shot at me, his eyes hard on my face as if he sought something in me.

It came over me with a rush that I did. I missed Salem Town, my father and my half brothers and sisters and Amity Wrenn. I wished myself there—even in Elizabeth's house. I was a stranger in England.

I owed my grandfather a reply. "Yes," I said.

"I know what cures that illness. Jerkum! Bring the jerkum, lad," and Sir Nicholas snapped his fingers at old Jonas, who came in with the tray and little glasses. Then my grandfather proposed the same health to my grandmother as the night before.

I pretended to drain my glass but secretly I left a bit of the stickish plum wine. It made me too giddy. Still and all, my head swam again—but not so badly as before. I was happy though to go to my bedchamber after supper, light my candles, and lock the door.

I would wait. I opened a book I had borrowed from Douglas and tried to read. But the words blurred. In a moment the book fell from my fingers and slipped to the floor.

I slept for a time and when I awoke I was surprised to see how low my candles burned. I must have slept for hours. My journey had been a long one and I was still weary but I had not slept so heavily at Bristol or Gloucester. Oddly, my head ached once more. It must be the jerkum. I looked out my window. It was still inky dark but dawn could not be far off. The shortness of my candles told me that. If I was to explore, now was the moment.

Catching up my candle holder, I unlocked my door. I hoped I would not need the candle long. Candle glow was a danger. If I was fortunate I might have a few moments of dawn light. I should be close to invisible in my oyster-colored gown. Quietly I stepped into the passage, shutting my door noiselessly behind me. Then I put my hand around the candle flame.

It was black in the airless passage, so black that I could have been at the bottom of a well. And then I heard it—a door shutting with a soft sound.

Who was it? My cousin Douglas? I blew out my candle with one silent puff.

Now I saw the light of another candle coming toward me from the last door at the end of the passage, the door opposite my cousin's. Whoever it was, it was not Douglas. The progress of the light was swift. Fear clutched at me. I had not a moment to lose.

I opened my door again and slid inside. The passage was not so wide that I could hope to remain in it unseen. Who else walked about Campion Towers at night? And for what reason? Afraid, I blew out the candle in my chamber.

I held my door open a crack and watched, my eyes close to the slit. Whoever it was must pass by me if he was to leave this wing of the house.

The yellow glow was close by now and, as I held my breath, my heart beating so fast that I felt I smothered, I watched Amabel Sutton pass rapidly, her footsteps barely audible. Her face was oddly disturbed. She seemed deeply concerned as she strode by my door, the black skirts of her riding costume sweeping the floor. She muttered in a worried manner to herself, "The first of September is it then? So soon. So soon to be ready!"

I waited until her footsteps died away and the blackness returned to the corridor. Then I relit my candles and peered out again. Mistress Sutton was gone but I could see where she had passed. Her trailing skirts had swept the dirty floor clean. On each side of her path there was a dark line. Her skirts were wet. I closed my door and locked it. I had no wish to encounter Mistress Sutton and be forced to make some explanation to her.

I went instead to my window. The rose-pale sky showed me that it was a new day. Now I had something to tell Mistress Cardwell. Something was to happen the first of September—something important, judging from the look on Mistress Sutton's usually masklike face. What could it be? It was now mid-August. Whatever it was, it was to come soon—very soon.

My window was not tight. A cold wind came from it, making me shiver as a new thought struck me. What was Mistress Sutton doing in this wing of the house? I suspected her chamber was in the other wing. Yet I *had* seen her here and I *knew* that she had come from the chamber opposite her daughter's. If she had come from Douglas, it would all have made sense. Perhaps Douglas had been taken ill, but I doubted that. I went over what I had seen: yes, Amabel Sutton had closed a door behind her and it *was* the door across from her daughter's. Before she came down this passage she had been out of doors or somewhere near water.

It was all very mysterious and somehow frightening. Who was in that room? How long had someone been there? This was something Dr. Moonjean would wish to know—but how was I to find out? Whatever, I was not about to rap on that last door. I would not have been surprised if the black devil, himself, answered my knock.

I did not go back to sleep. Instead I changed into Douglas' riding costume, reviewing my devise. I would go to Holt Heath to find a Bible. It was up to Mistress Cardwell now. I hoped she would send word to me soon. I had nothing to do but wait and, if possible, avoid the company of most of those who lived at Campion Towers.

There was no clock in my rudely furnished room, although I had seen fine clocks from France and Italy in other chambers. When I thought the time had come, I unlocked the door. I passed by one of the little maids in the passage. She dropped me a hasty curtsy and hurried on down to my cousin's bedchamber, her drab skirts fluttering. Why should a maid be here? I went to Douglas' chamber, noticing that the door was ajar. My cousin sat among the pillows in her bedgown, a fine garment of linen and lace. Her face was sullen.

She glanced at me. "I have a headache, Pen," she complained in a whine. She motioned to me. "Tell the cookmaid to bring me a cloth soaked in vinegar and I want a glass of wine, too. You must do without me today." Douglas turned her head to glare at the little maid. "You there. You plump up my pillows and do not take all day about it. Then you can rub my temples the way I like. Do not, any of you, speak to the physician about my headache. I will not be bled again. It hurts! If Mistress

Killingtree hears that I am abed she will send him here at once."
My cousin shot a venomous glance at me. "Close the door, Pen.
I am cold!"

I did as she asked, very pleased that this gave me the day to
myself. I tiptoed softly across the passage and put my ear to
the opposite door but I could hear nothing inside. I wished I had
the courage to stoop and peer through the large keyhole. I could
spy light.through it without stooping. But I dared not turn the
door handle.

I found my way, after only one false turning, to the steps
that led to the great hall. I crossed it and entered the smaller
room where we dined.

Sir Nicholas was at the table alone. His eyebrows rose at the
sight of me. He had not expected me so early. "Jonas," he
called out. "Ale, bread and cheese and hot porridge for Mistress
Penelope."

I sat down across from him. "May I ride Berry again?" I
asked him.

He liked my question. "Indeed, you may. I only wish I could
squire such a maid about."

Privately I felt a bit of triumph over Douglas but I remembered her message and spoke to old Jonas. "My cousin Douglas
has a headache. She wishes a vinegar cloth brought to her," I
told him. "She also wants a glass of wine," I added.

The old servant nodded and hobbled out to the kitchens.

"Headaches," grumbled Sir Nicholas. "I suppose you are
afflicted with them, too. Never knew a wench who was not!"

"No," I said. "I never had time for them, sir."

"And you do not like jewels?" he said almost approvingly.
"There is not much frippery in you, is there, girl?"

"No, I guess not, sir."

He leaned forward to peer at me. "Is it because you are a Roundhead, do you suppose?"

"No. I do not think so." I thought of my grandparents and great-aunt and then for some reason of the man who called himself "James Rowland." In some strange way he was like them. There was little foolishness in these people. "I do not think there is much frippery in you either, sir, and you are a Cavalier."

"Well said," he grunted, biting into a piece of yellow cheese while wagging a porridge spoon at me.

I grew bold. "I have noticed your foot, sir," I told him. "Is it gout?" Captain Enderby had once had gout and had his foot bandaged in the same manner.

Sir Nicholas exploded at my question. "Gout, be damned to it! What do ye take me for—a wine-bibber or a gluttonous fool? No, it was a horse that did this to me. Before that it was arthritis that crippled me so cruelly I could never fight for the old King in 1641. What else would ye like to know?"

His bluster did not frighten me much by now. "Was the horse Russet?" I asked quietly.

He seemed very surprised at this. He pulled at his little beard. "Aye, so it was. The mare stepped on my foot. Happened some time past. My foot was crushed. The doctor says the bones may never knit. I am too old."

"Was Mistress Sutton riding Russet?"

"Aye. We were in the stables. I was about to mount Rufus when Russet reared and came down onto my foot with one hoof."

I looked into my grandfather's thoughtful eyes. I would tell him, not Laurel. "Russet kicked Berry yesterday. You saw me fall, sir. Did you see Mistress Sutton put Russet to a gallop and leap the hedge a moment after? Did you see Cranberry run away with me? I had only ridden a horse twice before."

"The devil you say!" He was truly astonished.

"Sink me, sir, the devil I do say!" I was stunned at my speech. I had spoken like a Cavalier. I put my hand to my mouth but I could not recall the words.

Sir Nicholas had not even noticed. The words must have seemed natural to him. "And ye'd ride Berry again?"

I had finished eating, so I got up, curtsied to Sir Nicholas and said softly, "Yes, sir. Will Garth saddle her for me? I do not know how to go about it."

"Yes, of course. 'Tis what Garth is for. But will ye be safe, do ye think?"

"I believe so, but I do ask a thing of you, sir."

"Ask it then."

"I have no wish to ride with the Suttons again. I would rather ride alone."

"As ye choose—by daylight only. Go where ye will, except to the Aylmer farm. There are vagabonds about. I was not pleased to learn you and Douglas had been there alone. Where do ye ride today, Penelope?"

"To church," I told him.

He looked puzzled. "There is no Roundhead congregation closer than Worcester. Do you wish to go there? If so, I forbid it. It is too far."

"No," I said. "I shall go to Holt Heath."

He was still puzzled but he did not press me. "Take care with Berry or Cranberry—whatever it is you choose to call her."

"I will not harm the mare," I promised.

"Take care she does not harm you! I have Philippa to answer to. I cannot tell her of yesterday's runaway or of the other things you said." There was a mocking glint in my grandfather's eye.

I curtsied once more. "Do not fret yourself, sir. I will do or say nothing to harm my grandmother. The horse and I will get along now. She is my 'beauty,' too. I have told her so."

"Who told you the secret of the red horses? Garth? I shall wager Garth did. He babbles. So, ye know?"

"If I told you how I learned, sir," I said, smiling, "I doubt if you would believe it."

Now his eyes were merry. "I might believe it at that, Pen, my girl. Little goes on about here that does not come to my ears sooner or later."

I smiled to myself as I left the room—he had called me "Pen"!

What would my grandfather think if he knew of my conversation with Amyas Moonjean in Bristol or with Mistress Cardwell yesterday in his own house? No, Sir Nicholas Killingtree did not know everything.

Garth saddled and bridled Cranberry and brought her to me. To my joy the red horse knew me. She neighed and rubbed her velvet nose on my arm, asking for loaf sugar, but I had none. I caressed her in its place.

"I promise you two lumps tomorrow, beauty," I told her.

The stableboy helped me mount and Cranberry and I rode off at a trot. Once we were out of sight of the great house I put Cranberry into a gentle hand gallop. She behaved beautifully. I dared believe that my troubles with the red mare were over and I thanked James Rowland silently.

Holt Heath was only moments away. I rode up to All Hallows Church and dismounted at a nearby block of stone.

Master Meredith, a tall old man with mournful dark eyes and thin gray hair, who was dressed in a sober black coat, came to the cottage gate to peer over it at me.

"I am Penitence Hervey from Campion Towers," I told him. "Do you have a Bible here, sir?"

He seemed taken aback by my question. "I have a Bible, mistress." He looked at me as if to ask me something in return but then seemed to change his mind as he opened the gate.

I walked through the churchyard with him. The grounds about All Hallows were a tangle of roses, hollyhocks, trailing woodbine, and gray headstones. The damp English air was perfumed with the scent of many flowers but somehow the effect was melancholy rather than pleasant. I could not help but wonder if my Aylmer or Killingtree ancestors were buried near the church.

Master Meredith took me into the church and silently pointed to a group of figures carved in stone. He had almost seemed to know what I had thought. "The Killingtrees, mistress," he told me. "The first Killingtree to rest here was a Crusader. That is his effigy on the right. We know he went to the Holy Land because he has been depicted with his legs crossed. In 1191 he was knighted at Acre by King Richard the Lion Heart and given this land. Most of the Killingtrees are entombed here with their ladies. Some are buried beneath the church floor."

All Hallows Church was cool and gray in the morning light. I walked down its passages looking at the little effigies of my grandfather's family. Some lay along side passages. Others stood in niches. Many effigies were badly carved; others had been crudely painted, and the centuries had not been kindly to the colors. Even so, sometimes I believed I saw a face like that of Sir Nicholas or Laurel.

"Where are the Aylmers?" I asked.

"In the churchyard near the church door," he told me. It was as I had suspected. The Killingtrees had always been gentry, the Aylmers lesser gentry, but the Killingtrees were greater folk in Holt Heath even if in Queen Mary's time the Aylmers had reached for an earldom.

I glanced at the altar. The church was almost plain enough for Salem Town, although a rail was set up between the worshippers and the altar. I knew most Anglican churches had once been Roman Catholic. Papist masses had been sung at All Hallows. How many English churches were still Papist—in secret? Was All Hallows?

I felt as if the eyes of the long-dead Killingtrees were accusingly upon me as I set out on Amyas Moonjean's business.

"Where is the Bible, sir?"

"On the altar, Mistress."

There on a tall lectern lay a great black Bible. Master Meredith's voice was gentle. "May I help you, Penitence Hervey?"

"No," I said, "I came here only to find a text."

He nodded. "If you wish anything, please call me. I am working in my garden behind the cottage."

He turned to go but came back when I spoke his name. "Master Meredith, have you been here long?"

"For forty years, mistress."

"Did you know my mother, Nicola Killingtree?"

"Yes."

"What was she like?"

"Very like unto you, mistress. That is she looked like you but if you truly resemble her I do not know."

"Did you like her?"

He smiled. He had a sad, slow smile. "Yes, Mistress Hervey."

And then without waiting to hear the other questions that came to my tongue, he went away, his head bowed, his hands clasped behind his back.

I waited until he was out of sight, then opened the Bible, swiftly turned the many pages of the Old Testament until I had reached the first book of the New Testament, *St. Matthew.*

I found chapter 21 and ran my finger swiftly down the verses until I came to number 38.

I read it aloud: " ' But when the husbandmen saw the son, they said among themselves, This is the heir; come, let us kill him, and let us seize on his inheritance.' "

Once More, the Man from the Turk's Head

THE VERSE from *St. Matthew* baffled me. I pondered it as I rode back to Campion Towers at a steady trot. Cranberry was calm under me but her eyes followed every gay butterfly and each falling leaf. Who was the heir? Who were the husbandmen and what was the inheritance they were willing to kill for? Amyas Moonjean's text chilled me and filled me with fear.

An old crooked man with a heavy pack on his back trudged along the road ahead of me. I remembered what Sir Nicholas had said about vagabonds so I put Cranberry to a hand gallop. We would pass the stranger at the far side of the road and we would pass him swiftly.

Hearing Cranberry's hoofbeats, he turned, flinging up his hand. He was very, very old and very dirty. His hair hung in gray greasy locks under a battered velvet hat. His feet were wrapped in cloth, while his tattered coat fluttered in the August breeze.

"Mistress," he called out to me in a cringing whine, "will ye buy my pretty ribbons? If ye've no fancy today for ribbons, I've fine Flemish laces, too."

I shook my head. By now I was abreast of him and could see his thick-featured brown face and his flat dark eyes. He was nearly toothless. His voice was a cackle, "Buy a pretty, Mistress Hervey."

I had almost passed the peddler when I heard my name. Few people in Worcestershire knew me, but he knew! I rode ahead and turned Cranberry about to face the man. If he made a motion toward me, I could escape him easily.

"You know my name?" I asked him, eying him warily as he hobbled nearer.

"Aye, ye be Penitence Hervey, the maid from Campion Towers—the lass with the yellow locks. I've a message for ye—a text." He was closer now. His voice was softer and somehow different. "*St. Matthew,* mistress, a verse from *St. Matthew.*"

Now I was no longer afraid. I held the red horse quiet. As the peddler came up to us, he put his hand on the scarlet rein and Cranberry snorted. She did not like his sly face any more than I.

"What verse?" I demanded, looking into the old stranger's eyes.

"Chapter 21, verse 38, mistress." He whispered now, "A mile south of Holt Heath you will find a copse of elms. Be there at midday on the morrow. There is someone who wishes to speak privately with you."

"I shall be there," I promised. I tried to pull the rein from his hand. He was less ancient than I had thought. His grip was strong.

He clung to the rein even though Cranberry tossed her head, shaking her mane. Now he held up his free hand. In it lay a red ribbon—a ribbon the color of blood. "Take it, mistress. Who knows who lurks to see us? There are eyes everywhere. The ribbon will lull suspicion to sleep. Tie it in your hair. If it is rumored that you were seen speaking to a peddler on the highroad, say you bought a ribbon of the poor old man."

I took the red ribbon from him, nodded, and whirled Cranberry around as he released her rein. In an instant we were off toward Campion Towers.

Despite his soft and civil words, the man had frightened me. I hoped that Mistress Cardwell would meet me alone. I had no wish to see the peddler again.

Campion Towers soon loomed before me. I almost welcomed the sight.

I was alone for the remainder of the long day; I asked the servant for my midday food to be brought to my room. This time I truly read my borrowed book, for I had nothing else to do, but as evening came, I set it aside. I had been in England but a week. How far I had come, I thought, and how much had happened to me since I left Salem Town in June! It was now past middle August. It would soon be September. What was to happen the first of September? Perhaps Mistress Cardwell knew. I thought of what I would ask her and tell her, too, as I changed to Douglas' fine gown and dressed my hair.

As I left my room, I saw the little maid again, walking ahead of me down the passage. Was she put there to watch me—or did her presence have something to do with the third occupied chamber? Perhaps Douglas was still ailing? I called to the maid but she did not turn around.

I followed the servant to the great hall. I found Sir Nicholas, my great-aunt, and to my surprise Douglas already by the hearth. Douglas sat again at her crewelwork. She wore yet another gown, this one of pale yellow satin. My cousin gave me a cool glance and put her needle into the linen as if she would like to put it into me.

My grandfather hailed me. "Did ye see Master Meredith, Pen? Did ye find what ye wanted?"

I curtsied to him. "Yes, sir."

Douglas looked up sharply when he called me "Pen." She was not pleased with the friendliness he showed me. Now she jabbed her needle into the embroidery, cried out in pain, and popped her finger into her mouth as she eyed me accusingly.

"Have a care, Douglas. Do not be clumsy," Laurel warned her.

Douglas Sutton was not made any sweeter by the lack of sympathy. "Where is my mother?" she asked petulantly.

"She will not be with us tonight," Laurel replied in a matter-of-fact voice.

"What, again?" Douglas was piqued. "She never came to see me today at all when I was ill."

"She was not well herself. And you were not ill. I have had the experience of your headaches before this. They are the result of your nature when it is thwarted." Laurel spoke bluntly. "Your mother went to Worcester late last night to the apothecary to get a cordial for Philippa. Amabel was wearied today."

I seized upon this as Douglas pouted. But the physician had gone to Worcester to get a cordial and oil of St. John's wort for my grandmother! Why should Mistress Sutton go the same day? Surely Sir Nicholas would not send a woman alone at night to Worcester. Either Garth or Peter could easily have ridden to the apothecary. For some reason Laurel had lied to Douglas.

"Let us go to supper," Laurel said.

I walked in to supper with Douglas, who refused to look at me.

It was lonely at the big table. My grandfather and great-aunt were silent. Douglas was sullen. I would much rather have eaten in my room. I broke the silence at last. "Am I to see my grandmother tonight?"

"No." Sir Nicholas seemed depressed. "She is not well," he said. "The physician lets no one see her. The excitement yesterday was not good for her. The physician says that if he had been informed of what she had devised he would not have permitted the seamstresses into Philippa's tower."

"I am sorry," I said.

"It is not your fault. She wished to see the silks and satins from Worcester."

The meal continued in absolute quiet. I was pleased when Jonas brought the plum wine to mark the end of supper. I wanted to go to my chamber as soon as I could and learn who or what was in that room across from my cousin's. This time I drank less of the jerkum than ever before, for I had thought of a trick. I dropped a thick crust of bread into the glass, unnoticed. The bread sopped up a good deal of the wine—enough so my head scarcely swam at all.

Douglas and I climbed to our chambers without speaking. I pretended to yawn. Then I touched Douglas' arm. "Have I offended you in some way?" I asked her.

The yellow gown was a ghostly gold in the flickering thin candlelight. Her eyes were hard. "You want this house, too?" she flung at me.

"No, Douglas. I am content with what my grandmother has given me," I protested.

"I do not believe you."

"Douglas, what would I do with Campion Towers across the sea in Salem Town? I cannot take it with me in a trunk. For that matter, what shall I do with the Aylmer farm? I do not expect to stay in England."

My cousin twisted away from me, but her eyes held a question as well an accusation. "You make up to Sir Nicholas! Deny that if you can. My mother warned me."

"Why should I offend him? I think it is enough that my faith offends him. I do not wish to quarrel with my grandfather all of the time."

Douglas sniffed. She was not quite so certain now. "Well, we shall see," she said, and as I stood at the door of my room she put her nose into the air and flounced off.

Once inside my room I sat down to wait. When I knew my cousin had gone to sleep, I would steal out to learn what I could about the strange room. I sat waiting, trying to keep my eyes open. Thanks to the crust of bread I had put into the plum wine, the slight dizziness soon passed. Finally, I arose and took up my candle. If anyone saw me in the passage I would say I was looking for my cousin's chamber and was muddled with sleep. It was a bold devise. I put on my bed gown from Salem Town, a rough yellow linen homespun thing, and my nightcap, tying its strings under my chin. I had no slippers so I went barefoot.

I opened my door and walked down the empty passage quite as if I were sure of myself. The first thing I noted was that the air was less stale than usual. I sniffed at its fresh dampness as I hurried along my way.

To my amazement the door across from my cousin's was ajar. I shielded my candle with my hand to see better, but there was no gleam of light coming from the room. I rapped on the door, again part of my devise, and called out softly, "Douglas?"

There was no reply, so I pushed the door open wide enough

for me to enter and slid inside. Unlike other doors at Campion Towers, it did not creak. I held my candle high to look about me and then I sighed. The news I had hoped to have was no news after all. The last room in the left wing of the house was completely empty. There was little to report. There was a purple bed and one old purple chair. Other than that, the chamber was barren except for a ragged tapestry over one wall. The air seemed oddly cool and fresh—far better than the air of my chamber that made me so often drowsy. My candle flickered so badly that I was forced to guard it with my hand. Was the window open? I hurried across to it. No, it was not open. In fact it had been boarded up. The pure air must have been my imagination. The draft against my candle must come from the passage. Disappointed, I went from the room, careful to leave the door ajar as it had been.

I had seen no one. I went back to my own chamber and locked the door. The fact that the door to the purple room had been ajar must mean something. It had been closed that morning. Who had opened it? Could it blow open with the window boarded shut?

I climbed into my bed and sat for a time wondering if I should have seized my opportunity and searched further. But I had no notion what Dr. Moonjean wished to know. His agents in Worcestershire would have to tell me what to watch and look for. I worked alone—in the dark now. Why had Amyas Moonjean told me so little?

Now I truly yawned and in an instant I was asleep. My dreams were not happy. In the morning I told myself the hard truth. I was afraid of that empty room as I was afraid to meet Mistress Amabel Sutton face to face alone as I explored and spied. If she had not come to supper, perhaps she walked about the great house by candlelight at night. I felt certain she would like to put crooked pins in my bread and butter.

Shortly before midday Cranberry and I trotted through Holt Heath and at the appointed moment we were at the copse of elms the peddler had marked as the meeting place.

Mistress Cardwell, dressed in a long gray cloak despite the August warmth, came rapidly toward me out of the trees. I rode up to her as she beckoned. "Get down," the woman ordered. "Take that horse of yours into the elms. We want no watchers, mistress."

I did as she asked, somewhat surprised by her harsh, commanding manner. The droning of the bees in the wild flowers was the only sound to disturb the stillness of the quiet grove. I had not yet had time to look about me when I was startled by a man's soft voice.

"Penitence."

The tall, black-clad figure came forward to greet me. I dropped Cranberry's reins as I looked into the face of Dr. Amyas Moonjean. I curtsied.

"Ah, Mistress Hervey," he said, smiling, as he looked down at me from his great height. "We meet again. I am pleased to see you so soon. I had not quite expected it."

Mistress Cardwell did not give me a chance to speak in turn to Dr. Moonjean. "She lives in a sinful house," she said. She stood behind the tall man, her arms folded, her strangely colored eyes intent on me. "Look at the wench. Mark out her curls, her black velvet, and her fine green plume. Folly and vanity!"

I was angry. What right did she have to criticize me? And to think I had felt sorry for her because of the way Mistress Turtledove had treated her.

"If I am to watch for the cause I serve, Mistress Cardwell, it would not be wise of me to make Sir Nicholas Killingtree angry, would it? What I wear and how I dress my hair pleases him. He mislikes my cap and apron. You will remember that I chose but one gown—the pewter-colored one—one much like your own. Yours was of silk!"

Amyas Moonjean held up his hand. It was almost transparent. I had seen him before in a driving rainstorm and thought him pale, but in the light of day he seemed as fragile as the thistledown that drifted about us in the golden air of late summer. Yet I had detected a streak of iron in him before and I caught it again in his words to the seamstress, which delighted me. "Mistress Naomi, let me remind you that Penitence Hervey is also a soldier in our cause. Sir Nicholas is a difficult and choleric man I have heard. Penitence is wise to give in to him on lesser issues. Folly and Cavalier ways have not changed her heart, I am sure."

He took me gently by the arm and led me to a fallen tree. "Tell me, child, what you have learned." We sat side by side, Cranberry, cropping grass in a little glade not far away.

I began with Madame Gawdy's revealing herself a Catholic and finished with Mistress Sutton's nightly absences and her appearance from the unoccupied chamber. Dr. Moonjean's eyes never left mine. They saw to the bottom of my soul and I was glad that I held nothing back. Now and then he nodded, but he seemed most pleased when I spoke of my encounter on the hilltop with James Rowland. Once as I mentioned Rowland I heard him murmur, "Ah—returned so soon?" but he did not interrupt me. It was as if he spoke to himself. My poor recital had not been a long one. When I finished he closed his eyes and smiled. He had not been contemptuous as I had feared he might.

I glanced at Mistress Cardwell. Her look was sour and

disapproving. Dr. Moonjean spoke to her. "It is as we guessed, Mistress Naomi. The ribbon peddler will travel swiftly to the north now. He will bring you word in the usual way."

I was confused. "But what shall I do now, sir?"

"You are a clever child. You have done us a service, Penitence. Continue to watch—everything! I shall not come again. My work takes me elsewhere. Mistress Cardwell will send word to you."

"I do not understand all this," I said. "Will I bring danger to my grandmother Philippa? She is a Papist, I am sure, but she is old and very ill."

"She will come to no harm. No Roman Catholic at Campion Towers will come to harm because of you."

"I am to keep watch that no priests come?" I questioned him.

"Of course, Penitence. Watch for all strangers. Let us know of strangers who come."

"What does the text mean, Dr. Moonjean? I do not understand it."

"It is of no signification. 'Tis only a Bible verse which was chosen at random to identify those of us who serve General Cromwell."

I was nearly satisfied. I had had two of my most troublesome questions answered. Others remained. "What if I learn something? How will I get word to Mistress Cardwell?"

The woman herself replied. Her tone was biting. "You are not to approach me or seem to know me as other than a simple seamstress, Penitence Hervey. If you learn anything of great import, a message can be left for me at The Swan outside St. Martin's Gate in Worcester. The proprietress of the inn is my kinswoman. But do not go to her unless you feel you must."

Dr. Moonjean spoke to me. "Mistress Cardwell is correct,

Penitence. In this work of ours we remain apart as much as possible to avoid suspicion. You know me and Mistress Cardwell, and you have seen the ribbon peddler. You will know no one else. Every new-forged link in a long chain may weaken it."

The seamstress turned to Amyas Moonjean. "She must be told of the wine and of the other matter. Will you tell her, sir?"

"No," he said, "you are from Worcester. From now on you tell Penitence what she is to know. Her orders will be given by you. It is time for Mistress Hervey to return to the bosom of her family." He bowed slightly to me as I curtsied again. "Serve our Puritan cause, child. Do as you are bid and do not question further."

"I promise, Dr. Moonjean. I will serve our cause against the Spanish enemy and their allies, the English Papists."

He looked strangely at me for an instant, then I asked my last question. "What is to happen the first of September?"

"I do not know, Penitence, but I should like to know. If you can but learn this fine secret of Mistress Amabel Sutton's, General Cromwell, I am sure, would be forever grateful to you." As he spoke to me, I saw something that frightened me. The rising breeze had lifted Amyas Moonjean's long hair and I saw that his left ear had been cropped. He had truly suffered in the pillory for our cause! He caught my glance and smiled at me. Then he made a gesture of dismission.

Naomi Cardwell walked with me toward the red horse. She put her hand so heavily on my shoulder it was almost a blow.

"Hear me now! Exchange wineglasses with someone at supper tonight, Mistress Hervey. Laudanum has been put each night into your jerkum to make you sleep. Mistress Laurel Killingtree purchased it in Worcester the day after you came to her brother's house. One of the apothecary's lads reported it.

They give you jerkum because you could taste laudanum in anything but that heavy wine."

I gasped in surprise. My great-aunt did this to me? Papist poisoner! Sir Nicholas knew, too! Mistress Cardwell caught the anger rising in me.

"So, you are angry? Do not lose your head. You will have need of your wits. That chamber you speak of may well be meaningful. Somewhere in that house there is a secret passage, Mistress Hervey. This could be one of its entrances. Try to find the passage but take care. We know that the passage is in use. Mistress Sutton's appearance has told us that."

"So this is where they hid Edmund Campion—in a secret passage. It must be!" I cried out.

The woman seemed quite baffled for a moment. But then she nodded. "Ah, the priest so long ago? Yes, that is surely where they kept him. No one has ever found a way into the passage, although many have searched for it."

"If no one has ever found the passage at Campion Towers, how do you know there is one?" I asked her.

"In Queen Elizabeth's reign a carpenter found it by accident when he went to Campion Towers to repair a panel. He was killed a day later by a robber," the woman's pale lips twisted, "or so it is said, but before he died they say he spoke to his wife about a secret passage and a button. There have always been rumors about passages in Campion Towers."

"But how could I ever find it?"

"The carpenter's wife thought she knew. She kept her secret well, though. The guess is she feared the Killingtrees, and wisely so. She told this to my grandmother, her kinswoman, and my grandmother told me. If her story be true, there is a button in the paneling in a certain chamber. We do not know how the button works or how it is identified. It could be one of many similar buttons. The Parliamentarian soldiers could not find the passage when they sacked the house, although I told them what I knew. Now, Mistress Hervey, it is urgent that we find it. Dr. Moonjean does not come from London unless a thing is urgent."

I was silent. The secret passage frightened me. How could I find it at Campion Towers when no one else had ever found it—no one except the unfortunate carpenter? I repeated my question. "But how shall *I* find it?"

Her face was fierce. "You know more than any other seeker has ever known. *You* know the room in which to begin to search. We have reason to suspect that people will come to Campion Towers tonight—important folk. They call themselves 'The Twelve.' You have heard of them, too, for I heard you speak just now. We wish to know what you can learn for us about 'The Twelve.' You must find that secret passage tonight and enter it, Mistress Hervey."

The Twelve

THE LITTLE seamstress was not quite finished with me. Clearly she saw how little I relished the thought of the secret passage and I felt that she enjoyed my fear. I did not understand why she misliked me until I heard her words. "Rely on your pretty face, Mistress Hervey, if you find danger. You are fortunate that Sir Nicholas Killingtree had his dogs shot."

"Dogs?" I asked, swallowing my anger. Somehow I knew how Mistress Cardwell, scarred cruelly by smallpox, felt about my still-smooth face.

"Aye, he kept a pack of hounds for the hunt and house dogs, too—three mastiffs. They were trained to leap for the face and the throat."

"But why did he get rid of them?"

"If you cannot guess, I shall not tell you," and she walked swiftly away from me to rejoin Dr. Moonjean, who was at once in deep conversation with her.

I whistled very badly to Cranberry, but still the horse trotted to me. I mounted her and rode off. The man and the woman took no notice of my departure. I saw them walk through the grove together, and through the trees where a plain coach waited. I knew, then, that they had come secretly, for the coach was not Dr. Moonjean's fine one I remembered from Bristol.

I was alone and I was afraid. Only my gathering hatred toward my great-aunt kept my spirits up. Anger was a strong physick in itself.

I walked my horse slowly over the mile north to Holt Heath. I hated the thought of returning to Campion Towers. Only the knowledge that I aided Oliver Cromwell forced me back to that house of evil and cruelty. I could not pass over Amabel Sutton's attempt to have me killed or my great-aunt's putting laudanum in my wine.

Suddenly I knew what Mistress Cardwell had meant about the dogs. Laurel drugged me to keep me mewed up in my bedchamber because people came at night—surely dogs would have set up an alarm that would call attention to strange doings at Campion Towers. The wise thing would be to get rid of the dogs.

I passed the village at a faster pace but not before I spied Russet once more before the miller's house. I had no wish to fall in with Mistress Sutton so I urged Cranberry into a hand gallop.

My heart sank as I saw the gray foreboding pile of Campion Towers ahead of me. Its very stones were soaked in the blood of Protestant martyrs. Now that I had been told it contained secret passages within its walls I found it even more sinister and threatening.

I rode to the stables where Garth came running to catch Cranberry's bridle and help me dismount. He volunteered news, his brown face split by a wide grin. "The master rides out today, Mistress Hervey. He has a special stirrup now."

So Rufus, the red stallion, was gone, too? What errand would take Sir Nicholas away?

"What of the other horses?" I asked. "Is Pippin gone? What does Mistress Laurel ride?"

He shook his head. "Pippin is in her stall. Mistress Killingtree does not ride. She had a bad fall years past. She rides only in the coach. It has been called for today. They want ye at the house, Mistress Hervey. Jonas brought a message."

He let Cranberry go, slapping her on the flank. I gasped in anger. The groom had hit my horse!

Garth's grin was impish. "She likes it, mistress. Let the Berry go. She finds her stall."

Message or no message from Campion Towers, I stood watching Cranberry, who moved calmly, her reins trailing, toward her stall—the next to the last. She stopped for a moment to rub velvet noses with little Pimpernel and with her other friend, Pippin. Then she stopped at the open door of her stall. The red mare paused for a long moment and then, as Garth and I watched —Garth proud to show me how well she knew the stables—Cranberry ambled along to the last stall, the closed one. She put her nose to the half door and snuffled. Then she did a remarkable thing. The red horse lifted her right front leg and struck it against the wood hard, again and again.

I flew toward her. "She will harm herself." Garth ran behind me. I reached the stall first and caught at the mare's bridle. "No, Cranberry, this is not your stall," I cried out and tried to pull her away.

The horse would not budge. Garth's face was pale now as he moved between me and the stall. He pushed and I pulled. Cranberry snorted and moved in a circle, forcing me once again by the stall. There was a loose plank in the door and out of the corner of my eye I caught a flash of movement and saw a satiny red-purple hide. I heard sounds, too, of a horse moving about, agitated by Cranberry's wild behavior. I knew who the red horse was, for I remembered that the last stall belonged to the best of the red horses. Will Scarlet had come back to Campion Towers!

At last we quieted Cranberry and got her into her stall, bridle and saddle still on her. She turned to kick once more at the partition between her stall and the last one.

Garth was worried. "I cannot go in there now," he told me. " 'Tis not safe. She would kick me, she would."

"What horse is in there, Garth?" I pointed to the last stall. He lied. "One of the sorrel coach horses, mistress. The gelding is spavined. I've sent to the smith at the Heath. He could know what to do."

I let it pass. The horse had been no sorrel!

"Look after Cranberry well," I told him and left the stables, walking slowly, wondering. I caught up my black skirts to keep them from the drying mud.

My cousin Douglas met me at the huge door, opening one side of it to greet me. Her cheeks were rosy with pleasure, her eyes dancing. She wore a light traveling cloak of dark blue wool over yet another dress—this time of blue and silver brocade. "Pen, where have you been?" she cried. "We wait for you."

I went into the large echoing room as she stepped aside gracefully. "I have been riding south of Holt Heath," I told her, giving her the proper direction in case anyone had spied upon me or would bring news of my actions to the Killingtrees.

"Well, no matter," she commented. "You are here now. We go to Worcester—to the harvest fair. It will be very fine. Have you ever been to a fair?"

I had not. I was about to ask her something but she babbled on. "Go, don your oyster gown, Pen. Hurry, hurry! Mistress Killingtree will be here soon. She says she has business in Worcester. She sends us to the shoemaker. Hurry, before she changes her mind."

"Why do we go to Worcester?" I asked.

"To buy shoes, goose," Douglas chided. "Why else does one go anywhere unless it is to purchase something or to have a pleasant time?"

"I often went to the shoemaker to have my shoes made wearable for another year and I had no pleasant time," I said tartly as I crossed the room.

Douglas stuck out her lower lip. "We are not all sour starveling Roundheads, you know."

"Aye, that you are not." I started up the steps and was confronted on the first landing place by my great-aunt. I had nearly added that I found Cavaliers fat and huffed up with vanity but I was glad I had held my tongue. I thought of the laudanum the moment I saw Mistress Killingtree. I was hard put to keep my good temper and drop her a proper curtsy but I thought of my purpose and did so.

"Make haste, Penelope," she told me, "you have nearly missed the August fair."

I was not taken in. They were getting me away from the house more than likely—probably to prepare for "The Twelve," who were to arrive tonight. Perhaps we would enter the city by St. Martin's Gate and if my eyes were sharp, I might spy out The Swan Inn that Mistress Cardwell had mentioned.

I shifted to Douglas' gown and now I almost despised it for its gaudy green band at the neck. The shoes that matched it were equally obnoxious to me, yet I wore them and caught up the cloak I had brought from Salem Town. That, at least, was godly. I hastened back to the passage. I did not choose to make Mistress Laurel angry with me.

The fine coach was waiting and my great-aunt shooed Douglas and me out to it. Peter helped us up, and in a moment we were off, traveling the same road we had come that first night to Campion Towers. I was quiet. I glanced only briefly at the vale where Madame Gawdy and I had met the highwayman. In daylight it seemed innocent and peaceful, the red campion tall in its grass.

Douglas chattered away, while the coach creaked, and Laurel and I answered with the "yes" or "no" she seemed to find satisfying. The prospect of spending a golden angel or two at Worcester was so enticing to Douglas that she did not care if we listened to her or not.

I had a problem to ponder. How could I exchange glasses of jerkum with Douglas without being seen? It would have to be my cousin. She sat nearest me at the table and the others might suspect, from the swift giddiness that the laudanum produced, what I had done.

It would be difficult to change glasses. I would have to draw everyone's attention from me and from Douglas. How could I do this? How tempting to throw a pigeon pie into Mistress Sutton's sullen face or into my great-aunt's harsh one! Sinful or not, since I had been in Worcestershire, I yearned to throw things at people. I glanced at my great-aunt under my lashes. How straight and stiff she sat as we went along, the coach bouncing on its leather springs.

We saw Worcester far off in the south across the hop fields, the slender spires of its churches rising in the soft late August air. One spire was much taller than the others.

"That is St. Andrew's Church," Douglas told me.

I nodded, more interested than I would let her know.

"Two of Worcester's bishops were made saints—St. Oswald and St. Wolfstan," she added proudly.

We passed the old decrepit city walls, as old as King Alfred's time, Douglas said, and I stuck my head out to see better as we entered by St. Martin's Gate. I spied a great signboard with a strangely depicted white bird on it. I would not have known what the long-necked bird was if I had not been able to make out the time-weathered words above it: "The Swan." The old white-plastered half-timbered building with a sagging thatched roof, much like the Green Man Tavern of Holt Heath, was sheltered among tall feathery elms. It looked inviting but I shivered. I drew in my head. I knew where to find Mistress Cardwell now.

"Have you taken a chill, Penelope?" Laurel asked me.

"No, mistress," I said meekly.

"Night air is dangerous," she added, significantly. She knew all too well how very well I slept.

We went down New Street and then the coach's iron wheels rattled into Friar Street. Here Peter stopped and we got down. We were at the edge of the fair. The crowd was thick. Many were drunk. I could not describe the people—I thought of "rags and tags and velvet gowns." It did as well as any.

"The beer is free," Douglas whispered as a large woman pushed a small man down, laughing wildly.

I misliked the fair. We walked on, listening to the tabor, pipe, and fiddle. People danced in circles and sang—near the huge beer casks. Idlers and drunkards eyed Douglas and me and Douglas smiled. As for me, I frowned. Peddlers sought the three of us out. "Posies! Gloves! Garters! Ribbons! Fine laces from Venice!" I thought of the ribbon peddler and looked hard at the one who sold Douglas a half-dozen gay ribbons for her hair as Laurel waited impatiently.

The bear warden frightened me almost as much as his great brown dancing bear. He was a great hulk of a man with a brute's face and a tangle of hair. I walked behind my great-aunt. Even the bear warden and his bear moved away for her. We passed through the joyful crowd that came to Worcester's harvest fair and Douglas called to me over the din of the fiddlers that this was little compared with London's famed St. Bartholomew's Fair, which endured twice sennight.

A man on a platform, a knife in one hand, a pair of pincers in the other, bellowed to us, "Draw a tooth, mistress? Cut a boil or a corn? Swift and painless!" The crowd standing before him roared out teasingly and then set up a howl of approval when a little man with a bandage about his face stumbled up the steps and fell onto a stool.

"Come away," said my great-aunt and I went with her. Her face was a portrait of disapproval and I noticed how she hauled at Douglas who stood on tiptoe to see the tooth drawer perform his task.

Douglas was angry. She grew sullen now. She had no interest in the brisk young rope dancer who frolicked high above the crowd or the juggler who kept six gilded balls in the air.

Once we had made our way through the fair, Mistress Killingtree turned to face us. "I have business here," she said, pointing to a brick house with a carved wooden lintel. "Douglas, you and Penelope go to the shoemaker at the first turning. Do not tarry and do not pay heed to any drunken idler or bumpkin. I shall not be tardy."

Douglas nodded, her face growing more bright. She and I

hurried off as Laurel entered the house: "She visits Madame Gawdy, I think," Douglas confided.

"Oh," I commented, much doubting that Madame Gawdy kept to her house when there was free beer flowing in Worcester.

"Laurel brings Madame Gawdy money."

"Will Madame Gawdy come back to Campion Towers when I leave?" I asked.

Douglas shrugged. "Who knows, Pen? Laurel tells me little of such matters."

By now we had reached the shoemaker's shop. Of course it had the usual large signboard, this time of a woman's shoe, silvered over. For those who could not read, the signboards were as good as any letters. Many pairs of boots and shoes—from great leather jackboots to dainty slippers—were placed in the window. Douglas put her face to the glass like a child. She giggled and pointed.

"Pen, see the yellow ones."

I could not help but see them. They were bright as sunbeams and in minutes would be soiled by any floor.

We hurried inside because we spied a group of drunken, roistering, shouting men coming toward us. I was unpleasantly surprised to see that they wore helmets and cuirasses. They were Puritan soldiers. I had never dreamed such a thing could be and I was ashamed as I followed Douglas into the shoemaker's shop. I had only half believed what she had told me about the soldiers who had come to Campion Towers to pillage and plunder.

The shoemaker, an old man, bowed deeply to us, leaving a second old fellow who sat in a tall-backed chair. Both were soberly and decently dressed in gray. "Is there summat you lack?" the shoemaker asked.

"Shoes!" Douglas said gaily and seating herself on a stool, she pointed to me. "Shoes for both of us."

I wanted no shoes. I sat down, too, and waited while the shoemaker took our sizes, stripped his window of shoes, and then went behind a screen to bring out two dozen pairs of all colors and cloths—velvets, satins, soft leather, some with buckles, some with ribbon bows. I had not known such fine shoes existed. Douglas gleefully tried on every pair, sending the old shop-keeper away until she called. If I must have shoes I would have the most simple of all I decided, so I settled at once on a pair of black leather slippers with tiny gold thread bows. Bows could be snipped off and silver buckles put in their place. How I had changed! Silver buckles, indeed! When had I ever known such?

I shut out my cousin's babbling. The old men were speaking. I did not find their conversation particularly interesting but it was to be preferred to my cousin's. Their accents were difficult but I could now make out Worcestershire speech somewhat better.

The man in the chair spoke first. "They's news from the north. The Scots 'uv crossed the border, Arthur."

"Aye, I've had the news. Do ye know where they be bound? They come down oft enough," commented the shoemaker grimly.

"Naw, I know it not. They will fight though. Cromwell has come over from Ireland. He is past his sickness, curse the luck."

"They'll stand and fight at Durham 'less I miss my guess."

I was very interested now. I had not known General Cromwell had been ill. So he was to lead his army once more—and against the Scots this time?

"Who leads the Scots? Have ye heard for certain?"

"Who else but the King?" The shoemaker shook his head. " 'Twill be another Dunbar, I fear, Thom."

"Aye," the second man looked sadly at the floor. "Old Oliver allus wins. The devil fights on his side. I pray the murdering Ironsides come not to Worcester again. Their garrison is harsh and cruel enough. Their colonel chose to stop the August fair but our mayor won the day."

I kept my eyes on the heaps of shoes. Douglas had finally set aside three pairs—a scarlet, a violet, and naturally the yellow.

I heard the shop door open and then my great-aunt's voice. "Have you chosen?"

Douglas gestured to the shoes. "That—and that—and that!"

"As I suspected, fit for the feet of a butterfly." Laurel Killingtree looked resigned. "What have you chosen, Penelope?"

"Only the black, mistress."

"Sir Nicholas will not be pleased."

"I need no others," I said. "The green I wear will suit this gown and two of my new gowns my grandfather ordered. The black will suit the others."

"It pleases me to see you know the value of money," Laurel said grudgingly. She shot a glance at Douglas who looked blandly at her. Laurel reached into the purse at her belt and gave the shoemaker what he asked.

He called for his shop boy to carry our bundle of shoes for us and this time we hurried through the fair, which had grown more loud and bawdy as the harvest beer gushed into waiting tankards. Soldiers from the Puritan garrison danced with painted Worcester girls. I turned my head away in anger. I felt a hand at my waist more than once but it was no one who wished to dance with me. Pickpurses were about in the crowd. I had been well warned of them in Salem Town. It did the pickpurses no good. I carried no purse at my belt. My passage money to take me home was in my bodice and I had no jewels to steal nor earrings to tear from my ears.

Fleetingly I thought of the Aylmer diamonds and emeralds, the necklace and bracelets, and then a devise sprang into my mind. It might do if I played my part well and carried myself cleverly.

We got into the coach once more; the shoemaker's boy placed the bundle on the empty seat. I looked after him for a moment and watched him run toward the rope dancer. I had rather fancied the agile rope dancer myself.

As we shook out our skirts I asked my great-aunt, "Am I to see my grandmother Philippa tonight?"

"Perhaps, Penelope," Laurel replied. "If she is awake, mayhap the physician will permit you to see her for a moment. She sleeps a great deal."

I slept a great deal, too, I told myself, but I said only, "I would like to wear the Aylmer jewels tonight if I may. It pleased my grandmother."

"They were given to you," Laurel snapped. Then she added, "You may keep them. There are no thieves at Campion Towers. I will have them brought to you."

"Thank you," I said.

The first part of my devise had gone well.

The little maid brought me the Aylmer jewels not long after we returned to Campion Towers. I thanked her, locked my door, and put the necklace on my table to examine it carefully by candlelight. The emeralds and diamonds were fixed in prongs as I had remembered. The bracelets did not concern me; the earrings, because my ears were not pierced, were unwearable. I threw them into the table drawer. The gold prongs were as soft as I had hoped.

I took Bloody Mary's necklace to my door. The door latch was old and in need of repair. There was money for vain frippery but none for thrifty repairs. A piece of black metal had broken loose. Carefully I set the candle on the floor beneath the latch. I could just see to place one of the prong-set emeralds which was well toward the clasp of the necklace, under the bit of metal. I prized up two prongs and to my joy the jewel flipped out easily onto the floor. I caught it up, satisfied. Then I clasped the necklace about my throat and touched it. Good! The empty place was hidden by my hair. I put on the bracelets.

Now I unlocked my door, not a moment too soon. My great-aunt had come to take me down to supper. They wanted no dawdling about the passages the night "The Twelve" came, and they did not trust Douglas with secrets.

The loose jewel hidden in my hand, I followed Laurel Killingtree to supper. The others were there and Laurel took her seat. I pushed before Sir Nicholas to curtsy and as I passed behind him to my chair, I threw the emerald into the far dark corner of the room, praying that it would land on the Turkey carpet—a garden of garish colors, itself—and be lost among the other bright colors. Success! There had been no clatter as the stone fell.

Our supper was of roast fowl tonight. Again it was a silent meal. Mistress Sutton, dressed all in black and gold brocade, did not lift her eyes from her plate nor did Laurel. My grandfather was silent, seeming concerned. Douglas, for a wonder, was also quiet—but most comely in apricot satin. No one remarked that I wore the Aylmer jewels.

I was left to my own devices. "May I visit my grandmother tonight?" I asked Sir Nicholas. "I wore her jewels to please her." I touched the necklace.

"No," he replied, scarcely glancing at me. Then he called over his shoulder for Jonas to bring the plum wine.

I waited only a second. Then I cried out as convincingly as I could, my hand to the back of my neck. "It is gone! One of the jewels is gone!"

Everyone now looked at me. Laurel said coldly, "You are mistaken. I examined the necklace before I sent it to you, Penelope."

I rushed on. "The jewels were there when I left my bedchamber and when I came into the great hall. I must have lost the emerald when I curtsied. I remember touching the clasp just before I came in. It is one of the jewels near the clasp."

"Then it is in this room," Sir Nicholas said, unperturbed. "Jonas will search for it Do not fret, mistress." It was as if they lost an emerald every day.

He beckoned to Jonas who came in with the usual salver and glasses. Jonas moved with agonizing slowness around the table placing the jerkum at each seat.

"Mistress Penelope says she has lost a jewel, Jonas," my grandfather said. "Take a candle and look for it, lad."

The old servant took up a candle from the great sideboard and—as I had hoped—everyone's eye was upon him as he tottered behind Sir Nicholas' tall chair, examining the floor. I would have only a moment or two until he found it. As Laurel called out, "I see it. There it is!" and everyone stood or shifted himself to look, I swiftly exchanged glasses with Douglas Sutton.

No one had seen me!

The jewel returned and Jonas properly thanked, I drank to the health of my grandmother Philippa gladly.

Douglas would sleep very well tonight.

And so Douglas did. She said almost immediately she was not

well and then complained of pains in her head. Laurel put this down to exhaustion from the excitement of the Worcester fair, while Sir Nicholas suggested that she had had too much wine at supper. I helped Douglas to her chamber and left her sprawled across her fine blue and silver bed, already breathing heavily. I threw a coverlet over her and left.

I had work to do. I locked my door from the outside to make the others believe me asleep for the night, thanks to their laudanum, and then I entered the last room, terrified. Its door was closed but fortunately not locked. I had almost hoped it would be, coward that I was.

The air of the last chamber was now as stale as that of the passages. If there was an entrance to a secret passage in this room it was not open. I would have to find it myself. Holding my candle high I swung the old tapestry back. I had hoped that it concealed an obvious entrance, but I was disappointed. The oak paneling behind the hanging was solid. Everywhere I looked I saw buttons, tiny particulars in the panels that made up the walls of this room. They were flat and almost flush with the panels. I examined several of them carefully, touching them with my fingers. They were the same. All bore the symbol of the Tudor Rose. I had seen that curiously round flower often enough to know what it was—the symbol of the Tudor kings of the last century. Some of the cupboards in Salem Town bore it. Of the Tudors only Bloody Mary had been a Papist after Henry VIII, her father, had outlawed that faith.

I must have sighed, for my candle flame fluttered. I hoped as I moved about the room that no one from outside saw my light. The window was boarded up but I could not be sure how much light would show through the cracks. The empty chamber had scores of buttons—all of them the same—all the Tudor Rose, all a purposeless part of the oak walls. I could not push every button. What was I to do with the right button in any event? Was I to push it, pull it, or twist it? Except for Mistress Cardwell's words about a button, I had no clues at all.

Heedless of the dust, I seated myself in the window seat. I placed my candle holder beside me and then put my chin in my hands. How had the carpenter found the secret?

I gazed at the portion of wall lit by my candle. The wall was covered with buttons—all of them carved with the same flower, but I got up and looked at each one closely.

And then I noticed something! One button nearby was vaguely different—it carried the emblem of the fleur-de-lis, the lily of France, instead of the Tudor Rose. I thought. The fleur-de-lis was somehow familiar to me. In a moment I remembered where I had seen it—the arms of the Killingtrees bore two fleurs-de-lis. But this was such a strangely carved lily. The petals were so plump and rounded that the flower fit into a space exactly the size of the Tudor Roses. It was not at all like the tall, sharply defined lilies on the Killingtree arms. Had the wood carver tried to disguise the flower?

I could barely breathe for excitement. I put my thumb on the fleur-de-lis and pressed. Nothing happened. Praying, I then twisted the button. Finally I pulled it. I heard a faint click. The lower section of the large panel to the left of the button swung open slowly. I could scarce believe my luck.

I had found the secret passage of Campion Towers!

I peered into the blackness, as cool damp air flowed onto my face. Although my terror had deepened, I must go into the secret passage. There was no help for it now. I stooped and went inside, my candle holder gripped tightly, my free hand sheltering the flame. What if the candle should go out and I were left inside in that blackness? Yet there was no draft. Because of the damp the candle burned lower, but it burned steadily. I bit my lip, rose up, and held my candle as high as I could.

A blank stone wall lay about a foot in front of me. On my left a passage led into further blackness but on my right there was but a short space of stone floor. Even the feeble gleam of my candle showed that here the passage ended in the first of a long series of steps.

Praying again, I started swiftly down the steps. It seemed that they would never end but at last I came to the final step. Here a wall blocked my way. I searched for a button or pull or another fleur-de-lis. There was none. A huge stone at one place in the wall jutted out slightly. I touched it with my foot; it swung back.

Air gushed into the passage, and I protected my candle just in time as I bent over and went out into the night. I was in the little court I had seen from my own window. I had not noticed before, because of distance, but the floor of the court had been level at one time. The stones were now crumbling and the spaces between covered with grass. A small gate in a wall led out of the court. I felt I knew what the court had been—a tennis court. I had never played tennis. We Puritans misliked games. The court would give me a quick way out of Campion Towers whenever I chose it. I tried the gate and found it had long ago lost its latch.

Thinking of the "The Twelve" and my instructions, I re-entered the secret passage, shutting the stone door behind me, and climbed the steps. My heart hammered against my ribs from the climb as well as from fear. The secret passage was cold, so chill that I shivered. I considered carrying my shoes even though they were almost noiseless, but the floors were ice-cold and in places moldy. I had no wish to sneeze. I needed both hands to guard my candle, too. I hurried ahead, the pale skirts of Douglas' gown rustling, their sweep nearly brushing both walls of the narrow passage.

Under my breath I counted my steps. When I had taken sixty of them, the passage suddenly took a right-angle turn. Now it was somewhat wider. I guessed that I had reached the center of the great house. Several narrower passages branched off the main passage; they were filled with dusty cobwebs, spider webs so thick I could not peer into them.

I stooped to touch the floor. It was gritty and dusty. There were few spider webs in this central part of the passage—and these only at its top, which meant to me that this part of the secret passage was in use. Who else but Mistress Sutton walked this way? Had she swept the webs away? Such chars would not frighten her. I did not fancy spiders. I put my hand to my throat where the Aylmer jewels lay cold as death.

Still I must go forward. I quickened my steps. What joy it would be to turn my key in the lock of my own chamber again and be as safe as Campion Towers could ever be for me.

I came to another turning and went down it. I guessed that I was in the right wing of the house now. Now I walked more slowly. This was where my grandfather's chambers lay.

The passage ended suddenly but twenty paces ahead, and there were no steps leading downward here. I walked back ten steps and examined the stone wall before me. I could see no wood that marked an opening like that of the empty chamber in my wing of the house. But one of the stones again jutted slightly and I knelt to examine it. It was marked with a fleur-de-lis.

As my head came near the wall, I thought I heard something. Now I stood up quickly and put my ear to the wall above the marked stone. I heard the murmur of voices—several voices.

A Tall Black Devil of a Man

"The Twelve" had come to Campion Towers as Mistress Cardwell had expected, but how had they entered the house? They had not come in by the great hall. If they had I would have seen them. I did not believe that they had come earlier and waited. Perhaps they had entered by a back way and been conducted to this chamber, whatever it was, by one of the maids. No, that was not likely. The maids were young and no young person was overtrusted in this house.

"The Twelve" came through the secret passage, the passage in which I stood. But who led them this night? Certainly not Laurel or Amabel Sutton or Sir Nicholas—or even Jonas, for they had all been at supper. It must be someone who knew Campion Towers very well indeed. It was not Madame Gawdy. I smiled at the thought of the Frenchwoman's bulk in this narrow passage.

But there was one other person who might have guided "The Twelve." I had seen Will Scarlet at the stables. James Rowland might also know the secret of the Killingtrees. I suspected that he knew many of the secrets of Campion Towers.

I listened. The wall was a thick one. Few words came through distinctly and the voices were muffled. I knew my grandfather's voice but could not make out his words. And then my suspicions were justified, for I heard the voice of James Rowland as he spoke loudly—and angrily. "You all know the man who is to come. He will require your loyalty—and your aid."

A babble of voices followed these words. Some seemed murmurs of agreement, others were clearly mutters of mislike.

A stranger spoke up, " 'Tis not disloyalty on my part, sir. I fear danger from the Roundheads. I have a wife and children. If we fail, there will be hangings aplenty in Worcestershire."

"Aye," another chimed in, "what if we fail?"

"We will not fail if you do your part," my grandfather roared.

For a moment there was silence as I wished fervently for a peephole to see into the chamber and spy out the faces of the mysterious "Twelve."

"He approaches Worcester now. You know this. You have had the news," James Rowland warned. "The time grows short."

"I will not support it," said a strangely thick voice, unfamiliar to me.

"Then we shall bring no more grain for ye to grind," threatened another man.

I nodded. The miller was one of "The Twelve," then. I now knew why Mistress Sutton rode to the miller's house in Holt Heath. She was a courier to "The Twelve."

"I will come here no more," said the miller angrily. "I put my neck into no noose again. The Roundheads are too strong."

"The garrison in Worcester will crack for us like a nut," Rowland offered.

The miller spoke once more. "The poor squirrel who cracks it will be skinned and cooked in a trice by Cromwell's Ironsides, I tell ye."

"Do as you please," Rowland stated, his voice cold. "I take it I need not tell you to hold your tongue if you do not join us."

"No, ye need not."

James Rowland seemed to be the leader. "We shall soon speak together again—but not at this house. A woman lies ill here. You know the other meeting place. We achieve nothing tonight. Get you to your homes and ponder well. He comes! He expects welcome for his pains and the dangers he has run for your sake. He has faith in you. It is too late now for him to turn back."

I heard a crashing of chairs and stools and my heart leaped. They might disperse to their homes through the passage. I fled swiftly down the short passage, then down the longer one. Only when I reached the right angle that led to my wing of the house did I slow my steps. Here no one could see my candle glow. I counted my steps and stopped at sixty paces. The entrance to the empty chamber still gaped. I hurried inside. One swift glance told me that the room was still empty. I twisted the button with the fleur-de-lis, watching the secret door swing shut. Then I opened the outer door and peered out. Mercifully, the passage was empty. In seconds I was in my chamber, my door locked, and into my gown and cap, and abed.

I had found the secret passage, had entered it, and had heard the voices of some of the mysterious "Twelve." I might know their voices again. I knew James Rowland was in the house. By the manner in which he took command I felt he meant to stay. I scarcely closed my eyes all night for excitement. Who was "the man" they talked about—another Edmund Campion—another Papist, another Jesuit priest?

My civility was strained the next few days, knowing what wickedness was planned at Campion Towers. I drank my jerkum each night, always saving bread to drop into it first, but I was not affected by the plum wine now that there was no longer any reason to give me laudanum. There were to be no more night meetings at Campion Towers. There was no longer any cause, either, for me to go into the frightening secret passage.

Sir Nicholas frowned constantly and spoke little except to his sister or to Mistress Sutton. I knew of what they spoke and why all three seemed concerned. It was of the man who was to come. They ceased speaking the moment I was within earshot.

There was a second trouble in the house. My elders spoke of my grandmother freely enough; she grew steadily weaker. I saw her twice again. The first time she smiled at me and called me by name; the next day she did not seem to know me nor did she call me "Nicola." Like them, I was much concerned over her.

My grandfather and great-aunt spent their time with her. I wondered, too, if James Rowland went to her, but I could hardly ask this. Mistress Sutton absented herself, riding about the countryside on Russet, taking messages to "The Twelve," I suspected. I saw nothing of James Rowland, of course. I was left with the silly Douglas, who, to my amusement, had taken an entire day to recover from the effects of the laudanum meant for me. We rode together each day and each day I noted the closed stall next to Cranberry's. Sometimes the red horse was inside—sometimes not.

The company of my cousin was dull. I would have almost enjoyed an encounter with Master Rowland. He was interesting, although frightening. His peculiar profession did not concern me overmuch. If Campion Towers was to harbor conspiring Roman Catholics, why should it not harbor an outlaw, too— particularly a Papist outlaw? The two were nearly the same. He was a rogue but I almost liked him. More and more I suspected that I knew his true name. If what I thought were true, it would explain many things—his knowing I resembled my mother, his skulking about, his owning Will Scarlet, and his knowledge of Campion Towers. It would be quite unlikely that Master Rowland would wish to harm me—unless he knew I spied.

So I rode about the countryside each day with Douglas, never straying far for fear of vagabonds. We kept to the road that led to Holt Heath, avoiding the main road from the north. Sir Nicholas had told us that there were wanderers about on that road and we were not to take it.

I waited impatiently. As promised, Mistress Turtledove and Mistress Cardwell came, a week to the day, with the gowns and the riding habits. I stood patiently in my great-aunt's bedchamber while I was fitted. Mistress Cardwell did not speak to me and her eyes did not meet mine as she pinned the hems. All would be ready the next day. A lad would bring the gowns from Worcester to Campion Towers.

The gowns were very fine indeed. Douglas looked covetously at the gay red and the coral, but I was sad when I wore the willow-green. I wished my grandmother could see it, but she was no longer aware of people, Laurel had told me sharply. No, I was not to see her.

Mistress Turtledove was in haste. They had much work to do in Worcester if the gowns were to be ready, she complained while she fitted the shoulders of the dresses.

Finally Mistress Turtledove donated her attention to a preening Douglas, fitting her into the red velvet riding costume, while Mistress Cardwell was sent to adjust the skirt of my costume.

Douglas chattered with joy to Mistress Turtledove of the latest fashions from France. Laurel looked on disapprovingly at her over her crewelwork.

Naomi Cardwell knelt at my feet, her fingers adjusting the string of the skirt at my waist. No one took notice of us.

"I have news," I whispered. "I have found the secret passage. I heard 'The Twelve' speaking."

"Did you contrive to see their faces?" she asked softly, her face averted from me against the dark red velvet.

"No. They no longer meet here."

"Aye, we know. We watch them. They meet nearby. Do not go to the Aylmer farm."

That is where I had guessed they met. Owen, the shepherd, was their watchful sentry. The mystery of the warm ashes, the candle stub, and Holt Heath's "ghosts" was no longer a mystery. "But what of the man who comes? What of the priest?"

She pulled the string tight, hurting me, and hissed, "Watch for that one. Watch for strangers who come to the house! Keep to the house. The roads are not safe."

I bent my head to loosen the string. "The length is near right, Mistress Cardwell," I said loudly so everyone would hear me. With our heads close together I added, "James Rowland is here. Why did *you* come here today if there is danger?"

"I know of James Rowland," she told me. "No one sees two old women who make gowns. A pretty wench is a different matter. Watch—but do not seek me out."

She got to her feet and held out the long red coat to me. It fit perfectly. Mistress Cardwell was an excellent seamstress.

I would go into the passage again it seemed. I wished that I had time to tell Naomi Cardwell the secret of the button. But Laurel's eyes were now upon us.

I waited that night until I knew Douglas would be asleep and once more I entered the secret passage! All was completely silent in the great house. I was soon back in my chamber, satisfied that no one had come to Campion Towers.

At dawn I learned that my grandmother had died in her sleep an hour past midnight. All but Douglas and myself had been with her. Laurel Killingtree brought the news to me. Her eyes were wet as she sat on my bed—something she had never done before—while she told me of my grandmother's death.

I wept, too. If I had ever come close to loving anyone at Campion Towers, it was gentle Philippa Aylmer. But I dried my tears when I thought of what evil went on here and of the laudanum Mistress Killingtree had purchased for me.

"Penitence," Laurel said, using my true name, "your grandfather has taken to his bed. He is ill. His vigil was a long one. He scarcely left her side. You need not concern yourself with this. You may go now if you choose. You have our gratitude for coming so far and you have the Aylmer jewels and the farm. Sir Nicholas says you may go. We do not seek to keep you here. But we ask one more favor of you."

"What is that?" I asked.

"To attend your grandmother's funeral. It will be held in our chapel tomorrow."

I was shocked. They bid me, a Puritan, come to a Papist burial! I thought. I should do this. Perhaps here I would see the "man who came." The priest might very well be in the house already. He had surely given my grandmother her last rites. He would officiate at her funeral while he plotted with the Roman Catholics of Worcestershire against the Parliament.

"As you wish, mistress," I told Laurel.

"I thank you, child."

"I have no mourning gown with me."

"Your pewter-colored gown will serve."

I nodded. There was black mourning and there was white mourning.

"Will Peter take a letter to Swindon for me?" I asked. "I shall write my friends. I will return with them next month on the *Godspeed.*"

Laurel was agreeable. "In Swindon, do you say? Write *at once*, then. Peter will take your message to Worcester this morning. It will travel by messenger from there. Swindon is not far. As soon as you have a reply, Peter will take you there. It would be wise of you, I think, to go soon. There is unrest in the county."

They hoped to be rid of me, of course, but I did not wish Laurel to read my knowledge in my eyes. "Yes," I said, looking away. "What am I to do with the jewels and the farm?"

She shrugged her bowed shoulders. "They were given to you. The jewels you may take with you or you may sell them if you so choose. The farm cannot be sold, however—it would be impossible to find a buyer. Since the Civil War, Worcestershire has been poor."

"I would not sell it," I told her, "but if I were to live in England I would sell the jewels to repair the farm. Can I arrange that the farm goes to my grandfather? Would that please him?"

"Yes. He would favor that," she agreed, "but you know his pride. He would pay you rents and send you money." She got down slowly from my bed. I had not noticed how old she was. Her brisk, harsh manner had hidden this till now.

She left my room as I got out of bed and slowly dressed myself, putting on my cousin's riding costume. It was black and it would serve until my gowns arrived. I began to weep again, remembering the green gown my grandmother had wanted me to have. I would take that back to Salem Town with me—even if I must keep it in a cupboard. As for the red and the coral, I would never have to wear them now. Douglas was very welcome to them.

Jonas brought up my morning meal on a tray and as I opened the door to him I saw the little maid walk by with a second tray—this time for Douglas.

I ate and then I went to my cousin's room for paper, ink, and a quill.

Douglas was still abed. She wiped at her eyes with a lace handkerchief. She had been told the news, too, and she only nodded when I asked her for the things I needed. Then she spoke up. "I suppose you will be going away now, Pen?"

"Yes," I told her, "I shall leave soon."

She snuffled into her handkerchief. "There will never be anyone young in the house at all any more."

Clearly she had not spied James Rowland yet. I remembered the shattered hand mirror well enough to know she knew him.

"I am sorry, Douglas," I told her. "You have no other cousins? Perhaps someone else can come to keep you company here?"

She shook her head, the white ribbons on her night cap fluttering. "Not a soul, Pen. My mother had two young brothers who fought for old King Charles. One was killed at Edgehill, the other fell at Naseby. They had no children. My father had no brothers or sisters."

I was truly sorry for Douglas Sutton. She had nothing but her beauty and that was an empty vanity. "I wish I could help you," I said truthfully, forgiving her much of her past silliness. "You are my only cousin, too."

Douglas looked up, her eyes huge over her handkerchief. "No, I am not," she told me, "not, truly, Pen." Then she added to this odd comment. "Sometimes 'tis hard to remember you are a Roundhead. I never thought I could favor a Roundhead. When you first came here, Mistress Killingtree had to threaten to take a stick to me if I were not pleasant to you. She would have, too!"

I smiled. I doubted if Douglas had ever felt a stick across her back. "I thank you for favoring one Roundhead, at least," I told her. "I never thought I would favor a Cavalier either."

I closed her door and went thoughtfully to my bedchamber. Another cousin? What had Douglas meant? Well now I thought I knew.

I sat at my little table and took up the quill. I would get wax and a thread later. Mistress Killingtree would have such things. I wrote to Pastor Wrenn, telling him I would come to Swindon soon. I supposed I could leave now and arrive at Swindon unexpected, or spend a few weeks at the Turk's Head in Bristol, but I had business yet for Dr. Moonjean at Campion Towers. Until Amyas Moonjean dismissed me, I must remain.

I took my letter to Mistress Killingtree's bedchamber and left it there. She would seal it and give it to Peter. It mattered little to me if she read it—as I guessed she would.

At midday a lad came from Mistress Turtledove with a large bundle. My gowns and the two riding habits were in it. I took one of the cranberry red velvet habits to Douglas, who sat at her window seat, looking sadly out toward the grove of oaks, her cittern on her lap, red ribbons like streaks of blood across the black silk of her dress. I recalled how everyone in this house had worn black to mourn for King Charles I when he was beheaded. I doubted if her grief went deep or that she would long wear mourning.

I went back, then, to my chamber and put on the pewter-colored dress. Although it was somber enough, I was uncomfortable that I, the Puritan, was the only person at Campion Towers who did not wear true mourning for Philippa Aylmer. Now I was sad and felt somehow guilty as I thought of my purpose in her house. How did I repay her kindliness to me— by spying for her deadly enemies! I had even begun to like Sir Nicholas and to find my great-aunt Laurel admirable—before I had learned of the laudanum.

The priest, who was surely at Campion Towers, would be with my grandfather tonight. I was certain the chamber in which I had overheard "The Twelve" was my grandfather's. I would listen again.

I waited alone through that very long day in my room, while I prayed for my grandmother's soul, feeling that even though she was of an enemy faith, she would have been pleased by this.

Supper came to my room, as my midday food had come, on a tray. I ate without appetite. I understood many things now. I had learned today that Amabel Sutton had lost her family in the Civil War. I knew a second reason then for her obvious hatred of me. Because of her, I would be happy to leave Campion Towers. But what was I to do in Salem Town once more—take up my old life as a drudge for my stepmother? Nothing else lay ahead for me. I had no one in England who cared for me. I could not stay here.

The maid took my tray and bade me good night. My candles lit, I sat silent, waiting. My gowns hung on pegs in the clothes-press, making a brave show, but I took no pleasure in them.

When I thought it time, I got up and went to the empty room. I twisted the fleur-de-lis button and reentered the passage. Tonight I had little fear. I need not worry that I would meet anyone in the secret passage. Any Papist stranger would surely be with my grandfather, comforting him.

Boldly I walked along, my candle held high. I made the first angle turn and passed two of the smaller, even narrower, passages that led off. Suddenly I noticed something disturbing. Cobwebs filled one passage. But the other was now clear. I walked back to peer into it but it was deeper than I had thought.

I stepped forward into it and as I did, I screamed. Someone caught me around the waist and as I cried out in terror, a hand was put over my mouth. I kicked and tried to bite as my candle holder fell to shatter on the stone floor.

"Hold your tongue, mistress," came a deep voice. "I mean you no harm. Why do you come here?"

I stopped my struggling and waited, my heart pounding.

The man spoke again from the absolute blackness of the secret passage. "Who are you? If I take my hand away, will ye give me your word not to skreek?"

I nodded my head as hard as I could, banging my head against his chest. Whoever the stranger was, he was very tall.

He let me go at last and then I felt a hand on my shoulder, a hand which reached down to my own. "Come with me," the stranger said. "We shall converse in the priest's hole, snug though it be." He laughed. His laugh was a deep chuckle—and not unpleasant.

My thoughts raced. I must be clever now if I hoped to get

away safely. I was in grave danger. I let him lead me down a narrow passage and at his sharp command to wait, I stayed. I could have run, I supposed, but perhaps he knew the passages better than I. I had not known of a priest-hole—Edmund Campion's very hole certainly.

A flash of fire struck my eyes. The stranger knew his way to flint and tinder. I blinked at the second flash and then I opened my eyes wide to look about me. Even the few moments of blackness had disturbed my sight.

I was in a tiny stone chamber. There was nothing in it but a very narrow bed, rather like a ship's bed, along one wall and a small plain table with a single candle upon it. A plate of food, bread, cold meat, and cheese, lay on the table next to a book.

In an instant I shifted my gaze to the man who had caught me. He was tall, very tall indeed, and he was not at all old. His shoulder-length hair was thick and black, his eyebrows the same black, while his face was a deep brown as if he spent much of his life in the sun. His mouth was wide and merry, his eyes brown. He was neatly dressed all in black with a wide white collar. A plain black steeple hat lay on the bed. He looked like one of us—a Puritan—but I knew what he was well enough. Roman Catholic clergy wore black too.

"Who are you, mistress, and why do you walk about in secret ways by midnight?" he asked me, his eyes intent on my face.

"Who are you, sir?" I demanded, deciding to attack the stranger. "I *live* here at Campion Towers."

He bowed low, smiling. "I am William Jackson, mistress. I am at your service."

I hesitated. I knew I had to give him a name. My own was on the tip of my tongue but instead I came out with "Mistress

Douglas Sutton." I had told a deliberate falsehood—but my cause was good. I curtsied, but not deeply.

"Ah, Mistress Sutton, it is? I have met your mother. You do not favor her." He seemed quite amused.

"I am like unto my father," I said hastily. And then I added slyly, "It was kindly of you to come see my grandmother Aylmer. You must have been of great comfort to her."

He raised an eyebrow. "I have been of scant comfort to anyone in my life, Mistress Sutton. I do not think I comforted your grandmother overmuch."

He was clever, I decided. "I meant," I said, "that it must have pleased her to have received the proper last rites."

The stranger looked at me in a peculiar fashion. "I understand, mistress, that it usually does. But why did you come into the secret passage?"

I could not say I was a sleepwalker. I countered with a question. "What do you do here, sir?"

"I hide," he said simply. "This is where they choose to put me. This is a very strange house, I think. When I first spied you in the main passage, I thought you to be a phantom, but, by the gods, you are no phantom. In that gown you seemed ghostly. But you are a pretty wench, indeed." He reached out with a long brown hand and touched my hair. "Who spun that gold for you, I wonder?" he asked, and then he bent down. Before I guessed what he was about, he kissed me on the lips.

I drew back. Then I raised my hand, but before I could strike him, he caught my wrist and held it, laughing. "Ah, I have had much practice in that game, Mistress Sutton. It is one I fancy."

"You dare do this!" I cried out. "What would the people who believe in what you stand for think if they knew?"

I had caught him there. He looked puzzled. "I do not believe I understand you, mistress."

"You have come to read the last rites and the burial services, have you not?" I flared.

He sat down heavily on the narrow bed. "Aye, that is true enough, but you put it very oddly. Do you always speak in such a fashion, Mistress Sutton?"

"May I go now?" I asked angrily.

"Perhaps you had better," he agreed. "I prefer maids who do not speak in parables of what is to come and who would rather kiss than ask questions."

I swung about as well as I could in such a narrow place and started for the exit. I could find my way back without a candle by counting steps or by touching the wall. Whatever I did, I would ask no favor of the disgraceful William Jackson.

But as I left that small passage, William Jackson's light still glowing behind me, I heard limping footsteps and I found my way blocked by another man. He held a candle, too, and behind it I saw his face, his eyes, and his light-brown hair. It was James Rowland. I caught my breath. Here was a pretty situation. What was I to do?

His mouth fell open. Then he motioned with the candle for me to follow him. We went together into the main passage, away from William Jackson's lair. "Why are you here, Mistress Hervey?"

I tried the same tactics that had worked so well with Jackson. "And what are you doing here?" I asked. "You are an outlaw. I do not believe that your name is James Rowland at all."

"It is not," he admitted. He leaned against the wall. "I am not James Rowland. I am your cousin, Julian Killingtree. I am an outlaw by decree of your fine Roundhead Parliament—but I am no highwayman. I stopped your coach only to see you when I learned you came here to inherit. I knew your mother well when I was a lad."

"Oh," said I, think how Douglas had cajoled away what Julian should have inherited—Campion Towers. But he was no Aylmer so *I* took nothing from him.

"How did you know of the secret passage? What are you doing here?"

I lied once more. Lies were becoming easier for me, I was unhappy to say. "My mother told my father of it. He told me. I wished to see it." Surely my mother had known of the old passage and the priest-hole.

"Aye," he accepted my explanation. "She knew of it. Children have walked in it. Valuables have been hidden in it and animals have been sheltered within its walls." I thought of the red horses as he went on, "Did you speak with that man?" he asked, nodding toward the priest-hole.

"That priest?" I snapped, losing my wits for a moment. "He kissed me. What sort of priest is that? William Jackson is no fit priest, I think."

My other cousin began to laugh. "Oh, you little Roundhead! He shall laugh for a week at this. It will be the talk of the camp for a month. Someone may even make a ballad of it. 'Tis no priest who kissed you." He leaned toward me, his fingers under my chin. "It was King Charles who kissed you," and then my cousin, too, kissed me.

Charles Stuart at Campion Towers! My knees were like jelly.

Julian let me go. I was near to falling and leaned against the wall, too. "That was a cousin's kiss," he told me. "It was also the kiss of a loyal subject of King Charles the Second. What a jest! I doubt if the King has ever kissed a Roundhead before this. I know that I have not."

"I told him I was Douglas Sutton," I said, annoyed at him. Each time I saw him James Rowland, or rather cousin Julian

Killingtree, had the knack of putting me at a neat disadvantage.

"So you came into the passage and you found the King and gave a false name to him? Do you spy for Oliver Cromwell?"

He had hit the truth, but I knew from his tone that he jested. I could outwit him still. I shook my head. "Truly, I looked for you. I saw Will Scarlet in the stable next to Cranberry, so I knew you were in the house. I half-guessed you were my cousin. They all spoke here of someone who had been wounded. Some said you were dead, but others contradicted this. I thought you might be here. But what I found was a stranger I believed to be a priest who had come to my grandmother."

"And why did you tell the King you were Douglas Sutton, pray? And why did you seek me out?"

"You use a false name. So does that man—if he truly is Charles Stuart," I pointed a trembling finger at the priest-hole. "Why should I give my true name? I wanted to see you again —to tell you I leave England soon. I wish to thank you once more for helping me with the red mare. I have known little kindliness here."

"I know you go away. Otherwise—I do not believe you," he told me. "I think you eavesdropped and learned the King was here. Priest, indeed? What Puritan would know a priest? You came to see the King. Wenches have been known to do many things to catch the eye of Charles Stuart, who is all too ready to see. He must be protected from them."

"Protected from them—indeed!" I protested. "He is a wicked tall black devil of a man!"

Julian grinned. It took the harshness from his face. "So some folk say. Yet I know him well. I have been at his side off and on for years when I have not been doing his work elsewhere.

He would share his last crust of bread with me and I with him.

"I have not been satisfied with your answers nor do I know why you walk here at this hour. If you were English-bred, I would think you spied on us. But you come from the New World and have been in England only a few weeks, so it is unlikely. In any event, Mistress Pen Hervey, it matters little. I have no time for clack.

"Charles Stuart leaves tonight. He takes the red horse, Rufus, with him. On the morrow he will be in Worcester with his army of Scots. Since August 6th he has marched three hundred miles from Scotland. The Roundhead garrison at Worcester will surrender. Even now the news travels like the wind throughout England that the Cavaliers stand and fight at Worcester once again."

My eyes must have grown wide, for he spoke more kindly. "No, you have not been told. They do not speak of this at Campion Towers. It was a well-kept secret. Your grandfather did not want to alarm you or Douglas with the news. Your General Cromwell marches even now on Worcester from the east. You are the last to know in Worcestershire—you, with the King, himself, at Campion Towers, at twenty paces away!"

"If everyone knows," I asked sharply, "why does Charles Stuart skulk in a priest-hole?"

My cousin shrugged. "There is a Roundhead about who might be offended, Sir Nicholas thinks."

"What Puritan?"

"You!" he told me. "Sir Nicholas considers you overmuch, I believe, when you creep into the passage to see the King, like any other silly wench in England. But cheer yourself, Mistress Hervey. You have been kissed by the King. I shall wager you kissed him back. You have something to tell your grandchildren."

I sniffed and bent to pick up my candle. The holder was broken but the candle, for a wonder, whole. "If 'tis not too much to ask, may I light my candle from yours?"

"Aye," he said, "and then go back to your bedchamber. Keep out of the secret passage. Return to the colonies. If you are wise you will not speak of this; you will not be believed."

"You will not tell Sir Nicholas or my great-aunt or anyone else?" I asked. "I would not want Douglas, who has done nothing wicked, punished by her mother, either, if that man speaks." I was badly frightened. Would the others believe me to be the silly maid my cousin Julian did? I was not so hopeful of Mistress Amabel Sutton. She, of all here, would suspect me, I believed.

"They have more important matters to concern them now," he told me. "No, I shall not tell anyone that either you or some-one calling herself 'Douglas' had been with Charles Stuart alone. If Sir Nicholas knew you had been with the King, I would not vouch for what he might say to any one of the three of us—the King included. He knows the King's reputation. Sometimes I even believe he has his misgivings about the King, but I tell you that this Charles Stuart will someday rule this land wisely and well."

I lit my candle from my cousin's and curtsied. By the double light I saw that he had a sheaf of letters in the cuff of his same brown coat. Messages for the man he called a "King"?

"If I do not see you again, Pen, think of me sometimes," he asked, his voice softened. "I shall not forget you. You are greatly like your mother." He smiled. "Do not confide in your cousin Douglas, whatever you do, about this business tonight. She would be envious and her mother would think she missed her opportunity."

He brushed past me. As for me, I walked a few steps beyond the entrance to the passage that led to the priest-hole. Then I set my candle upright between two stones and softly I crept back into the passage.

I could hear perfectly well while my light could not be seen. My cousin was speaking. "I have a fine jest for you, sire."

"What could that be?" Charles Stuart's deep voice asked.

"It can wait, sire. It will crown your victory at Worcester. I will save it for you and tell you then."

"It is as well. I fancy no jests now, Sir Julian. Did you see that pretty golden-haired maid who was here just now? Odsfish, she was a strange one. I did not know what to make of her. At first I thought her to be a ghost. I have been pondering on it. I believe she thought me someone else—someone she had expected to find here. Is Mistress Sutton crazed?"

I smiled into the blackness. What would Julian—Sir Julian Killingtree—have to say to this? His answer did not please me. "No, sire, but at times she takes strange notions upon her. It is her Aylmer blood. Do not speak of her to anyone, I beg you. She will be punished for coming to see you."

I bit my lip. Strange notions, indeed! He painted me a "flirtgill."

Julian went on, changing the subject. "What plan do you follow, sire, if you are defeated at Worcester?"

The words of Charles Stuart were grave. "Aye, Julian, you have the right of it and as always a cool head. Last year's defeat at Dunbar would have taught one to have a devise even if Cromwell's other victories had not already done so. I must face the possibility of defeat if the men of Worcestershire do not rally to me. My Scots are wearied from their journey—as am I. I have seeming friends here at this house, so I shall make my way to this fine hiding place if Wilmot has no other course of escape planned. As yet I do not know that he does.

"From here I shall go to France—to my mother's land—to gain strength for another attempt to wrest my throne from the Roundheads. I will not return to Scotland to be scolded and eternally preached at like a small child."

His voice became more brisk. "Now when am I to see Sir Nicholas Killingtree? I have waited long enough in this priest-hole, I think. His food is excellent, but his books are dull and intended to make me a soberer man than I am. As for his descendants on the distaff side, they are too confusing for my poor head."

I had heard enough. All England might soon know that Charles Stuart was at Worcester and would fight. What they did not know was where Charles Stuart would be when General Cromwell had beaten him—as Cromwell surely would.

I had something to tell Mistress Cardwell at once—something that would surely interest her.

General Cromwell

I FAIRLY FLEW back to my chamber, so excited I could scarce breathe. What great things had happened to me tonight! I knew I would never know such adventure again. I even laughed aloud. What would Amity Wrenn say to this? Would she believe that I had been kissed by Charles Stuart? How shocked she would be! Better yet, what would Elizabeth say? All Salem Town would have me stand in their pillory with my tongue in the cleft stick for a liar. Like Julian, I must keep my silence and I did not for a moment think my cousin would betray me.

So much had happened so swiftly to me in one day. As I said a prayer for my grandmother's soul, my cheeks still burned. I could not forget my cousin's kiss, far sweeter than the King's.

But I must remember my purpose. I had no way of knowing how much time there was before Cromwell's Ironsides and the King's Scots clashed in battle. I must get a message to Mistress Cardwell very soon.

I blew out the candle beside my bed and lay back on the

pillows. Was William Jackson, or Charles Stuart, still in the great house, I asked myself? The very thought was exciting. I would have something, indeed, to tell my grandchildren. I had never been kissed before tonight, but my first kiss had been from a man many called the King of England, and my second kiss, although a kinsman's kiss, had been very little like a brother's kiss. I thought hard, trying to remember what my great-aunt and Douglas had said about Julian Killingtree, the outlaw, the wounded Cavalier hero, who would now fight again for the Stuarts. He was the son of my grandfather's younger brother. That made him a second cousin, I reckoned, of no very close degree to me. I was unaccountably pleased at this—even if he was a Papist. Perhaps before I left Campion Towers I would see Sir Julian again and match wits with him. I thought about the "sir" before his name. I had not heard "sir" before. Charles Stuart must have knighted his faithful follower.

What would Cromwell think of tonight's events? What excited me most of all was the knowledge that Oliver Cromwell came, too, to Worcester!

I found no one else at the table for the first meal of the day. Jonas served me. "They keep to their chambers, mistress. You will see them at the services." Perhaps I should not have come down, I told myself, but I did not know what to do or how to behave. I knew nothing of Papist mourning customs.

I wandered out to the stables after I had eaten. I took sugar with me. This was not the right thing to do, I was certain, but I was lonely, and was pleased to find Garth currying little Pimpernel. I supposed I should not make a friend of a stable-boy, but a cooper's daughter could enjoy few illusions regarding her station in life. Once I left Campion Towers I would be a cooper's daughter first—and a Killingtree no more.

Garth grinned as I went along the stalls, giving sugar to each horse—even gingerly to Russet, and stopping at last at Cranberry's stall. I broke off the two last fragments for her but not before I noticed that two stalls were empty. Rufus and Will Scarlet were gone. Charles Stuart and Julian had ridden off together, I guessed. I wondered when they had gone.

I went back to where Garth stood and Cranberry neighed softly to me as I left her.

"She fancies ye mistress," Garth said, turning his head to look at me, his hand busy with the curry comb.

"I shall miss her sorely, Garth. I go away soon, you know."

"Do ye now?" he asked. He wore a frown. "The Berry will miss you, Mistress Hervey. She will be lonely. She takes to few folk. Peter and I are leaving, too."

"Oh? Where do you go?"

"To Worcester. They'll be a battle soon. They need grooms for the king's horses. Sir Nicholas sends us."

I nodded. The secret was really out, then. I wondered if Douglas knew by now.

"What will happen to the red horses?" I asked.

"Naught to these," he gestured toward Pimpernel, Pippin, Russet, and Cranberry. "They be mares, mistress. Mares never go to war—but the geldings and the stallions."

I was happy to hear this. I hoped that Rufus and Will Scarlet would not be harmed, but I was also glad that not all of the red horses would be ridden into battle. Ungodly, wicked men made wars. Horses harmed no one—except for the unusual vicious animal like Russet. I gazed at Mistress Sutton's horse. Yet she had not tried to nip me when I gave her a sugar. Russet might mislike Cranberry but she behaved badly only when Amabel Sutton was her rider.

Several dozen horses—chestnut, gray, sorrel, black and white —stood before Campion Towers when I returned. I entered the great house warily. These men were Cavaliers. The fine red plume in 'the hat of the soldier who guarded the horses proved this clearly.

At the door I edged past a handsome young soldier in a bronze cuirass, a white scarf across his chest, and a lobstertail helmet. He looked very martial even when he smiled at me. I looked quickly away. How bold the eyes of these Cavaliers were!

My grandfather, looking more aged than I had ever seen him, sat before the black-draped firehearth. Despite the heat of late August he had had a fire built. Laurel sat opposite him and Douglas stood before the blaze in her black gown. Her eyes were fixed on the three tall soldiers next to Sir Nicholas and her checks were rosy with excitement.

One of the three, a very tall brown-haired man, said loudly, "Sir Julian Killingtree sends his compliments, sir. He is at your service. He asks that you strictly confine the ladies who live at this house. The highroad is used by the army from Scotland. The savage Highlanders now straggle in to Worcester."

"This is a house of mourning. Have you no eyes to see? The ladies of Campion Towers do not need to be told such things. Do you think they would ride out to see a group of wild, bare-kneed Scots?" My grandfather had not lost his fire.

"Nevertheless, I have conveyed to you what I was told to convey," the soldier said.

Laurel Killingtree looked harshly at Douglas, who was gazing at the youngest and most handsome Cavalier from under her lashes. "Aye, Julian knows you well enough, Mistress Sutton."

This was not truly fair. I knew whom Julian meant. A fine opinion he had of me! But I could not speak up for my cousin without revealing myself. At least Douglas knew what was to happen. The arrival of the Cavalier army had taught her that.

Laurel spoke to me, "Peter could not get away with your message for Swindon after all. I am sorry. There is much confusion on the roads. It seems you must stay with us for a time."

I nodded. "Until the battle is won. I understand."

"Who told *you* of a battle, if I may ask?" my grandfather demanded, as the soldiers stared at me in frank curiosity.

"Garth."

"You have been to the stables?"

"I took sugar to Cranberry. I am sorry I displeased you."

My grandfather turned away. He stared into the fire. I knew what went through his mind. He thought of Rufus and Will Scarlet—of the red horses. He had lost so much he loved in two short days.

"King Charles will fight Oliver Cromwell at Worcester," my great-aunt explained quietly as if I had not known it. "This may pose a difficulty for you, Penelope. The Puritan garrison at Worcester has surrendered."

"It will not be over-difficult, Mistress Killingtree, if you do not make it so," I told her. "I am what you call a 'Roundhead.' I have not pretended to be anything else. I will not take a musket and join General Cromwell." I held out my satin skirts and let them fall.

One of the soldiers roared. He clapped a comrade on the shoulder. "Would that we fought such fine lasses—not ugly cropped-haired Roundheads. Come join *our* cause, mistress!"

I kept my temper while my grandfather glared and Douglas hid a giggle. The soldiers left quickly under Sir Nicholas' hard gaze, shuffling their feet like my half brother Obedience when he had been tongue-lashed by Elizabeth. Their leader called out from the door. "Sir Julian Killingtree will send word to you soon about another matter." In a moment they were gone, and everyone heard my cousin Douglas sigh.

Before the funeral took place, I spent long hours thinking. I was blocked from riding to Worcester. I could go, I supposed, at night by way of the secret passage, but it would be dangerous for a girl alone. If I must, I would brave it. But for a time I would wait. I wanted to learn what message Julian sent to my grandfather if I could, and perhaps Mistress Cardwell would send someone to me to take what news I had.

I followed Douglas and my great-aunt down through the great hall at the hour for the funeral. We passed along the black-draped hall and walked through the massive wooden doors at one end, doors always shut before this time. I had not known if I should, but I had worn one of my linen caps from Salem Town to cover my hair. It went at odds with the satin gown but Laurel nodded her approval. Douglas, Laurel, and Amabel wore black veils, which hung from small velvet hats.

We moved slowly into the Killingtree chapel below the empty bell tower. I looked about me swiftly. The servants, what few there were, sat in back pews. They, too, wore black. Sir Nicholas had bought them suits of mourning. My grandfather and—my heart leaped—Julian sat before the rail near the black-draped catafalque on which my grandmother's coffin lay. Sprigs of rosemary, gray-green and fragrant, were strewn upon it.

Laurel motioned for us to seat ourselves and as we did, others entered—the people of Holt Heath, I suspected, for I marked out the miller's wife, the miller's son, and the blacksmith.

Master Meredith, clad in an odd-looking embroidered garment over a long gown of white lawn, stood at the end of the chapel.

I moved into my pew, wondering at the appearance of this Papist chapel. The pew was of plain oak, but a low bench before me was covered with worn green velvet. We Puritans did not kneel in church, but to show respect to my grandmother I had bobbed a sort of curtsy, as did Douglas as we had entered the pew we were to share. Laurel and Mistress Sutton sat in front of us.

The chapel was very simple, but I remembered what Douglas had told me. The stained glass had been broken and could not be replaced. The ancient stone walls were unadorned save for candle sconces, while the altar held only a silver crucifix. There were no statues of saints, no burning lights, and no incense. I thought this strange as I sat quietly and harkened to Master Meredith. Listening civilly was the least I could do if I were to stay in peace at Campion Towers and repay my debt to Philippa Aylmer.

The service went on and on. I had expected this. Pastor Wrenn preached stirringly for hours in Salem Town, but this service was vastly different. Sometimes the Killingtrees read from a little book; Master Meredith answered them or they answered him. I did not quite know who replied and who questioned, but the Killingtrees found the responses easily enough. I did not even know where to look, although there was a book, identical to the one Douglas used, in front of me.

Suddenly Douglas closed her book and Master Meredith bowed his head to pray as did everyone else but myself. I stood staring at the altar and its rail, waiting. I had heard no words of

Latin. I had smelled no incense. I had found no stranger priest. In this house I had not once surprised anyone at Matins or Evensong.

The Killingtrees of Campion Towers were not Papist at all! They were Anglicans! The Anglican service was always said in English.

I felt as if the vanished bells of Campion Towers clanged in my ears as the others left the chapel. "Come along, Penelope," Laurel said to me, not unkindly, as tears ran down my face. She took me by the hand. "Your grandmother will be entombed in the floor of All Hallows tonight. We must have the funeral feast now. It is not a custom I approve, but the people expect it of us."

"Yes," I replied and followed along. I did not know what else to say or do.

I took a black funeral ring, a gift from my grandfather, but did not put it on my hand as the others did. The willow-green gown was my remembrance. Silk stuff endured for a very long time. I held to this thought while I silently ate and silently drank the canary wine. Julian—I still called him "James Rowland" in my thoughts—spoke only to my grandfather, who leaned sadly on his cane and listened.

It was as well that Julian did not speak with me. I was numb with shock. The others took my peculiar behavior for grief, not shame. I could see this in Laurel's glance and in even Douglas' cool blue eyes.

How very wrong I had been—ever since my conversation with Dr. Moonjean in Bristol. I had believed Campion Towers to be a nest of Papists. I had been so certain. And I had been so wrong! I scarcely took notice when my cousin Julian kissed Douglas, Laurel, and Mistress Sutton. I realized afterward that by this gesture he included me in the family of Campion Towers, but at the moment I was so dazed by my new and terrible knowledge that I could think of nothing but my grievous error.

There had been no danger of conspiring priests and of future Protestant martyrs at all. The idea had been mine alone. Ever since the *Godspeed* had entered Cádiz harbor I had been obsessed by the thought of Roman Catholics. Madame Gawdy had been one isolated Roman Catholic—and she was not an English-woman.

My fancy led me to Dr. Moonjean and Mistress Cardwell and I felt a stab of anger toward them. They had known what I believed but they had let me persist in my error. It was not fair of them. They should have told me I was to watch for treason against the Parliament and General Cromwell. They should have told me Charles Stuart was the man who came! I was tempted to abandon my watchfulness. To think I had found the secret passage and braved its dangers. They cared nothing for my life and left me in a lie.

At this moment General Cromwell was marching on Worcester, while I stood in the great hall of Campion Towers, a goblet of funeral wine in my hand. I had no quarrel with Oliver Cromwell—only with his agents, who had treated me scurvily. General Cromwell would gain the day at Worcester, and follow Charles Stuart in his flight—if he did not take the young King prisoner in Worcester. Cromwell would not tell me lies. He was a man of honor.

I knew what I would do now with my information. I would ride to Oliver Cromwell, himself, and tell him where Charles Stuart would lie after his defeat at Worcester. As a true Puritan saint, I must do this for England.

As I went to my chamber, I wondered how I was to get out of the house. How was I to learn where General Cromwell could be found? I could listen to talk in and about Campion Towers. Everything was open now. But Sir Nicholas did not look with favor upon soldiers at his house. If soldiers did not come here, how was I to learn what went on near Worcester? This August day I knew only that Cromwell marched from the east while the last of the King's Scots came down from the north.

Two days passed as we waited. Garth and Peter had gone to Worcester, dressed in fine new clothing, suits of sober brown wool, gifts of Sir Nicholas, as were the brown geldings of Campion Towers. Only the red mares and some of the nags, the coach horses, remained. I went to the stables often to take sugar, or an apple that had escaped the cider press, to Cranberry and her stall companions.

As for "The Twelve," I heard nothing of them. My grand-father did not journey to the Aylmer farm. I suspected "The Twelve," whoever they were, met in Worcester with Charles Stuart. I had come to a decision about them. I had never seen their faces and could not be certain who they were. Even if I saw Mistress Cardwell or Amyas Moonjean again, I would say no more about "The Twelve."

I knew what mysterious thing would occur the first of September—the battle! All that morning I waited for some word but all was silent. Finally I went to the stables as usual and stood at Cranberry's stall. How I wished I could ride her out into the golden countryside. I could tell by the way she stamped her hooves and arched her neck that she, too, would like a run in the fields near Holt Heath.

As I caressed her, my ears caught a sound, a faint scuffling it seemed, and I caught up a pitchfork from Will Scarlet's open stall. It was a rat. The stable was infested with them even though Garth and Peter tried hard to keep them down. The sound had come from the stall Rufus had once occupied. I went noiselessly toward it and pushed the door open. If a rat came out, I would kill it.

But it was not a rat. It was a man, who lay in the shadows. He jumped to his feet as I waited, my pitchfork held ready. It was a vagabond or a horse thief or perhaps a savage Scot. What could I do? Could I call for help? Who would hear me? Only Jonas or my grandfather, old men.

I sounded much braver than I felt. "What do you want here?" I demanded. "Come out of there." And I stepped back.

The man now crawled out of the deep stall. I let the pitchfork fall with a sigh of relief. It was the old ribbon peddler.

He cringed. "Mistress Hervey! I am in luck. 'Tis ye I came to seek. I guessed ye'd come to the stables sometime today. I heard they's been a death at the manor. They'd turn me away if I came to sell them laces now."

"What do you want with me?" I asked him. "I need no more red ribbons."

"I sell no ribbons to one of us," he pointed to his pack in the straw. "I have come from the north."

"Do not go to Worcester. Charles Stuart is there," I said, misliking the man, a sly creature of Dr. Moonjean's. I wondered if he was lied to also. I doubted it.

"I know that, mistress. I have all of the news."

Not *all*—I thought!

"Have you news for me?" he asked.

"No," I said shortly. Now my news was only for the ears of

General Cromwell. Then I asked a question of him. "Where do you go from here?"

"To Worcester despite your kindly warning," he said with a smirk. "Who would suspect a poor old peddler? I might sell much ribbon and many fine laces to the gaudy gentlemen who serve Charles Stuart and flock to his banner.

"If ye need to ride out I am bid to tell ye summat." How he constantly changed his manner of speech I thought! "I am bid to tell all of our people I meet. The battle begins day after tomorrow. The Cavalier army is twixt Holt Heath and Worcester—and in that city. Cromwell is at Evesham or soon will be there. He comes on apace. The watchword for Cromwell's army is 'This is the heir'."

He stooped to take up his pack. I did not know why I asked it, I tested him, I supposed. He was so proud of his prowess as a spy. "What is the watchword for the army of Charles Stuart?"

The peddler laughed. "Far simpler, mistress—but one word—'Dunbar'."

And then he left, passing behind the stables fearlessly, a harmless dirty old peddler.

Now I knew what I must do. I must ride to Evesham—and very soon. I walked with the pitchfork to the stable door and stabbed it into a pile of fodder. An old rust-colored coat of Garth's hung on a peg on the wall above the hay. A thought came to me. Garth and Peter wore new clothing. I hurried out of the stable to Garth's little cottage and pushed open the door. Had he left his clothing behind? I was in luck. His old leather breeches and vest lay on his pallet, his worn boots on the floor beneath. Even a hat, a shapeless old hat, lay on his table near the pallet. With the shirt from Douglas' riding costume, it would do. I would go to Evesham as a boy!

I went back to the stables and into the harness room. I believed that I could put the bit into Cranberry's mouth and I found her saddle. It was all I could do to get it an inch or two off the saddle block. Then it fell back with a thump. I could never throw it onto the mare's back, and I doubted even more if I could tighten the girth.

There was no help for it. I must ride bareback, and if I was to keep my seat, I must ride bestride like a boy. I had never done this. It would be dangerous. It would be very dangerous. I would ride through a strange countryside into a camp of soldiers. How pleased I was to have General Cromwell's watchword. That and a swift horse would be my only advantages.

Tomorrow night I would leave by the secret steps. I would wear Garth's clothing. There would be a half-moon, and the weather promised to be fine. I would ride to Evesham, seek out the General, tell him my message, and return by dawn. I would be safely in my bed by the time the battle began—even if the armies clashed at sunrise.

Evesham was twenty-five miles from Campion Towers, but to be safe I had better take a roundabout way to the west to avoid Cavalier scouting parties. I would be forced to stay to the roads, given my ignorance of the countryside. How I wished myself Worcestershire-bred so I could cut across the fields and take lesser-known paths. Cranberry and I could do it—but it would be a wearying trip.

Most of the next day, the second of September, I spent in the stables with Cranberry, but I spoke briefly once with my grandfather, asking him if there was any word from Worcester. Sir Nicholas would know what went on. Because I was a Puritan I hesitated to ask him and I felt guilty before him because I spied and because I had wrongly thought him a Catholic, but I took up my courage and asked. He had not treated me in any different fashion recently.

"News?" he said, looking at the floor. "Aye, Pen, there is news. There's no battle yet, but they skirmish outside the city. The Roundheads will bring up cannon. Many brave men will die."

"Yes, sir."

"Many brave Englishmen will die," he went on soberly, and I noticed that he did not now say "Roundhead" or "Cavalier."

"Will Sir Julian come back here?" I asked.

My grandfather caught the note in my voice. "Ye like your cousin? I see that ye do by your face," he commented. "You know he is not a highwayman—even if he is an outlaw. You know his history, then?"

"Yes, Douglas and Mistress Laurel told me something of him. I pieced it together."

"It is a sad tale. If the Roundheads win, he will be an outlaw once more. Everyone's hand will be against him. He will be a hunted man again. He ventured his life to stay near Campion Towers when he came down from Scotland."

I nodded. "He cannot inherit, can he?"

"No. An outlaw has no legal rights."

"Why does he not come to the New World?" I was quite surprised at my own question.

"He follows the fortunes of the King. He has been in the Low Countries, France, and Scotland with young Charles. I have spoken to him of Virginia more than once, but I do not know what he thinks of the idea."

"I wish he could have the Aylmer farm," I said. "I would give it to him. 'Tis of no use to me, sir."

Sir Nicholas looked at me from under his eyebrows. His eyes

were no longer fierce. "Aye, I believe ye would. Ye have a good heart, child. I must speak to you of your leave-taking now. I shall miss ye, but it would not be wise for you to remain in this house longer than need be. As soon as the battle ends and the countryside grows more quiet, I shall ship you off to Swindon. If the Roundheads take the city, they may wonder at your being here. They will come here to search for Julian. They will not forget this is his home. If the Cavaliers hold out and defeat Cromwell, a Puritan maid may not be well treated."

"I wish to see you all again someday." I meant my words.

He sighed. "Aye, perhaps ye shall if ye have the stomach for another long voyage. What will ye do in the New World, Pen? You are a wealthy maid—a catch for any man. I shall send you rents from the Aylmer farm."

I replied truthfully, "I do not know."

"Well, there is time to reflect upon it, child—on your return voyage."

He rose from his chair, and leaning heavily on his cane, left me alone in the great hall. I felt his affection, strange and harsh as it was, and I suffered guilt and shame for the betrayal I plotted of the King my grandfather served.

I waited until full dark, took up my candle, and locked my door behind me. I had complained of a colic at supper and had left the table. I would not be sought out, I was sure, and my grandmother's physician had gone from the house. By now it was easy for me to find the button with the fleur-de-lis, twist and pull it, and enter the secret passage. Tonight I shut the door behind me. I would be gone for hours. I wanted no one to see the gaping entrance. Swiftly I went down the steps and out into the court, closing the stone behind me. A slight kick would force it open again before dawn.

As I ran in the windless night the dust rose in soft pale clouds about the hem of my ghostly gleaming skirts and the new black shoes from Worcester. The half-moon was rising, golden but chill in the night sky. A handful of stars had been cast across its path as if by a sower of grain.

I reached Garth's cottage where I stripped off my gown and petticoats. Like a fool I had forgotten Douglas' shirt, but, no matter, an old dark flannel shirt of the stableboy's lay in a dusty corner. It was a deep green color. I shook it out and put it on; then I got into his breeches and finally hauled on his boots. I smelled strongly of horses—as a man should. All that remained was the hat. It fit snugly, more snugly when I tucked my hair beneath it. Even for a foolish Cavalier my curls were overlong. In an instant I had thrown my gown, shoes, and petticoats under Garth's pallet and was out the door, running for the moonlit stables.

Garth's hat may have fit; his boots were far too large. They carried me at a stumbling run of their own and I burst into the harness room nearly tripping over my own feet. I snatched Cranberry's bridle from its peg and turned to hurry to her stall.

But all at once a voice came out of the warm, hay-scented blackness. "Stand as you are, Mistress Hervey, or I will kill you."

I stopped in mid-stride, my mouth open, the bridle in my hand.

"Do not take another step," the voice ordered me. It was a woman's voice. Amabel Sutton's voice.

"What do you want of me?" I managed to croak. I searched for her in the blackness. Where had her voice come from? I could make out only the tines of the pitchfork with which I had threatened the peddler. They gleamed in a slender shaft of light.

Now Mistress Sutton came out into the moonlight. She held a pistol, its mountings a delicate tracing of silver. She stood not ten feet from me, her hate-filled eyes fixed on my face.

She bit off her words. "So you have stolen the stable lout's shirt and breeches, have you? They become you well. I thought you would ride out tonight to join your Roundhead friends. You wish that devil Cromwell to win. Roundheads—your folk —murdered my brothers. Perhaps the others at the house can forgive you, Mistress Hervey, but I do not. You hie yourself to the Roundheads to be safe, and you take the Aylmer jewels with you."

"No," I cried, "I have no jewels with me."

"Do you spy on us, then, Mistress Hervey?" she demanded with a sharp laugh. She took a step toward me.

I was silent. How had she known this? I had done nothing to make her suspect me and I did not believe Julian Killingtree, who held no affection for the greedy Mistress Sutton, had told her of my presence in the secret passage. She guessed at it, then.

I lied to her. "I am no spy. You have guessed why I leave Campion Towers. Sir Nicholas told me today that I would be in danger if the King wins at Worcester. If Cromwell wins, I might bring trouble to my grandfather's house. I go to Swindon to friends. I shall sail for the New World soon. I will not trouble you again."

Mistress Sutton grinned. It was a fearful thing to see—as if a cat skinned its lips back from its teeth. Her heavy silk gown rustled as she came another step closer. "It matters not. I do not care what you say. You probably lie. What matters is that you skulk off without a word. You take the jewels with you. I know you do! You would not leave Campion Towers unless you had the jewels. That is why you came here—to get the Aylmer inheritance. Give them to me and I shall let you go. Otherwise, I will surely kill you and take the jewels. It will be simple. They will believe that you hoped to run away to the Roundheads and were killed by a thief who came to steal the red mares. They will not even hear my shot."

I hesitated. She wanted the jewels. Her eyes told me she had no thought of letting me go. The moment Mistress Sutton had the jewels, she would shoot me.

"Will you let me go?" I asked.

She nodded, her grin fixed. "Aye, I shall let you go."

I reached toward the pocket of Garth's old breeches and made as if to pull something from them. Her eyes went greedily to my hand. Then I flung the heavy bridle into her face, hoping she would not fire the pistol. I took the woman by surprise. She stumbled backward, her hand flung up to protect her eyes. I caught up the pitchfork and, praying that my aim be good, brought its side down, hard on her hand. The pistol went flying through the air.

Mistress Sutton came at me like the great tawny cat of our New World forests, her fingers curved to claw at my face. I leaped back, ran my hands down the shaft of the pitchfork, and struck at the woman. It caught her alongside the head. She fell at my feet.

I dropped the pitchfork and bent to stare at her. Dark blood welled from a wound on her forehead. I had killed her. But she would have killed me! I had no time to lose over Amabel Sutton. I snatched Garth's coat from its peg and put it on. Mistress Sutton's pistol lay only a short distance from her. I picked it up and dropped it into the coat pocket. Then I dragged the woman into Rufus' empty stall, the nearest one, and shut the double doors tight.

Finally I ran back for the bridle. I took it up and hastened to Cranberry's stall. The red horses were stirring. I could hear them moving about, stamping with excitement. I threw open Cranberry's dark stall and darted inside. The puzzled mare put her nose against Garth's familiar coat and sniffed. She knew me in a moment and nuzzled me for sugar. The horse obediently opened her mouth for her bridle. In an instant I had the bit inside and fastened the buckles tightly. So far—so good.

I ran, hauling at the mare's reins, as she followed me at a trot. We went to the stone horsetrough at the stable's end. Here I steadied the mare and mounted from the side of the trough.

Praying, I clucked to Cranberry. At a trot we left the stables. My teeth chattered, half from fear and excitement and half from Cranberry's jolting gait, as we passed behind the stables. I was most unsure of myself riding bestride, but the moment I urged the horse into an easy, steady hand gallop all was well. We had far to go. We would save the galloping to pass through open countryside.

We swept west, skirting Holt Heath. The moon was bright enough for me to see roadside signs and I believed I knew my route. Mistress Sutton's pistol lay heavy in the pocket of Garth's coat. I knew how to use it. My father had taught both Obedience and me to load, prime, and fire a pistol to protect the house when the pirate ships from Tortuga came to Salem Town. But would I have the courage to use it? I did not lie to myself about the dangers that might lie ahead. I leaned far forward over Cranberry's neck as we rode on into the night. The wind, which had risen since I set out, was warm and sweet on my face, while the darker tops of trees tossed against the dark sky.

We went swiftly through Leigh and then south to another hamlet where a solitary dog came out to snap at the mare's heels and to race beside her, barking. I had feared the town of Severn Stoke, for I knew that I must cross the river there and I was afraid that the bridge might be held by soldiers. But no one blocked my way and Cranberry's hooves made a thunder on the bridge across the river.

Now I walked the red horse for a time to rest her. We now traveled east. She was scarcely lathered and pulled still at her bridle. She wanted to run but I checked her. We still had far to go tonight.

Finally I urged her into a hand gallop again. We went through yet another sleeping town and now turned northeast at its crossroads signpost. It pointed northeast toward Pershore. Beyond Pershore lay Evesham and General Cromwell! I turned Cranberry's head and once more we rode into the night. The moon had climbed higher into the sky but I guessed it was not quite midnight.

Pershore was only a hamlet, too. I stopped at the end of its highroad, but I could not make out the signpost, which had been broken off. Roads stretched away in all four directions. Which way should I take?

As I hesitated, I heard the jingle of bridles and from the south I saw horses and riders coming at a hard gallop. It was too late for me to ride off or to hide behind the tall roadside hedges. I had been seen. I turned Cranberry to meet the newcomers. Moonlight glinted on helmets and breastplates. The riders were soldiers. My heart raced as they came up to me. They wore no white scarves or fine plumes. They were Cromwell's men.

The soldier who rode at the head of the troopers called out for the others to halt. They reined up not far from me, every eye upon me. Trying to show no fear, I rode Cranberry to them.

"What is the watchword? Where do ye ride?" the soldier demanded.

"The watchword is 'This is the heir'," I told him. "I ride to Evesham to speak with General Cromwell. I have a message."

"Do ye now? Ye will find naught at Evesham, boy," the soldier said with a laugh. "Cromwell has broken camp. He is on the march. I shall take your message to the General. I am Cornet Tomlinson." There was scorn in his words and a man behind him laughed, too, at my presumptuousness.

"My message is for Cromwell's ears. It concerns the man they call 'Charles Stuart'."

"Aye, ye have come to tell old Oliver that Charles Stuart is in Worcester, I warrant?" The Cornet was unpleasant.

"My news is more important than that." I was angry. "I serve General Cromwell and Dr. Amyas Moonjean."

This interested the Cornet. He was silent for a moment. I could scarcely see his face under his helmet and I knew that under the brim of Garth's hat he could not see mine. He could not know I was a maid.

"Fall in behind, lad," he ordered. "We ride to Worcester. We shall catch up to Cromwell in a mile or two. I will take ye to him. God help ye if ye jest with him or make sport."

I did not thank the officer. I moved Cranberry in behind the last soldier and at the rude Cornet's shout, put her into a swinging stride that kept pace easily with the cavalry horses.

We heard the army before we saw it. The rumble of cart

wheels, the jangling of harness, and the calls of the men who whipped the dray horses on to Worcester drifted back to us on the air as we rode. We rounded a hillside bend and suddenly the rear of Cromwell's great army of thirty thousand men lay before my eyes, strung out along the moon-washed road below.

We rode past the army—past the supply carts, the cannon and the straining horses that pulled the huge guns, and past troop after troop of marching men, who carried muskets and trailed pikes. I had heard great praise of the musketeers and the pikemen of the Parliamentary army. Now I saw the famous soldiers marching grimly and silently toward Worcester. I was proud as Cranberry and I passed them.

As we went through the village of Whittington, the Cornet reined up beside the road and stopped to speak with a second officer who listened and then pointed wordlessly to the north. Now I heard the Cornet order the man behind him to take command. He trotted his mount back to my humble place at the tail of his troop and spoke to me.

"This way, lad. I shall take you to General Cromwell. Have a care what you say. I hope for your sake that Cromwell finds your news as important as you claim. Old Oliver has no time for folly. If ye had not said ye came from Dr. Moonjean, I would take a whip to your hide and drive you home to your mother."

I kept my tongue. This was not the courtesy I had expected from my own people. Cornet Tomlinson and I trotted by yet another troop of horses and then drew rein, together, near three men, who walked their mounts calmly, surrounded on all sides by cavalrymen, the renowned Ironsides.

My breath caught in my throat. One of these men was Oliver Cromwell! Which one?

Battle

—————◆—————

"General Cromwell?" I asked, scarcely daring to speak.

"Yes," the man on the white horse replied and he added, "I am told you bring a message for me from Dr. Moonjean. Come ride beside me." His voice was high and thin.

I did as he asked, hoping that Cranberry would behave herself and not disgrace me by misliking Oliver Cromwell's horse. Cranberry had not liked following the troopers. Now she eyed the unfamiliar white horse and sidestepped a bit but behaved well enough otherwise.

"Who are you?" Cromwell asked as we traveled side by side. "Where do you come from?"

"I am Mistress Hervey—Penitence Hervey. I come from Salem Town in Massachusetts Bay Colony."

He turned his head to look at me. I could not see his face but I caught his surprise. "Then, what, in the name of all that is holy, do you here, Mistress Hervey? Has no one told you that we march into battle? Has no one told you in the New World that women do not go to war? There are no ungodly Amazons

221

in my ranks. Do the women of Salem Town dress in men's clothing?"

I was taken aback by his severity and was hard put to reply. "No, sir. I know of the battle. I do not go to war. I wore breeches only because I have ridden far and swiftly. I needed to attract as little attention as possible. Besides," I added lamely, "I could not lift the sidesaddle."

I heard him snort. Cromwell was contemptuous of me. Let him wait until he heard what I had to say, I thought.

"Take no more of my time, Mistress Hervey. The Cornet has told me of your master. Amyas Moonjean sometimes chooses strange instruments for his work. You knew the watchword. I accept you as one of his creatures—one of his spies. What news does Dr. Moonjean send by you?"

"I am not sent by him. I have not seen Dr. Moonjean for some time, but I come with great news, sir. I have ridden tonight from Campion Towers to the north."

"I do not know of such a place. I have much to ponder now. You say Dr. Moonjean did not send you? What news, then, has a maid like yourself learned that could concern me? Speak quickly."

I was frightened. I stammered out, "Charles Stuart was at Campion Towers but days past."

"Charles Stuart has been in Worcestershire for nearly twice sennight. He attempts to raise the county against me. Worcestershire will not rise for him. He shall fail. So he has been to this Campion Towers and you have seen him? So have hundreds of people."

"But I know where he hopes to hide after the battle, General Cromwell."

This took his attention. He was silent and then said, "How do you know this thing?"

"I listened. No one saw me. I heard him tell my kinsman that he would return to Campion Towers to hide in the secret passage if you won at Worcester."

"God willing, I shall win the victory. So he goes to this Campion Towers? Where is this place?"

"North of Worcester nigh to Holt Heath."

For a long moment Oliver Cromwell was quiet as our horses walked. Behind us the two men who rode with him spoke together in low tones. After a time the General commented again. "I suppose I should give you my thanks, Mistress Hervey, but I mislike spies. Your news may be important at that. Who is this kinsman you speak of?"

"Sir Julian Killingtree," I said. I had not wanted the General to ask me this.

"Ah!" Cromwell touched his chin. "I know of that one, although I have never seen the man—a gallant soldier and a slippery devil. Why do you betray your kinsman?"

"He is a Cavalier. I am a Puritan," I replied simply. "I wish you to win at Worcester."

"Reason enough, I suppose." I felt an unspoken rebuke in his words and felt that General Cromwell did not like me.

I heard the galloping of hooves and a rider carrying a blazing torch came up to us. "A dispatch from General Fleetwood for General Cromwell!" he called out.

"Here!" said Cromwell loudly. I waited while the officer gave him the dispatch, a rolled sheet of paper, and held his torch close so the General could read. I looked for the first time on the face of Oliver Cromwell.

Under his plain hat his face was long and severe—as severe as his words to me. His nose was long and hooked; his upper lip heavily indented, his lips taut and firm. His chin was long, too, above his high white linen collar and his red-shining half-armor. He lifted his eyes and gazed for a moment at me as he finished reading. His eyes were heavy-lidded, his eyebrows thick and arched. I could not tell the color of Cromwell's eyes, but his look was one of patience and of strength. I had expected to see contempt in his gaze when he looked at me, but I found none—only a sadness, and then instant dismission as if he had shut a door on my presence. His gray hair was shoulder length and, like a girl's, it curled. Although he was the greatest Puritan of them all, he was no "Roundhead" with cropped hair. But what struck me most was the fact that Oliver Cromwell had bit his lip with strain. Blood streamed over his chin. The effect was terrible. I remembered what Captain Enderby had told my father about the awesome Cromwell. It was a legend among us saints how he had ridden about his camp in the night hours before he fought at Dunbar in Scotland, the blood pouring, unnoticed, down his chin.

The general spoke to the courier with the torch. "A moment." He gestured to one of the men who rode with him. "I write a dispatch," he commanded. Cromwell, his two companions, the courier, and I moved without further command to the side of the road, where we halted.

One of his companions took an inkhorn, a flat board, a sheet of paper, and a quill from a leather bag at his side. He put the paper onto the board and waited expectantly.

Cromwell spoke. "The order is for General Lambert. He is to take his men across the Severn and to go up then to the River Teme. A Royalist division lies north of the Teme. This division must not be permitted to escape me. Tell General Lambert that I shall send more particular orders later."

He finished and the secretary reached once more into his bag, sprinkled sand from a box over the dispatch, rolled it up and handed it to the courier.

Cromwell addressed the courier. "Ride swiftly and take care. Lambert must be at the Teme by dawn." The messenger nodded. The flames of his torch now fluttered in the damp night air. In a clatter of hooves he was out and away and I watched his torch spark across the sky in an arc as he threw it into a brook at the side of the road.

I spoke to Cromwell, who frightened me. I saw both his greatness and his ruthlessness. He would triumph at Worcester because he willed it. Oliver Cromwell did not need the help of God—or any man. "I must go back," I said. "They will look for me. If I am not at Campion Towers in the morning, they will suspect something."

"Go then, Mistress Hervey. Remember well what you have done tonight and what you have seen here. Ride east to Alcester and then ride north. The way should be open for you. You have our watchword if you meet my men. It has not changed."

Oliver Cromwell urged his white horse forward to fall into the line of march.

I was dismissed.

I put my heel to Cranberry and we went at a hand gallop along the side of the road, soon passing the fore of the New Model Army. I was ordered to halt by another officer there and I gave him the watchword and asked the way. He pointed ahead. "The maps say there is a road ahead over the next hill, lad. It runs east. My advice to ye is get home. We do man's work today."

So it was past midnight? I thanked him, put the red mare into a hand gallop once more, and rode up the hill. In a matter of minutes I had turned Cranberry onto the east road and was on my way to Alcester and then to Holt Heath.

The moon had reached the zenith of its night journey. So had I. As it began its descent in the sky, we rode on at a steady pace. We had time. I would be in my bed before sunup.

I thought of all that had happened to me since I had stolen out of the secret passage. I had taken a life. I had spoken with Oliver Cromwell. I had not loved him as his men did—but a Cromwell dwelt beyond my knowledge, even if I did understand his mislike of spies, for I did not fancy my work for Dr. Moonjean and was ashamed because of it. I had felt joy when I heard Sir Julian praised by Oliver Cromwell. It was the only pleasure I had taken from my speech with the greatest Puritan of them all.

I rode through a little vale lined on each side of the road by tall, funereal black trees. They were frightening and I looked toward the moon-drenched open heath beyond as I clucked to Cranberry.

Suddenly I heard the neigh of another horse and a shot rang out. The bullet passed before my face and I ducked my head, racing with my cheek against the red mare's neck.

"Stand or we fire on you again," came a shouted command.

I reined Cranberry in. She reared, terrified by the pistol ball and by the shout. I kept my seat with difficulty. As it was I slid backward, and as she came down with a jolting crash on her front hooves, I slid forward, my arms clasped around her neck.

"Rise up, whoever ye be," came a hard voice.

I raised my head and cautiously unwound my arms from Cranberry's neck. The horse quivered beneath my quivering knees, but I sat up as I had been ordered.

I looked at the two men beside the road. Both were dressed in dark clothing. Each rider wore a helmet and each had a broad white scarf across his chest. These were Royalists—Cavaliers.

The man nearest me spoke sternly. "The watchword, boy? Give us the watchword and tell us where ye ride so swiftly on that fine horse or I shall blow your head off your shoulders."

"Dunbar," I blurted out. "The watchword is 'Dunbar'."

The other man laughed. " 'Dunbar' it was—yesterday. If ye know that, 'tis not likely ye be a spy. All the same 'Dunbar' is not the watchword. We ride to Worcester. We shall take ye with us. Let them decide what to do with ye."

"That is a very fine horse you ride," the first Cavalier said. "The King rides one summat like it. I warrant ye stole that mount from Worcester and ye ran away?"

"I ride to the physician at Alcester," I stammered. "I stole no horse. I was told to take the mare. There is illness in my house."

"A likely tale from a lying lad. No more of your clack now. Ye go to Worcester with us—and no tricks, mind ye. I would not care if I shot ye. I have a fancy to that horse, myself."

I let the Cavalier catch Cranberry by the bridle. I could not use the pistol in my pocket. I had been taken unaware and had no time to bring it out. I must go to Worcester with them. With luck I could convince someone in that city that I meant no harm to anyone. Conscience pricked me—I had already done what harm I could to the Cavalier cause. Perhaps I could still be on my way to Holt Heath and Campion Towers before daybreak.

We trotted in silence to Worcester. The roads were clear, and we saw only one other scouting party, made up of two more Cavalier soldiers, who fell in with us and who laughed when they were told my story. I now began to wonder if anyone would believe me.

We came into the moonlit city by the Sidbury Gate. I thought of the seamstress spy. Could Naomi Cardwell help me now even if I could go to her kinswoman at The Swan? I doubted it.

I felt faint as we made our way through the narrow crooked streets and drew rein before the Guildhall. At a harsh command, I slid down from Cranberry and stood beside her.

All four soldiers dismounted. Three climbed the steps, their spurs ringing, while the fourth took Cranberry's reins and the reins of the other horses. He sagged down on the steps, yawning, as his comrades paused at the top.

The tallest soldier called out to me, "Get along here, lad. I shall take ye to Colonel Robbins. He may find your tale amusing if ye make it brief. But ye had better tell him the truth about that horse of yours!"

I followed unwillingly through the great wooden doors of the Guildhall. A crowd of people milled about inside. Candles dripped in floor sconces. Men wearing white scarves, their uniforms a blaze of different colors, stood in little groups arguing and laughing.

Someone had placed a long table at the far end of the lofty old hall. A brown-faced man with a scarlet plume in his hat sat behind it. Before it stood a line of men and women, most of them humble-looking people in sober clothing.

The soldier with me explained, "They be folk who seek to leave Worcester before the battle, boy. If ye can tell a story that convinces and if ye can prove ye own the horse—or if someone vouches for ye—they will give ye a pass to leave the city."

My thoughts sped as we took our place at the end of the line. How could I prove what I had said? I watched hopelessly as people were granted passes and were identified by those Worcestershire Royalists who occupied benches behind the Colonel. A woman in a black riding cloak with its hood drawn about her face now stood before the Cavalier officer, who looked weary and yawned often.

"Your name, mistress, and your occupation?" he asked sounding annoyed by this task.

"Mistress Naomi Cardwell," came the reply. "I am a seamstress." I started violently at this.

"Why do you wish to leave the city?" the man droned on. "Where do you go?"

"To Kidderminster," she replied. "My Mistress, Mistress Turtledove, has gone there to make gowns for a rich family. I am bid to bring her the stuffs." She gestured toward a bundle at her feet. "If I am mewed up in the city I will lose my place in her employ."

Without raising his eyes the officer crooked a finger and a burly man came up behind him. "Do you vouch for this woman?" the officer asked.

"Aye," the man replied. "I have known Mistress Cardwell for many a year. She does no harm to any man."

"You may pass," the soldier signed the paper.

I looked at Garth's boots as she took up the bundle and pushed her way through the crowd. Naomi Cardwell had not seen me at all, but I had seen her face. It bore a look of sly triumph at having hoodwinked the people of Worcester so well and so long. How I wished I could wipe that from her face!

The line moved slowly. Finally, the little man ahead of me approached the officer. He took his hat off and held it before his breast. "I am a capmaker from Bewdley, your lordship. I did not think there would be a battle so soon. I come to Worcester to buy wool." He mopped his forehead with his sleeve. " 'Tis all in such confusion here. My business took longer than I'd a thought. My cart is loaded and at the gate. And, it please ye, let me pass, or my wife will fret."

Another man now came from the benches. "I vouch for him,"

said the citizen of Worcester. "He bought his wool from me. I have never heard him say a goodly word for any Roundhead."

"Pass," said the officer, who scrawled his name on the paper and gave it to the capmaker. The little man from Bewdley had put an idea into my head—a good thing, too! It was now my turn to stand before the Cavalier officer.

The Colonel stared at me for a long moment, his eyebrows drawn together. "You cannot be more than twelve years, boy. By the look of ye, ye have never had a razor to your face." He spoke in a softer, more interested tone. "What brings you here? Is your father with you? I cannot give a pass to a child."

The soldier who accompanied me bowed to the Colonel. "There is a bit more here than meets the eye, sir. We caught the lad riding hard for Alcester tonight just a few miles ahead of the Roundhead army. He gave us yesterday's watchword, so we brought him in."

Colonel Robbins leaned back in his chair and put his finger to the side of his nose. "Is this all? Did he shoot at you or threaten you? Is this the green fruit of a night's scouting when Roundheads are about? You were to bring in a Roundhead officer—not a child." He laughed.

"There is more, sir," the soldier explained hastily. "You should see the horse he rides. We all knew it at once. 'Tis of the same breed as the King's own horse. There are no others like them in the army—only the King's and Sir Julian Killingtree's. The boy rides one of the red horses."

"Are you a horse thief, lad?" The officer had gone from jesting to sternness in an instant.

This was the moment I waited for. I whipped off Garth's hat. My hair fell to my shoulders in a tangled mass but it would have to do. The Colonel was clearly astonished.

"I am not a lad," I told him. "I am no horse thief and the red horse is not stolen. She was given to me by Sir Nicholas Killingtree of Campion Towers. I am his granddaughter. I rode to Alcester to find the physician. There is sickness at the manor. There was no one else at the house to go. Sir Nicholas cannot ride far because of his broken foot. All of the younger servants have been sent here to Worcester. I would have come here for the physician but I was not certain I could come into the city. I knew 'Dunbar' was yesterday's watchword. I knew no other. I hoped it would serve."

"How come you by those?" The Colonel pointed at the stable-boy's clothes.

"They are borrowed, sir. It was safer on the roads at night to ride out as a boy."

"It is strange but sensible," he agreed. "I fear we cannot accommodate you in the matter of a physician, mistress. We shall need every doctor of physick in Worcester, ourselves. I shall write you a pass. A physician will come as soon as we can spare one."

I was relieved. I sagged against the table. How easy it had been. If I rode hard, I could yet be back before dawn.

"Who lies ill at Campion Towers?" Colonel Robbins asked in a friendly manner, drawing a sheet of paper toward him.

"My grandmother," I replied. I still found it difficult to think of Philippa as dead.

All at once I heard a woman's voice call out, "She lies, your lordship. Hold her!" and as I looked on in terrified amazement, Madame Marie Gawdy, as fat as ever, got up from the bench and waddled forward.

"Who are you?" the Colonel demanded.

"The widow of Hinchingbrooke Gawdy," she told him. "Her

grandmother died two days past. *Mon Dieu,* I would have kept my silence until I heard the wench lie. She is up to mischief. She might possibly have ridden to Alcester for Sir Nicholas. He suffers from illness as does my friend, his sister, Mistress Laurel Killingtree. I would have let it pass had the maid said this, but Mistress Laurel sent me a message, telling me her brother's wife had died. The wench is a Roundhead from the New World. I know her well."

The Colonel looked at me in some surprise. He sighed and pushed the paper from him. "Well, mistress, what am I to do with you? You have not told me the truth, it seems. If you were older, you would be put on trial and perhaps hanged as a spy. We have hanged Roundhead spies before. It seems this woman here marks you out. Can no one else come forward to vouch for you? You must realize this—before a battle all liars become suspect as traitors and spies."

I shook my head. Mistress Cardwell had gone. The peddler was not there—not that I thought any of Dr. Moonjean's agents would attempt to save me. I was weary and ached from so much hard riding. The Cavalier Colonel made an impatient motion to the soldier who still stood next to me. "See to it she is put under guard. This is a matter for those above me. Let the King's advisers decide what is to be done with the maid. It may go hard with you, mistress, if no one can vouch for you."

Now a man's voice rang out through the throng and every head turned to see who called. For a moment I thought it was another accuser. Then my tears spilled over. It was Julian Killingtree, limping through the Cavaliers, who respectfully made way for him. He was very fine in a lobstertail helmet and half-armor over his buff-colored breeches. The other Cavaliers paled beside him, although his clothing was far less gaudy than their ruby-red, purple, green, and sky-blue coats.

"I vouch for Mistress Hervey," he said as Madame Gawdy looked reproachfully at both of us and then rolled back to her bench. She did not approve of Julian, although Colonel Robbins clearly did.

"You know this girl, Sir Julian?"

"Aye. She is my kinswoman. I spied her red mare outside just now, so I believed someone from Campion Towers was here. I could not guess who it might be or why someone rode to Worcester. I came at once to satisfy my curiosity."

At my cousin's words my tall guard had melted into the crowd. Julian took me by the arm. "There is no harm in the girl. She is a Roundhead no more. She has seen the error of her ways. I shall take charge of her and see her back to Campion Towers."

"She has come for a physician, Sir Julian. I told her there was none to be had."

"Is someone ill?" Julian asked in surprise. "I had not heard it."

I looked at him through my tears and saw his mouth tighten, the old harsh line reappearing. I was not sure that I could take him in with another falsehood.

"It must be Sir Nicholas Killingtree's arthritis," Julian said to the Colonel. "The pain comes upon him suddenly in the middle of the night. Is that it, Pen—his arthritis?"

He pinched my arm as a signal and I nodded miserably. How weary I was of lies! And I had hoped to be done with them. Julian let me go, went around the table and stooped to whisper into the Colonel's ear. The man raised his eyebrows and looked strangely at me in Garth's old rust-colored coat, his ragged breeches, and overlarge boots.

"No, I do not dispute the matter, Sir Julian." He grinned as Julian took me by the arm again. Then the Colonel turned to the old man who stood waiting behind me. "Next!" he said, sounding annoyed once more.

Julian propelled me through the interested Cavaliers so swiftly that he almost carried me. Some of them laughed, but most stared coldly. "You fool," my kinsman spoke through his teeth. "What are you doing here? Must I spend all of my life looking after you? The hangman's rope was not more than an inch from your neck back there. 'Tis fortunate for you that Will Scarlet spied Berry as we rode by. I did not mark her out. My horse nearly tore the reins from my hands going to her."

"What did you tell the Colonel?" I gasped out as we reached the steps of the Guildhall.

"What he would believe, of course. I told him you were the King's latest light of love and that, unbidden, you hied yourself to Worcester to be with Charles Stuart before the battle. You quarreled with the King and you ran from him. I told him you were half-crazed with love and proud as Lucifer. You would not tell anyone the truth because you would not wish anyone to know the King was angry with you and might cast you aside. I told him further that your wits were somewhat dim, despite your beauty, and that you were an empty-headed flirt-gill."

We went down the steps to where Cranberry and Will Scarlet stood side by side, waiting in the moonlight.

Julian shook me. "Now, tell me why you were on the road to Alcester alone at night and in Garth's clothing. Tell *me* the truth."

My head ached from weariness. I could not think up yet another tale, so I would tell him what I had told Mistress Sutton. "Sir Nicholas spoke with me today. He said I was a danger at Campion Towers. No matter who wins at Worcester, I could bring danger to my family or be in danger myself. I only waited at Campion Towers until I could go to Swindon and then to Bristol safely. But how long before it was safe to travel? I decided I could save myself and everyone else trouble if I left before the battle."

I took the pistol from my pocket and gave it to Sir Julian.

"So you stole one of Sir Nicholas' pistols? Did you know how to use it?"

I nodded unhappily. "I killed Amabel Sutton."

"Good God!"

"She was waiting in the stables to catch me," I went on. "She had the pistol. She thought I had the Aylmer jewels with me when I ran away."

"Did you?" He shot the question at me.

"No. I have only the passage money I brought with me from Salem Town. I had nothing to give Mistress Sutton, but she was set to kill me because I was a Roundhead."

"How did you come by the pistol?"

I told him of the pitchfork and of my taking up the pistol. "She said they would think it was a vagabond who killed *me*," I explained, "so I guess they will think a vagabond murdered her."

He shoved me down to the horses and lifted me onto Cranberry's back. His face was sober as he gave me her reins.

"I am sorry you were forced to kill Amabel, but she was evil. Others have thought of killing her. Her greed has destroyed her as I knew it would."

He mounted Will Scarlet easily, for all of his lameness.

"Where do you take me—back to Campion Towers?"

He shook his head. "No, Pen. The city will be sealed off within the hour. I take you where you can find a cup of wine and a bed. You are in no condition to ride alone anywhere. You will stay in Worcester tonight. You will remain here until the battle is won.

"The King waits for me now. I shall send for you in the morning, for you will be safest with me. Some of the King's Englishmen are rogues and thieves and his Scots are wild and fierce. Many of them speak only their own tongue and will obey only their own commanders—when they will obey them. Bar your door tonight. Open only to my voice. There should be no plundering and burning in the city. The King sees to its order, but that order is not easy to enforce."

We turned off into a narrow little street in the eastern part of the city. The huge black bulk of the cathedral, which stood on the bank of the Severn, loomed above us. Julian reined Will Scarlet before a brick house. "My godmother once lived here," he told me. "She has been dead for five years, but her old servants, who now keep the house, have often taken me in and hidden me when I asked." He rapped thunderously with the knocker until the door was cautiously opened by a stooped old man, who held a candle in one hand and a pistol in the other.

"Oh, Sir Julian," he spoke with a tremble in his voice. "It is good to see you—even at this hour. What can I do for you?"

"I have a friend from Campion Towers with me. Do you have a place where she can rest?"

"Aye, we do. Come along, mistress." The old man gaped at my strange attire, but he put his pistol away and stood aside.

Julian did an odd thing. He returned the pistol I had taken from Mistress Sutton, but before he gave it to me, he checked to see that there was powder in the firing pan. "If anyone tries to force himself on you, Pen, fire this. I mean what I tell you." He clapped me on the shoulder. I was so exhausted that I wavered until he steadied me. His voice was more gentle now. "I shall take Berry with me. Garth will rub her down and feed her." He smiled at me by the candlelight. "Ye make a pretty lad, Pen. Garth would not believe how his clothing becomes ye, but how any man took you for a boy, even at night, I shall never know! They must be blind. Sleep well."

I caught at his armor, my hand slipping on the silvery steel. "You would not tell Charles Stuart of this."

My kinsman laughed. "Difficult as it may seem for a maid so comely, the King now turns his thoughts to greater things. He thinks of old Oliver tonight—not of kisses. He does not even know your true name. Now, good night, Pen. I cannot delay further."

"Must Sir Nicholas know the truth about Amabel Sutton's death?" I begged.

Julian paused at the door. "He could be told. Laurel could be told also. It would not affect them overmuch. They would tell Douglas it was a vagabond."

As he rode away I went slowly inside the house Julian had found for me. I was too weary to feel anything but shame and a sense of loss. The young King was doomed. And my words could easily be the instrument of his death. With all my heart I wished I could call them back.

I do not know how long I slept the sleep of exhaustion. The sun was high in the sky when I opened my eyes and stepped down from the high bed. I had been too weary to eat last night. The bread and cheese the man and woman had brought me was still untouched. Sir Julian's old friends were kind. They had been concerned when I ate nothing but relieved when I drank some wine. I wondered how kindly they would feel toward me if they knew I had betrayed their king?

I found a basin and a pitcher and hurriedly washed my face and then did what I could to my hair with my fingers. I went to the window and looked out. The street was a quiet one. I saw no guards before the houses, but as I watched some men in skirtlike garments, which stopped well above their knees, marched by. A man playing a peculiar-looking musical instrument strutted before them. I flung the casement open and heard the wailings of a bagpipe for the first time. I closed the casement hastily and silently. I guessed these were some of the King's savage Scots; it would not do to attract their notice. I sat down and munched the dry bread and the cheese morosely, wondering what this doom's-day would bring to me.

Julian came as he had promised. I saw him from the window as he rode up on Will Scarlet, Cranberry trailing happily behind the great red horse.

My cousin called to me from outside my door and I unbarred it at once. "Come along, Pen," he ordered. He grinned and shook his head at my costume.

"Where do we go?" I asked. "Can I leave now?"

"No, 'tis past midday. We join the King. He is in the tower of the cathedral. He knows you are in the city. You should hear the wild tale I told him to explain your arrival here. I did not know I could create such stories. It must be the Killingtree blood —either that or my association with you. Your mother was the finest tale-teller a small boy ever knew."

I must have looked dismayed, for he laughed and said, "No, I did not tell King Charles that you had conceived such a passion for him that you ran away to Worcester nor did I tell him you had gone stark mad. He still does not know you are a

Roundhead. Colonel Robbins will not inform him. The King thinks you are a devoted follower of his cause."

Relieved, I took up Garth's old hat and hurried down the stairs after Julian to our horses. In a few minutes we dismounted at the side of the great ivy-covered cathedral, leaving Will Scarlet and Cranberry tethered.

There were soldiers everywhere now in the streets of the city. The kilted Scots sat in doorways. Horsemen sat on steps— even on the cathedral steps—throwing dice and talking. Some looked up curiously as we passed. A few called out to Julian. More men seemed to recognize him at the cathedral doors and in the cathedral grounds. They bowed or nodded and all stared at me. Some smirked openly. I knew what they thought and I blushed.

I overheard one short man dressed all in deep green velvet say, "I trust the wench does not distract or divert the King overmuch today."

I was angry. Julian put his hand to his sword for a moment but let it fall at my murmur. "I have brought it on myself," I said.

"Aye, that you did," he agreed. "This is not the time to give a challenge, yet I mark Henry Wilmot out well enough."

I searched my memory. I had heard "Wilmot" before. His name had been mentioned in the secret passage. This man advised the King.

We walked into the cool dim cathedral. It was a pleasant relief. The day promised to be hot. Hastily we strode through the nave. Cavaliers sat in the pews, some reading, others talking quietly, while a few put their heads together over maps. Three or four, wisest of them all I thought, were on their knees before the altar praying.

We entered a little door at one side of the great church. A narrow winding stairway led up and up, and we climbed it without pause. My chest ached and my heart pounded when we reached the top and I stumbled out into sunshine.

The tower of Worcester Cathedral was not large. The stone gallery had openings in its walls. Men stood at these openings; all told there must have been twelve men in the tower. I recognized Charles Stuart at once—by his great height and by his sober clothing, for he still wore the black coat and breeches he had worn at Campion Towers, although now he wore a soft wide-brimmed black hat with an immense white plume. Another man stood at his elbow talking, seemingly arguing, while the King shook his head.

Julian went boldly up to his king, calling him "sire." Then my kinsman went to one knee. The King named him "Julian" and lifted him up. Then he spied me behind my cousin. He began to laugh. He roared with laughter. So did his companions and advisers a moment later.

I stood, my cheeks hot, Garth's hat in my hands. I did not know what to do but the King beckoned for me to come forward to him. I came a half step at a time while he laughed at me still. Should I curtsy? But how could I in such clothing? Should I bow? But I was not a man. I was a Puritan. I would not kneel to Charles Stuart. I felt foolish standing there, twisting the hat in my hands.

Charles Stuart solved my problem. He stooped and kissed me chastely on the brow. Then he took my hand and lifted it high. "This is Mistress Sutton from Campion Towers," he cried out in his great voice. I was certain most of Worcestershire heard him. "The county will not send its men to aid me, but its fairest has joined me, as you see—although she comes in less than seemly garb."

I caught his words for all that his gallantry overwhelmed me. As Cromwell had predicted, "The Twelve" of Worcestershire had not come out to him.

I still blushed and was tongue-tied, but as the soldiers turned away I grew a bit more at ease. Evidently the King thought me a true partisan of the Stuart cause.

"How fares the day, sire?" my kinsman asked him. "The lady wishes to know," Julian glanced at me meaningfully.

"Yes, will you fight today?" I ventured as boldly as I could, my voice trembling all the same.

"Aye, so it seems. Hear that sound?" Charles Stuart asked me.

I listened and heard a faint sound—a far-off crackling.

"That is musket fire," the King explained. He took me by the elbow and led me to one of the slits in the tower wall. I looked down for only one giddy second and was glad that the King held my arm even though the parapet on which I leaned was breast high.

Sir Julian stood behind the King. He nodded approvingly to me.

The King pointed to the south. "Look there, mistress—off to the right. See that line of tall trees? They mark the River Teme." He handed me a telescope. "Take this. Mark the troops this side of the Teme. They are mine."

I took the glass from the King's hand and put it to my eye. Yes, I could make out the men who wore white scarves standing in readiness at the river's edge. Now and then one of them fired across the Teme. Other troops, less easily discernible, lay across the river.

"The men on the far side of the Teme are Roundheads," Charles Stuart explained. All at once I remembered the order Oliver Cromwell had sent last night. Those were General Lambert's men. I nearly said this but caught myself in time. *I must know nothing!*

"Where is Oliver Cromwell?" I asked.

"South of the city, mistress. My main force is still in Worcester."

"What do you think Cromwell will do?"

Charles Stuart laughed bitterly. "Who knows which way the old fox leaps? They think he will attempt to move around our right flank to put himself between me and Wales. He hopes to cut me off to the west. But that is a dangerous game even for Cromwell to play."

I did not know what to say. "I must not take your time," I told the King. "It is kindly of you to speak with me of the battle, but it may not please your officers."

Charles grinned. "Let me be the judge of that, mistress. I would rather talk to a pretty maid any day than to sour faces and sober heads like Wilmot's—eh, Sir Julian?" The King added mockingly—"not that Julian approves any more than Wilmot does."

Julian Killingtree nodded. "I do not approve, sire."

Now the King chuckled. "An honest man, Sir Julian. I have all too few about me. I shall have to make ye a baron, Julian, one of these days, to reward you—not only for your sword and to repay you for the wound you took at Naseby in my father's service, but for your kindly but generally unfollowed advice."

Charles Stuart's face darkened. "To speak in a sober vein, Mistress Sutton, I do not like to do battle. My men are brave and loyal. They have suffered much for me and for my father before me. I do not glory in war nor do I fancy bloodshed. I pray that we can gain the day, few as we are, with as small a loss as possible. At Dunbar, a year ago to this very day, I lost faithful friends, humble loyal men who loved me and who served me without hope of reward. I could ill afford their loss.

"If it were only possible to fight without losses on either side." He motioned toward the army of Parliament, Cromwell's army, across the Teme. "There are men out there who are staunch Englishmen, too. They fight for what they believe. I do not like to see my kingdom divided. God made me king over all. Proud, stiff-necked men move against me. I know their ambitions. They wish to rule, themselves—those proud men in Parliament in London—safe in their seats in the House of Commons. I wonder how many of those fat, proud men come here to shed their blood at Worcester—few of them, I warrant —except for old Oliver, a brave man. But these men shall fall someday. England has ever had a king. I may be beaten today and again and again, but I *will* take back my father's throne. England *shall* have a king again!"

I was surprised at this speech. Charles Stuart had seemed the godless Cavalier to me before, but now I saw a different side of him. His affection was for England; his desire, to end the Civil War after near ten years of strife.

But what did Cromwell want? I felt his determination was greater than the King's and I recalled all too well the text from *St. Matthew*—kill the heir and seize upon his inheritance, upon England. I looked at Charles Stuart's face. He leaned his chin on one hand and gazed out at the countryside south of Worcester, a beautiful soft country, green and golden in the autumn air, ringed by purple-blue hills.

"How comely my kingdom is," he said quietly.

His eyes were sad. His face, I noticed now, was yet the face of a boy for all of its Indian-like swarthiness. The King had been fat at one time. The childish plumpness had not quite vanished from his face. He reminded me strongly of young Obedience, my half brother, who still carried much of what my stepmother called his "puppy fat." Although the King was twenty-one, I felt like an older sister to him. Then I remembered how I had betrayed him to Oliver Cromwell—it was as if I had betrayed little Obedience. But how could I tell the King not to go to Campion Towers when he must surely flee before Cromwell's soldiers?

I could not meet the King's eyes. I turned away as I heard footsteps on the tower steps. A soldier burst out into the gallery with papers in his hand. These would be dispatches. I rejoined my cousin at another slit, the King's telescope still in my grasp.

Suddenly a follower of the King who also had a glass shouted unexpectedly. "Sire, sire! The Roundheads are moving. 'Tis old Oliver, himself!"

Julian snatched the glass from me and ran with it to the King.

"Where does he strike?" the King roared.

"They cross the Severn. They bring up bridges made of boats. Look there, sire. That is Cromwell—the man with the scarlet cloak! He leads his men across. They come on us like ants."

"They will face our Scots," the King said, his eye to the glass. "They are going to fight among the hedgerows. I pray the Scots can hold them."

I could still see the mass of men without a glass. They were like ants, indeed, tiny black ants. I could make out the bridge of boats and the other ants who came streaming forward to fire. Some of the ants crossing the Severn fell into the river and I knew that they had been hit. But from the tower it was unreal to me even as I thought of the men I had marched with last night, the sober-faced, silent men.

The King swung his glass to the south. "God, they come across the River Teme, too, now! My division is in danger."

Sir Julian spoke shortly to the King who beat his fist softly on the parapet. "By God, you have the right of it. We shall do it now! This is my hour. Cromwell has committed himself. The Scots *must* hold him at the Severn. He leaves his Ironsides without a leader. I shall snatch the advantage. We shall ride on Cromwell's army and his cannon on Red Hill. My cannon on Fort Royal will protect our attack."

The men in the tower shouted. One by one they left at a run for the steps. The King led them down.

Julian Killingtree went last, but not before he kissed me— no kinsman's kiss at all this time—and said, "Remain here, Pen. There is less danger for you in the tower. I shall come for you soon as I can. I must ride with the King now."

I stood mute, leaving him without a word, although I thought I had seen a question in his eyes. In a moment I was alone in the gallery. The King's glass lay on the floor. I picked it up and held it.

I went sadly to the parapet where the King had watched and looked down, not dizzy now. The cathedral grounds were a scene of chaos. Men everywhere mounted their horses amid cursing, yelling, and shouted commands. I searched for the red horses and then remembered that I held the glass. I looked through it, scanning the cavalry massing below.

All at once I found Will Scarlet and my grandfather's Rufus standing together. Julian was bestride Will Scarlet, who tossed his head and danced. The King was still afoot, a man buckling on his half-armor while a second held his helmet. Wilmot, the man in dark green, sat a fine bay horse behind them. In the sun his half-armor twinkled with points of light.

I swung the glass. Cranberry was still tethered, but as I watched, she reared and neighed. She wanted to follow Will Scarlet into battle.

I looked back to Sir Julian and the King. Charles was in the saddle now and I saw him turn his head, the white plumes on his helmet fluttering in the breeze. He rose in his stirrups and held up his .hand. His deep voice boomed and came up to me as he spurred Rufus and galloped out and away. Julian glanced up once at the tower and I waved but I did not think he saw me. Then he followed the King. The others, by some last-minute miracle, had formed into orderly pairs as they rode behind their King. I watched the Royalist cavalry twisting and turning through the city. Foot soldiers leaped for safety to the wall as the horses clattered by. The cobbles rang with the sound of many hooves. From side streets other horsemen moved into place. I saw the cavalry divide and charge out of St. Martin's Gate and Sidbury Gate and watched them as they blended together once more outside the city and were swallowed up in a great cloud of dust.

The Cavaliers had thrown up an earthwork southeast of the city wall. I saw the black smoke and the belches of fire as the booming of cannon commenced. This was Fort Royal.

East of the guns the dust cloud moved on.

With the King's glass I swept the horizon. The army of Cromwell had crossed the Teme successfully and they still poured over the Severn. I looked down at Worcester, itself, quiet as if it waited. The glass picked up Cranberry. She stood, her head drooping dejectedly, alone in the cathedral grounds.

I put the glass inside my coat and stood for a long moment looking out toward the east. The cloud of brownish-yellow dust had stopped at the slope of Red Hill. I heard the sharp sound of musket fire through the constant roar of the cannon from Fort Royal. Now other cannon, Roundhead guns on Red Hill, added their ugly voices. From somewhere I heard the whining screech of the Scottish pipes, and all too often the scream of a wounded or dying horse came to my ears.

All at once I lost my courage and burst into tears. I could not wait in the tower until Julian came for me. Perhaps he would never return. He could die there below Red Hill under Cromwell's guns and Will Scarlet could die with him. I ran down the steps, through the cathedral, and out the great doors to Cranberry.

She lifted her head and neighed to me as I slipped her tether and scrambled onto her back. The way to the north had seemed clear. Everyone in the city had gone to the walls on the south and the east to watch the battle. As I went through the empty streets, I had but one thought—to go home!

We halted at the northern gate at the shout of a sentry. Guards came tumbling out of the shadows while an officer ran toward me, pistol in hand.

"Who leaves the city?" he demanded.

I did not know what to say. I was not able to think or choose my words with care now. Frightened and lonely, I stared at the officer, hardly believing my good fortune. He was the very man who had questioned me in the Guildhall last night. I whipped off Garth's hat again to permit him to recognize me.

The officer called out, "So, the King sends you away? You need no safe-conduct from me, mistress. Where do you ride?"

"Home—home to Holt Heath and Campion Towers!" I shouted to him.

"Take care. You may find deserters on the roads," he bellowed to me as I passed through the gate, which two guards had leaped to open for me.

"God be with you all!" I called back over my shoulder as I gave the red mare her head and she broke into a gallop on the road that led to the north.

"*This Is the Heir*"

THE TERRIBLE sound of cannon and muskets soon faded away behind me, drowned out by the steady drumbeat of Cranberry's hooves.

The Cavalier Colonel had been right. The road was filled with deserters, mostly Scots. They called out to me as we swept past. Some threw stones which missed us by a hairsbreadth. I knew they wanted the horse. They would kill me for Cranberry if they could. A freckle-faced little man in a ragged kilt leaped from the hedges and snatched at the red mare's bridle as we slackened our speed and turned onto the road that led to Campion Towers. He tried to claw me off, but I was ready for him. I had my grandfather's pistol in my hand and as the grinning Scot reached for me, I fired. I knew only that he fell back, and in an instant Cranberry and I were gone.

We met no more deserters. As we raced through the vale where I had first met Julian Killingtree, my eyes filled with tears.

Cranberry and I paused at the top of the hill where Madame Gawdy had first shown me the great house and I had seen the light in my grandmother's tower. That time had not been long past. I did not know how I would be received at Campion Towers now. But this was where I chose to be.

Cranberry raced for home. I did not try to keep our arrival secret. They would have forced the door of my bedchamber by now. They surely knew that I had gone, but they would not know that I had used the secret passage.

I had not decided what I would say or what I would do. If my grandfather chose to drive me away with a curse or a blow, I richly deserved it. Cranberry trotted into the stable yard and I slid down from her. Then I led her to the stable and into her stall. The red mare had earned her rest. I removed her bridle and started toward the harness room with it. Even if the Killingtrees would not be pleased to see me, the Roundhead, back again, they would want their Berry with the other red mares.

Sir Nicholas Killingtree's shadow fell almost at once across the stable door. I braced myself and stood waiting, taking a deep breath. I had feared his temper always. I dreaded it now. He came inside and in his hand he held the match to the pistol I had taken from the stable floor. When he saw me, he let it fall.

"Pen," he said calmly, "you have come back. We had not thought to see you or the mare again. I saw you ride by just now. Or rather, I saw a lad ride by on the Berry. I had not known it was you." He sat down on a covered barrel and put his pistol into his pocket. "Garth's clothing, eh? Did you steal those from the stableboy?" He leaned on his cane, his eyes fixed on my face.

"Yes, I suppose I stole them," I said, "but I only meant to borrow them, sir."

"Where is your gown?"

"In Garth's cottage."

"If I asked you to exchange those sorry rags for your gown, would you do as I ask?"

"Yes, sir."

"Well, do so."

I hung Cranberry's bridle in the harness room and then went to Garth's cottage. I hauled my pewter-colored gown, petticoats, and shoes from under his pallet, blew the dust from them, and shook them out. I hung Garth's clothing neatly on wall pegs and put his old hat carefully on his bed. Then I hurriedly put on my own clothing and rejoined my grandfather. I found his manner strange. He had not mentioned Amabel Sutton.

My grandfather still sat on the barrel. "Do you want to talk here," he asked me, "or do you wish to speak before the others?"

"I would rather talk here—to you."

"Where have you been, Pen? Why did you leave us?"

I told him the truth. I had had my fill of lying to the Killing-trees. I no longer cared what happened to me. "I rode to Evesham, sir."

"The Roundhead army was at Evesham?"

"Yes," I replied.

"You are a Puritan." He looked sadly at the hay-strewn floor. "You have never pretended to be anything else, have you?"

I shook my head.

"Why did you leave, Pen?"

"I rode to General Cromwell with news."

"You are a spy for Parliament?"

I nodded. "Not willingly, sir."

"Were you paid?"

I shook my head again. "No, I was not paid."

"Tell me, then, why did you spy?"

"I thought you were all Papists and tools of Spain at Campion Towers. I believed you would bring the stake and the martyr's fire back to England."

Sir Nicholas Killingtree laughed dryly. "The last Papist Killingtree died fifty years ago. Did no one tell you?"

"No, I knew only you were not of my faith, sir. I believed when I saw Madame Gawdy cross herself in Bristol that you all were Roman Catholics."

"Did the people who asked you to spy tell you we were Papists?"

"No, it was my idea." Then I added, "But they let me go on believing it."

"Devils!" he thundered, striking the ground with his stick as he did when he was angry. "Look here, Pen, what did you tell the Roundheads?"

"Very little," I replied, "I had been told of 'The Twelve,' but I never saw their faces. I said nothing about them. As far as I am concerned, they are safe. 'The Twelve' were watched here and at the Aylmer farm though."

"We know that," he said wearily. "We took care. We came in disguise. They cannot identify us for certain. What else do you know?"

"The secret of the passage."

He started visibly at this. "Who told you?"

"One of the people who asked me to spy. A carpenter from Worcester had learned it many years ago."

"I know the history. They still say in Worcester that a Killingtree had him murdered to keep the secret safe. That is possible, but it was long ago. So ye found our passage when no one else could? How did you accomplish this, Pen?"

I told him of the fleur-de-lis-carved button in the empty room at the end of the passage. He seemed almost proud of my achievement.

"You spied upon 'The Twelve,' I take it?"

"Yes, I went into the secret passage. I heard their voices."

"What else did you see or hear as you skulked about?"

I was ashamed at his words. I hung my head. "Charles Stuart, sir, and my cousin, Sir Julian Killingtree."

"So you found the King, did you? I had hoped you would not know he came to Campion Towers. I wished to spare you, as a Puritan, as much as I could. And how do you repay me? You spy on us and you run away on the Berry?"

"We did come back," I said quietly.

"Pen, what *did* you tell the Roundheads?" his voice was gentle again.

"I spoke with Oliver Cromwell himself." My grandfather's mouth opened at this, his face twisted, and he closed his lips grimly. "I told him Charles Stuart comes here to hide if he loses at Worcester."

"You told such a thing to Cromwell? Where did you learn this? *I* had not known it—the King did not tell me."

I told him how I had learned it. Now he looked gloomy, as well as sad. But I felt as if a great stone had been lifted from my back. I knew now why I had come home to Campion Towers. I could redeem myself by warning Sir Nicholas.

"The King must not come here, sir."

"You have the right of that, mistress," he told me. "But when did you leave and where have you been? A trip to Evesham should not take so long as this. Your great-aunt is crazed with concern. If she had known that it was you who rode Berry and not a farm lad, she would have come to the stable, too. I could not have kept her in the house."

I found it difficult to believe anything I could do could shatter Laurel Killingtree's calm. "I went out at dark by the passage," I confessed. "I rode to Evesham but found Cromwell gone.

I found him near Whittington and for a time I rode with his army."

My grandfather shook his head in disbelief. "Did he know ye for a maid?"

"Not at first. I told him who I was and where I lived." Then I told my grandfather most of the wretched story—of my capture by the Cavalier scouting party, of my rescue, the lonely minutes in the tower gallery of Worcester Cathedral, the Royalist attack on Red Hill, and of my flight from the city.

"And so you came home to us here?" he said at the end of my tale. Now he did smile in a morose fashion. "You have some affection for us after all? You are sorry for what you have done and you hope to make amends?"

"Oh, yes, I have a vast affection for you all. I did not will this. I fought affection. I was at the point of loving you and my great-aunt until I learned you both put laudanum in my jerkum."

He was surprised. Now it was his turn to be shamefaced. "It was to keep you safe," he muttered.

"No matter now," I went on, and, hoping to cheer him, I said, "The King rode Rufus into battle today."

My grandfather was proud. His eyes blazed. "Tell me of the battle later," he said. "Would that I could have been there riding beside my nephew. Now, Pen, what of Amabel Sutton? You do not speak of her. She says you tried to kill her."

My spirits soared. I had not killed the woman after all. "No, I did not try to kill her. She came at me with a pistol." I gasped. I had forgotten. "The pistol is in the pocket of Garth's coat still. She believed I ran off to the Roundheads with the Aylmer jewels. She would have murdered me to get them."

Sir Nicholas inclined his head. "Aye, she might have at that, Pen. I found the jewels in your bedchamber this morning. If they had been gone, too, I would have truly believed you would not return."

"I did not return for Bloody Mary's emeralds," I protested. This was unjust.

"Well, why did you come back?"

I wept now. "I do not really know. I am so confused. I want to set things right if I can. I saw Julian ride off on Will Scarlet with the King. Cranberry and I were left alone. I wanted to come back here. It was all I could think of. I did not know if you would have me back, but I came home." And I buried my head in my arms and leaned against the rough stable wall, weeping.

"You like Sir Julian?" my grandfather asked, getting up.

"Yes," I said through tears. " 'Tis a cruel, unjust thing that Parliament says he is an outlaw."

"Do you know, Penitence, you were well named after all? I believe this is truly why you came back—in penitence. You have given me fair warning and I think you have done the King a true service."

I shook my head. "I hope so."

He touched my shoulder. "Well, come along, Pen. When did you eat last? If we do not go to the house now, Laurel will think a horse thief has got the better of me. You look pale as a phantom. Tell me of the battle."

"What of the others?"

"Douglas and Mistress Killingtree wait in the great hall for news. Mistress Amabel lies abed with a cracked skull. Do not fear her. I took her measure long ago as I took her daughter's. I am not the doting old fool you so clearly think me. I shall not tell them your real history. They would never forgive you. I shall tell them that you went away because you feared you could be a danger to us here, no matter who gains the day at Worcester. You were caught by the Cavalier scouting party and spent the night in Worcester; then you changed your mind and came home to Campion Towers. They will believe what I tell them. Now, tell me of the battle."

I had one request of him. "Sir Julian does not know I was a spy. You would not tell him?" I begged.

"No, you have my promise. He did not tell me that you saw the King in the priest-hole, so I shall keep a secret from him. Now, Pen, about the battle . . . ?"

We walked slowly together across the stable yard and to the house. I spoke of the army of General Cromwell, a disciplined, experienced army, far larger than that of King Charles. I told him I felt the army of Parliament would triumph.

He nodded. He had expected this, too. "Aye, I must prepare myself, it seems, for a locust swarm of Roundheads. They would come in any event. They would search for Julian once more— even if they had not been informed the King comes here. What do you suggest?" He looked at me questioningly. "You have much practice in successful deceit and the making up of believable stories."

Even though the rebuke had stung me, I thought hard. "If the King is not here, sir, show them the secret passage. Once you have done this and they have entered it and found nothing, I do not believe you will concern them further. I spoke with Oliver Cromwell"—the name which had once had trumpets in it now seemed a dirge. "General Cromwell is a harsh man but a just one, I believe. He did not like me nor the work I did for him. He thinks me a foolish maid and will resent me more when he finds nothing for his pains. Tell him I returned here; and because I was a Roundhead and you feared for me if the King won, you packed me off at once to take ship for the New World. He knows I am from the colonies, so he will believe you. He will know, too, why I went so hastily." I added shyly, "I hope I do not offend you, sir, but I think you and Oliver Cromwell could understand each another. He is somewhat like you."

"Do not say that to me, Pen." He shook his head. But I could tell by the way his lips twitched that he was not unpleased at the comparison with the great soldier. He went on seriously, "If the news from Worcester is bad, you must leave us again, but this time you will go with our blessings. Cromwell must not find you here to ask questions of you."

Mistress Killingtree and Douglas Sutton sat before the fire-hearth. Both stood as we entered the hall. My great-aunt cried out and opened her arms. "Thank God you have come back. I thought you dead somewhere along the road."

I embraced Laurel Killingtree and kept back more tears. I had not realized that she had grown to like me. How little I deserved her affection! Even silly empty-headed Douglas was happy to see me. She had not been fully taken in by her mother's story, for the Aylmer jewels were still at Campion Towers. No one at the manor house, except perhaps my grandfather, seemed to understand how little I valued the gems.

Jonas drew up a chair for me and I sat down next to my grandfather. How my legs and back ached from my ride. Swiftly he told them the story I wished him to tell—that I had fled for my sake and for theirs and that I had been captured by the Royalists and by own wish had come home.

I added, "The Colonel in Worcester believed I was a boy who had stolen Cranberry."

Douglas was aghast, while my great-aunt hid a smile. Had Laurel ever thought of riding bestride? I suspected she had. Her eyes had shone with pride when I told her of the King's interest in the people of Campion Towers and his respect for Julian, but when I spoke of the cavalry charge out of Worcester to take Red Hill, she looked at her folded hands in sorrow. Laurel was not cheered as her brother had been when I added that Charles Stuart had ridden Rufus.

My cousin Douglas was openly envious. "I wish I had seen King Charles, too," she said. "You have all the good fortune, Pen."

"If you call danger of the hangman's rope 'good fortune,' I suppose I do. I do not relish watching battles either. I have seen men killed today, Douglas." I faced my grandfather. I had news that might please him. "If you want a relic of the King, sir, I brought his telescope with me from the Cathedral. It is in Garth's coat."

"Aye, I would like that well, Pen," he said, "but I mislike your choice of words. 'Relic,' do you say? I trust it will not be that. You say you saw the King's cavalry reach the slope of Red Hill and go no further?"

I nodded. "I could not see for all the smoke and dust, but I am sure they had not taken Red Hill by the time I rode out of Worcester. How long do battles go on?"

My grandfather pulled at his little beard. "I think we should have news by nightfall. Julian, Peter, or Garth will come to us or send us word. I asked this. Waiting is cruel and hard— hardest of all."

I looked at an ornate clock behind my cousin's head. It was now close to six of the clock. The battle had begun sometime in the early afternoon. It was dusk now. Were they still fighting?

What had become of Julian Killingtree? I twisted a fold of my skirt in my hand with fear and noticed Laurel did the same. Must I leave Campion Towers never knowing what had happened to my kinsman?

My thoughts went out to the King. Would he come here to Campion Towers for refuge and be sent away because of the danger I had brought upon him? Or would Cromwell capture him in the city? "If General Cromwell wins and captures Charles Stuart, what will happen to the King?" I asked Sir Nicholas.

"I do not believe the Cavaliers can win, Pen, from what you tell me of Cromwell's great army," he replied soberly, looking over my head to the nails where the weapons of Campion Towers had once hung. "Worcestershire has lost heart for the King's cause. The men of the county fear Cromwell and his Ironsides more than they love the Stuarts. As to what you ask, I believe they would try the King for treason to the Parliament in London. They would behead him as they did his father."

This is what I suspected but I could not understand how Parliament could so twist its thinking to execute the King for treason against *it*. I said as much and both my great-aunt and grandfather laughed.

"That is no Roundhead sentiment," Laurel stated. She got up. "I will see to Mistress Sutton's headache and then I will tell Jonas to set our supper early. When did you eat last, Pen?"

I had forgotten. I had not even had the wine I had meant to ask for when I came into the house. "I had wine last night and bread and cheese today."

"As I thought," she said briskly and was gone. I marveled at Laurel. She rose to great troubles but drooped under personal sadness such as my grandmother's death. My cousin Douglas got up now and went to the virginal to pick out a tune with one finger. She was still petulant because I had seen the King and been noticed by him. I went to sit beside her. "Shall I tell you about King Charles?" I asked.

She tossed her head. "No—perhaps I shall see him, too. He will come here again. He must. I wish it!"

"If he gets safe away from Worcester, he will return to England someday. I know Charles Stuart will."

"That is not what I have in mind. He *must* win at Worcester. I cannot see him losing. He must not lose. What is Charles Stuart to you. Pen? You are a Roundhead. What do you expect to get from him? You are an enemy. I am surprised that he did not put you into prison in Worcester. Had I been the King, I would have put all my enemies into prison. I certainly would not speak with them and be kindly to them."

The King meant more to me than I could ever tell her. My loyalty was a divided one. I did not want Charles Stuart caught and executed, but Cromwell, the protector of our faith, must not be defeated. Would the young King persecute us as his father, Charles I, had done? I did not know. Old wrongs and old hates could run far deeper than the Severn.

"I liked him," I said simply. "I liked the King. I was sorry for him."

Douglas glanced at me out of the corner of one eye. She did not believe me, but she did not speak again. What she had to say was said.

Laurel came down the steps now. She looked hopefully at her brother who shook his head. These two understood each other without words. Laurel had hoped that news had come in her absence. Now she knew there was none. Jonas, too, looked sad as he lit the candles in their sconces.

I went with her to the kitchens. I had never been in them before and the large, low-ceilinged rooms surprised me. I had never seen so many cranes and jacks in one firehearth until now. What a great house this had once been! The maids, the cook, and old Jonas sat at a long wooden table, but they got up at once when they saw us.

"We wish our supper now," Laurel told Jonas. "Cold meat, bread, cheese, and wine will do."

He bowed as we left. I was famished. The sight of a wheel of cheese and a round loaf of bread on the table had made me feel faint.

I could scarcely wait for supper—but, as it turned out, I was not to eat again at Campion Towers. Just as Laurel and I came back into the great hall, we heard a banging at the huge doors.

My grandfather got up swiftly, for all of his bandaged foot, and hobbled to them. "Who is there?" he called out. "Who knocks?"

"A messenger from Worcester. I seek Sir Nicholas Killingtree!"

I held my breath as Sir Nicholas withdrew the bolt and opened the door. I noticed that my great-aunt's face had gone white as she stood beside me.

A man in half-armor, a helmet, and black and silver brocade breeches burst into the great hall. He wore the white scarf of the King's army across his breast.

"I am James Stanley, Earl of Derby," he said hastily. "Viscount Wilmot of Athlone"—I remembered the man in dark green velvet who had disapproved of me—"sent me here as did Sir Julian Killingtree."

"Julian is alive?" Laurel cried out.

"Aye, mistress—not even scratched—a miracle. Someone godly

must have prayed for him." The Earl of Derby leaned against the wall. I stared at him. He was a small plump man with a soft drooping mustache, mournful eyes, and dark shoulder-length hair. His face was full about the chin and his mouth open with exhaustion.

"Douglas, fetch wine," my grandfather ordered.

In a whirl of black skirts Douglas hurried to obey and in a moment had returned. In the meantime the Earl had made his way to a chair and fallen into it. He drank deeply of the wine.

"What is the news?" Sir Nicholas begged him.

"We were beaten," the Earl said thickly. "There were too many of them against us. We quarreled among ourselves again, of course, and Worcestershire would not rise for the King. We fought under the King for three hours at Red Hill. When our powder and shot ran out, we fought with pikes and musket butts, but they pushed us back into the city like dogs into a kennel. It was a taste of hell. We died by the thousands—horses and men. The Roundheads took our cannon from Fort Royal and turned our own guns on us. Many of the Scots deserted or fled. The Roundheads pursue them now. Cromwell gained the day."

"What of the King?" I asked.

"When I left him, he was not yet taken. His officers were with him. He has abandoned the city to the Roundheads. Viscount Wilmot sends to you for help."

"The King does not come to Campion Towers now?" my grandfather asked anxiously. I knew what he meant. He could not give shelter to the royal fugitive in the secret passage, thanks to me, but how could he turn the King away? Both my grandfather and I suffered as we waited for the Earl of Derby to answer.

"No. He hopes to leave the country."

My grandfather's eyes closed with relief, while I steadied myself by holding onto the back of his chair. It had been a terrible moment.

"What can I do? I can send money with you now." Sir Nicholas recovered faster than I and was ready to help.

The Earl of Derby shook his head and waved the suggestion away with his hand. He took another deep swallow of wine. "No. He has money. He has enough, he thinks. He asks only for Mistress Douglas Sutton to come to him at once."

We were all thunderstruck. Douglas stood frozen, her hand to her cheek as if someone had struck her.

We were silent with surprise while James Stanley went on. "Asking for the maid is Wilmot's idea, but Sir Julian agrees. The King must travel in disguise. Tomorrow the county will swarm with Roundhead searching parties. They scour the city of Worcester now. The King scarcely fled in time. If he travels with a maid, he would not be so easily marked out than if he rides with his officers. Most of them have already refused disguises. The King asked for Mistress Sutton, himself. Charles Stuart asks your permission, Sir Nicholas. If you give it, he will travel only with her, Viscount Wilmot, and Sir Julian. So small a party will not attract attention."

"There will be grave danger for the girl," my grandfather reflected. He was frowning.

"Aye, that there will be—grave danger," the Earl agreed.

Sir Nicholas turned to my cousin. "Will you go, Douglas? Will you do this for your King?"

Before our eyes, Douglas Sutton's pretty face dissolved. She burst out with a wail of fear, "They might hang me." She darted to my grandfather and buried her face in his shoulder. "I'm afraid! I could not do it. I would fail the King and betray him. I could not help myself. I know it." She lifted her face to him. "Do not make me do it."

I saw her very real fright. No, Douglas could never carry it off. I saw my chance to redeem myself. I spoke to Douglas. "It is not you Charles Stuart sends for, Douglas. The King asks for me. He believes I am Douglas Sutton. I gave him your name. It was wrong of me, but yours was the first name that came to my mind. I will go. If you went to him he would not know you. He would send you back."

The Earl of Derby sat up surprised, but I had eyes only for my grandfather. "It is true, sir. Do not concern yourself. I make up for much this way. Let me go. If you have any doubts, be sure that Sir Julian will keep watch over me—and over the King."

"Aye, do as you wish, Pen," he said, as Douglas, relieved that she would not be in danger, turned her back on me and sobbed. It would be hours before she had time to reflect and become angry with me because I had given the King her name.

"Mistress, whoever you are, you must hasten," James Stanley warned. "Take little with you." He spoke to my grandfather. "I must beg a horse of you, sir. I brought your red horses back with me—the King's and Sir Julian's. Both are spent and the King's horse is wounded. With care though he will recover, although he will not go to battle again."

As Laurel and I started for my bedchamber for my cloak, I heard my grandfather say, "I have some sorry nags in the stable now. Except for the red horses I have no others. I sent my other horses to Worcester with my coachman and the groom days back."

"Take the King's horse and Will Scarlet away from here. It would go hard with you if they are found." The Earl's words came faintly up to me as I climbed the steps.

"Aye, sir, I shall hide them. If they are found, I shall say they were stolen from me. No one will believe it, but no one can prove otherwise."

My great-aunt and I were out of earshot now. We hastened to my bedchamber and reached it out of breath. Its door hung loose on its hinges. It had been forced as I had guessed it would be when they had found me gone. I caught up my black cloak from the clothespress and then started for the door, but Laurel stopped me, unfastened the purse at her waist, and gave it to me.

"Penitence, the Aylmer jewels are in the table drawer," she said. "Take them with you now. I doubt you will come back here."

"If I take the King safely away, I will go to Swindon or to Bristol. I do not know which," I told her honestly.

"Then I shall send your trunk somehow to Bristol. Sooner or later you will go there. Our agent, Master Quentin, will watch for your ship. He will write up any news."

"The coral gown and the red gown are for Douglas—to make her remember me. Please put the willow-green and the cranberry-red riding costume into my mother's trunk. I cannot wear them, I know, but they will make me remember my grandparents."

"What will make you remember me?"

I smiled and held up her purse. Then I opened the drawer and scooped the jewels into it. "This purse—and the fine letter you wrote me at my grandmother's bidding."

I paused at the door. I had to know one thing more. "What will happen to Amabel Sutton and Madame Gawdy?"

Laurel sighed. "Nothing, I suspect. My brother is a stubborn and an over-charitable man. Mistress Sutton will have a home here as long as she chooses it, but I do not know how long that will be. She has a little farm, a small inheritance, in Surrey.

Perhaps she will go there now. I shall try to see to it that she does. As for Marie, I do not believe the Roundheads would harm her. She will remain in Worcester where I shall see her often. Sir Nicholas cannot abide her company, although it will be even more lonely here now with Philippa gone. I shall ask Nicholas to invite Master Meredith here to live. Perhaps he will come to comfort us." She caught me by my cloak. "Stay a moment. I ask your pardon for my rudeness to you." As I shook my head, she went on, "Still and all I must ask it. Carry yourself cleverly, Pen, wherever you go. Let us hear from you and do not concern yourself about your cousin Douglas. Sir Nicholas will find a husband for her, but I do not think now he will give in to her every notion. I saw your eyes when we spoke of Julian. Douglas shall not have him—even if she so chooses. I promise you that. Douglas does not deserve a Killingtree."

I kissed Laurel on the cheek and fled down the passage for the last time. I kissed my grandfather at the door of the great hall. My cousin Douglas was gone. I looked about hastily for her, and he gestured toward the chapel. "She prays for you. We shall all pray for you, for Julian, and for the King. Take care, Penitence. The horses are ready. We shall wait to hear from you. You are a brave lass. I am proud of my granddaughter."

I put my hood up over my hair and went out the door. It had grown full dark. The Earl of Derby sat bestride one of the nags which had pulled the old coach that had met me at Bristol. Another brown horse waited for me, its sidesaddle ready. Jonas helped me mount and I turned about for my last look at Campion Towers. I hated the leaving.

The great door was empty but both sides had been thrown open to the night. It did not matter who came to Campion Towers now. Everything was open. No one stayed to wave farewell to me. I knew where they were, praying for me, for Sir Julian, and for the King. We would need their prayers. I looked at the stables. How I wished I could give Cranberry a last bit of sugar and say farewell to her. Would I ever see her again?

I refused to weep. I had not completely left my family at Campion Towers, for I rode now to Julian. I was still a Killingtree and would ride into danger with a Killingtree. I could not ask for better company than my kinsman and the King of England.

"You must discard your armor and your scarf," I cried out to the Earl of Derby, our horses neck by neck, as if we raced under a rising moon, although the red horses would have thought our gait but an easy hand gallop.

He reined up, and with unskilled fingers I helped him undo the knot of his scarf. Then I unbuckled the sides of his half-armor, which shone in the moonlight. He threw it behind a tall black hedge and sent the helmet after. I rolled up the scarf and sent it flying, too. We were some distance from Campion Towers. Even if the armor and scarf were found, no one would think of my family.

James Stanley spoke. "Aye, you have got a cool head, mistress. I owe you much already. I trust someday I can repay you."

"You can repay me now," I told him. "Do not tell Charles Stuart that I am not Mistress Sutton. Let me play the game out. I fancy the jest."

He nodded, then spurred his horse. There was no time for idle clack.

Escape

THE Earl of Derby knew the Worcestershire countryside well. We rode through Kidderminster unchallenged and to a village a few miles beyond. Here my companion swerved left from the main road and I followed him. We rode more slowly now. We walked our horses up a hill and out onto a barren heath as the moon climbed higher into the sky.

From under deformed wind-shaken trees, a little group of horsemen came to meet us. In the cool light they were but outlines.

"Stanley?" a man called out. It was a strange voice to my ears.

"Aye," the Earl of Derby replied. Then he added, "Dunbar forever!"

"God be praised!" another man said. "You have come. Is the maid with you?"

"Yes, I have Mistress Sutton here."

"Good. She is to come with me."

I followed the man who led the way to the trees and dismounted. He lifted me down after he put a pistol back into his belt and he had seen my face by moonlight. I had already noticed that the other men held naked swords as they approached us.

"The King rests," I was told. "Sir Julian is with him. He says you are kin to him. You are a brave girl—would that all Worcestershire were like you." His words touched me more than he could ever know. I walked into the trees.

It was dark, but I could make out the King by his white plume. Somehow he had retrieved his Cavalier hat. He sat on a fallen tree, as Amyas Moonjean had done. Other men, dark shapes, clustered about him. One of these got up and moved away from the others as I approached.

"Pen?" he called softly. There was a note of anxiety in his one word.

It was Julian. I ran to him and he held me close for a moment. "I guessed you would come."

"What would you have done if the real Douglas Sutton had come? I am an impostor, you know," I whispered.

"Sent her home to Campion Towers. The King's cause needs courage now—even if it is Roundhead courage. I pray you will serve him well."

"You have my word. What are we to do?"

"We travel north and if we have luck we turn to the east and then down through England to the sea. They expect us to ride west—to Wales, or north to Scotland, but we are aware of that. Some of us have ridden ahead. Small parties will not draw attention. The Earl of Derby and the others will leave us now. You and I go with Wilmot and the King. The others will go alone to take their separate ways to France. God help us all."

"What folk are we to be? Who am I to be?"

"The King is William Jackson. You ride pillion behind him. He is your servant. You are Mistress Ann Grimstone. I am your brother, John Grimstone." He smiled in the moonlight. "Viscount Wilmot is our uncle. He does not fancy the part. We are farmers from Knightwick at the moment. God knows what we shall be tomorrow."

"But I have a sidesaddle," I protested, frightened at the prospect of riding behind Charles Stuart.

"No matter, we shall leave it and lead your horse. We will say we travel to Boscobel to sell your horse at the September fair. The King's horse is our very finest. It will carry you both easily." Julian laughed. "You shall see what I ride, Pen. I did not know there was such a steed. It is a pity Garth cannot laugh at it."

"Garth? What of Garth?"

"Dead. He did not know what hit him. It happened when they turned the cannon from Fort Royal on us. Garth was with Peter and some horses. He brought a fresh horse to a soldier who had had his mount shot out from under him. One cannon ball killed all three—Garth, the soldier, and the horse. Peter knows. He will take Garth back to Campion Towers tomorrow."

I buried my head on Julian's chest. We had all lost a friend.

Julian led me to Charles Stuart. As usual, I was speechless before the King. He got up slowly and I noticed that he was lame. He was not wounded but had wrenched his foot dismounting Rufus.

"It was kindly of you to come to me, Mistress Sutton," he said softly in that deep voice I would know anywhere. "I trust this is not one of your gamesome notions."

"No, sire, it is not." I curtsied and found my tongue. "You have reason to complain of my frivolousness, but I know of the danger that lies ahead. The rope does not amuse me. I am not noble enough to merit the ax."

"Scant comfort that," the King granted. "It is a damned dangerous game you play and it is well that you know it. If you did not, I would be forced to send you back. Even by moonlight I like you better in this costume than what you wore to visit me at Worcester, but I warn you—Wilmot, here—" he jerked his thumb toward the man beside him, "Robert Grimstone, my beloved master, your beloved uncle, Mistress Ann," his voice was mocking, "says that I have no notion of how to play a serving man. You must teach me. You must forget I am Charles Stuart. Order me about, upbraid me before others, strike me if you must. The role is new to me. I have been preached at and insulted, but until now I have served no master."

I laughed. "You have no idea, William Jackson, how well I play a role or the tales that I tell."

"Sir Julian tells me that you are a remarkable teller of tales. I believe that is one of the reasons he wished me to send for you—the other reasons I begin more strongly to suspect all the time."

Henry Wilmot cut the King and me short. "There is no time; we must ride. They will soon sweep north from Worcester. Hold your clack now. Seem like dullard farmers and you, young William, do not speak to the maid behind you. A servant speaks only when spoken to."

"A damned difficult part," Charles muttered and caught me by the hand.

We four went to our tethered horses. Julian tossed my sidesaddle under a tree and hoisted me up behind the King, who had groaned as he swung himself into his saddle. I was frightened but I caught the King around his waist. He had chuckled as I obeyed Wilmot's harsh order. I hoped that Charles Stuart controlled his horse well. I had a very uneasy seat, sitting sidewise behind him as a country woman should.

Julian held the reins of my riderless nag as Wilmot mounted his horse. Then Julian mounted his "steed" and rode it out into the light. The horse was everything he had said it was, a big-nosed horror, great-kneed, sway-backed, and of a color impossible to distinguish by moonlight—or by the light of day, I suspected.

We were a sorry-looking group as we left the heath for the road. Men waited as we rode by. Some murmured "God go with you, sire." Others bowed and removed their hats. Soon they, too, would take their chances on the highroads of England as hunted men.

If we four were to be judged by our horses, we would be considered poor farmers, indeed. Wilmot's black horse was a gaunt shadow of an animal; the King's was a gray cart-horse, so broad across the back that even the King's long shanks stood out stiffly at an angle. Beside them, my horse brought from Campion Towers was a tearing beauty.

We moved calmly out onto the road. We went at a walk through another northern village, a sleeping village, which would never awake to know that the King had passed. Julian found ale, bread, and cheese at a dirty little inn miles beyond. Then we entered the small winding paths that led to Brewood Forest. As the sun rose, we came into White Ladies.

Here we stopped for a time to rest inside the ruins of the old monastery. Poor people, true Papists who lived in the ruins, aided us. Now I was truly among Roman Catholics—and unafraid. I smelled no fires at White Ladies—unless it was the mutton chop on the hearth. William Jackson had a boy's appetite. I wondered how these good people would feel if they knew who I truly was. They called me "Mistress Sutton" and treated me as if I were a princess, although they did not feed me overmuch.

It was at White Ladies that Julian, Wilmot, and I transformed the King over his violent protests. Clothing was brought to him and how he looked with disgust on what the Papists of White Ladies had to give, but Wilmot prevailed. I left the little inner room while the King shifted his black coat and his shirt for a noggen shirt, a greasy leather doublet, and a green coat, much torn at the elbows. His hat was a tall one. Only his breeches were his own. The King left his white plume to the people who gave us refuge and then flung his hat and other garments into the fire as I came in at my kinsman's call.

Servants had cropped heads. Lord Wilmot went at the King's long black hair with a knife. He did such a hopeless job of work that I called for scissors and, seating Charles Stuart on a stool, I cut his hair. Then I suggested that he shave off his mustache. The King did not fancy this but he did as I asked.

"What now displeases you, Mistress Sutton?" he asked in a good nature but with a frightful frown.

"You are too clean, I think."

"Easily remedied." He put his hands up the chimney and rubbed black soot on his face. "Satisfied?" he asked.

"Yes, William, but *I* would not hire you," I told him.

"See, Wilmot," the King, who seemed a little startled at my words, called out, "I told you. I have not the merit in me to make a proper servingman."

"Aye, it is difficult, William," Wilmot said gravely.

It rained that day. We stayed at White Ladies to rest ourselves and our horses. This would be no swift journey to the sea. We could not gallop, for nothing drew notice so much as a galloping horse, unless it was three galloping horses.

We learned from our hosts at the ruined monastery that the Roundheads had already come to White Ladies. They had searched already for the King.

The next day we rode on and once more found Papists who would give us shelter. I admired them for their loyalty and courage. They knew the peril they ran and so did we, for now there was a price set on the King's head. Anyone who betrayed him to the searchers would receive a thousand pounds from Parliament. Such a prize would tempt many.

We moved on, sometimes stopping to rest or to confer with Royalists in the neighborhood of northern towns. Often we put our horses with our hosts' animals, while Wilmot, Julian, and the King hid in an attic and I was mewed up in a long-forgotten priest-hole. I was surprised to learn how many manor houses had priest-holes.

Sometimes we were stopped by soldiers who demanded our names and our business. Wilmot, "Robert Grimstone," usually spoke for us as the oldest member of our party. He had a ready tongue and quick wit when he chose. I kept my eyes lowered modestly as a country maid should and, for a wonder, Charles Stuart kept his tongue. Always we rode on to another village to sell the chestnut horse. In the last hamlet we had always found our offers too low.

In a week's time we had turned south to make for the sea. Wilmot's pride had refused a disguise, so he lorded it over the rest of us as an authoritative uncle who had a right to green velvet clothing, dirty as it now was. Julian had shifted his clothing for a suit of gray wool and a steeple hat. My pewter-colored gown had been left behind for a plain dress of brown wool. I had been glad to see the last of it, for it was too rich for a farmer's daughter. The brown dress had been the property of a milkmaid at a farm that gave us shelter for the night.

At Bromsgrove we had an evil moment. The King's fat gray horse cast a shoe and we waited at the blacksmith's shop while a new one was fitted. As bad luck would have it, the smith, who referred to Cromwell's latest victory as a "crowning mercy," singled out the King for conversation. Charles spoke soberly with the man of the trouble at Worcester and of the escape of the wicked and worldly young King. He agreed that it was a vile thing, indeed, for Charles Stuart to bring an army of wild Scots into England and said that for this crime the King should be hanged. As we left I heard the King chuckle. For a moment I had thought we would be asked to share a cup of wine with the blacksmith and drink to the health of Oliver Cromwell. Charles would have done it easily enough.

By September ninth we had doubled back northeast of Worcester—not far from Campion Towers. I wished I knew what had happened there. Had Cromwell come? Had he searched for Charles Stuart? I was sure that he had.

We passed through a troop of Roundhead cavalry in one town and afterward I wept with fright. In the next town I chastened the King loudly because he was rough when he lifted me down before an inn door. Sir Julian boxed the King's ears as an old Puritan soldier reined his horse in to grin at us.

"Give it to him," he urged Julian. "The insolence of serving-men is exceeded only by that of serving wenches." He leered at me and trotted past.

When we stopped at Cirencester at another inn, I spoke to my cousin privately. I had had little time for this, but I had always been aware of Julian's nearness. While the King slept, guarded by Wilmot, we talked together in my little room.

"Where do we go?" I asked Julian. "Do we four go to the south coast to the sea?"

He shook his head. I thought in the candlelight he looked weary. "It is the eleventh of September, Pen. We shall be in Bristol tomorrow at sundown. You will leave us there. We shall leave you money. You can wait at some reputable inn for your ship if it is not at the wharves."

I asked, "What of you? Where do you go? What do you do?"

"I go with the King for a time. I am to leave him at Trent—so Wilmot tells me. I will make my way alone to a port and find a ship for France. Wilmot and the King will pass on to other hands in Bristol. They will make for another seaport farther to the east. Wilmot feels we have stretched our fortune far enough traveling together as we have."

"What will you do in France?"

He reached for my hand and held it. "I shall wait for Charles Stuart to become King in deed—as well as in title. I may take service with the army of the Prince of Orange in Holland or with the armies of France. I do not know."

"Have you ever thought of coming to the New World, Julian? Do you so fancy becoming a soldier?"

"Aye, I have considered the New World. I would like to see the colonies—if I could be certain of my welcome—aye, I am weary of soldiering."

"You would not be known as an outlaw there. I think you can be certain of your welcome." He would catch my meaning.

"Well, then, I shall come. Soon if I can. I shall even visit Massachusetts Bay Colony, harbor of psalm-singing Roundheads that it is," he grinned and squeezed my fingers. "I shall come if I can, but we are exiles and poor in France. We take service in foreign armies in order to eat. The King has little money. Lack of money is the true curse of the Stuarts. He knows he will never have money."

I withdrew my fingers from his and pulled Laurel Killing-tree's purse from my belt. I loosened its strings and dumped the Aylmer jewels onto the rough wooden table before me as if they had been nothing more than seashells or pebbles.

"Philippa's jewels!"

"They are mine now. She gave them to me," I told him. "You speak of Charles Stuart as poor." I took up the necklace.

The emerald was still missing. I did not know where it had vanished and I did not care. I dropped the necklace into his hand. "When I am gone, give this to him."

Julian was overwhelmed. "You cannot do this, Pen. It is worth hundreds of pounds."

"Do you expect me to wear *that* in Salem?" I pointed to it. "I do not value jewels. I think my grandmother would wish the King to have it."

"What of those?" He pointed to the earrings and the bracelets.

I picked up one earring and gave it to Julian. "This is your passage to the New World. Can you sell the other earring and the bracelets here in Cirencester for me? I would sell them in Bristol, but I could easily be cheated. I know nothing of gems."

He nodded, taking them. "Aye. I shall do it—if you wish. I know of a goldsmith here in Cirencester. He would have sheltered us except for a suspicious, talkative wife. We dared not trust her."

Julian got up. "You will be rich, Pen. What will you do with this money? Will you catch a husband with it in Salem Town?"

"There are no men in Salem Town I look upon with favor," I told him directly and boldly.

He was openly pleased. "I doubt if you would be a suspicious, talkative wife, Pen."

And with these words he left me. I waited for some time. At last he came back and now he had a hundred fifty pounds in gold with him. "I sold the bracelets," he told me. "The goldsmith did not cheat me. We had great good fortune. He had money on hand to buy some plate, but the owners decided at the last moment not to sell."

Julian took the earring from his pocket. "I could not sell this without its match. I did not choose to sell it in any event. Take one earring to Salem Town with you. I shall keep the other and work my passage to France as a sailor. Philippa's earrings will be a bond between us."

I counted out fifty pounds and shoved the coins across the table to Julian. "Keep back ten pounds of this for your passage to the New World. Use the rest as you see fit. Keep the earring —as I shall keep mine."

He took the money, but from his face I saw that he did not wish to do this. "I shall come. I promise you." Now he asked, "Tell me of your life in Salem. Somehow I do not think it has been happy."

He listened while I spoke of my father's poverty and of my stepmother's nature, made harsh by necessity. He pointed to my pile of coins. "Will you take advice from me, Pen?"

At my nod he went on. "Put most of this money with a reputable goldsmith in Boston. I have heard it is a goodly sized town. Put it there yourself, Pen—and in your name. Let no one else touch it. If I gauge this Elizabeth right, and I think I do, she will not mistreat you long as she thinks you to be rich."

His devise was a good one. I would follow it. Julian took my chin in his hand and kissed me. "I shall say 'good night' now, Pen. We have a long journey ahead in the morning. You leave the King just outside of Bristol. I shall give him your necklace when I leave him at Trent. Shall I tell him, then, who you truly are?"

"If you wish. It might amuse him to know he has traveled so long with a Roundhead. But tell him in secret. Milord Wilmot will not be pleased."

Julian laughed. "Bar your door well, Pen. The King sometimes sleeps very lightly."

I did as he told me and then hid my money away in a knotted handkerchief. I would put the handkerchief into my dress in the morning. Then I undressed and got into the hard, none-too-clean bed—we stopped always at humble inns, farmers' inns, but tonight I fell asleep with a diamond and emerald earring in my hand, for the first time valuing it.

We put miles behind us as we rode to Bristol and I leaned my cheek against the King's green coat sadly. For a wonder he was silent, too. His unfailing good humor had been astonishing. He passed through danger; he hid in attics; spoke jestingly with Roundhead searchers, forded streams to avoid guarded bridges, took abuse from Julian and Wilmot and sometimes from me, and never lost his temper. His courage was admirable. I had realized at last that his bravery and spirit matched Cromwell's, although the King's was of a different stamp—gay and lively. In my heart I knew that Charles Stuart would someday come into his own. Perhaps then, I would come back to England.

The King spoke to me over his shoulder guessing my thoughts once more. "I am told that you leave us at Bristol, Mistress Sutton, and take ship for the New World. Do you have family there?"

"Yes, I go to Massachusetts Bay Colony," I replied. I lied a little to him. "I have kinsmen there, sire. My mother bids me visit them. It would scarcely do for me to return to Campion Towers now. My kinsmen in the colonies have asked me to come before this and I had half-promised them sometime past."

"I do not think you will be content in that nest of Roundheads, mistress. Why not go to my colony of Virginia or to Maryland? They are more lively places, I am told. A pretty maid of your spirit will not long be content among Roundheads. You will be no more content in Massachusetts Bay Colony than I in Scotland."

I looked at Julian who rode close by and smiled as I put my

finger to my lips. Julian's amused glance was knowing and tender.

"I much doubt if Mistress Sutton will be long among the Roundheads, sire," he told the King.

Near Bristol we parted. We drew up our oddly assorted horses at a bend of the road and walked into a secluded little wood. Here I took leave of King Charles. He dismounted, his lameness gone by now, and took my hands. I would have curtsied but he would not permit it. Instead, he bowed to me and kissed each of my hands in turn.

"You have guarded me well, Mistress Sutton," he spoke in a serious fashion. "I hope someday we shall meet again. When you hear I have regained my throne, come back to England. There shall always be a place for you in my affections and at my court—even if you have eyes only for another." He glared roguishly at Julian. "As an old hand at the game of hearts, I see clearly where others do not see at all. I am somewhat piqued, you know. I cannot thank Mistress Sutton for preferring another, but I shall comfort myself as best I can. I shall thank her though for her trouble and for the love she bears my father's cause," and now the King did kiss me truly—long and hard.

He let me go and bowed again. He swung up onto his ridiculous horse and addressed Wilmot. "Where do we ride now, Master Grimstone?"

"To a place I know. Julian knows it, too. He will come there after he has taken Mistress Sutton into Bristol." Viscount Wilmot of Athlone swept his hat off to me. By now his Cavalier hat was as sorry and as dirty as his rain-matted velvet coat and breeches. He had given his fine plume away, too, long ago, as a remembrance of his King. "Mistress Sutton, England owes you much. Would that we could repay it."

I curtsied. "I have been repaid by your company and by your constant devotion to the royal cause."

Henry Wilmot understood. For the first time I heard his laugh.

The King looked puzzled for a moment. Then he frowned ferociously at me. "Aye, he has been a most irksome watchdog, mistress! I call him privately 'Henry Will-not'!" and with this jest the King left us, Lord Wilmot's horse ambling behind the King's gray, plain countryfolk on their way to Bristol market.

Julian held out his hand once they were out of sight. I caught it and he pulled me up behind him. Wordlessly we rode out, too. I clasped Julian close around the waist. I was sad. I prayed silently for the King and wished him fortune on his journey. How I wished I did not have to leave Julian soon, too, as we walked through the streets of Bristol, moving to one side to let the familiar dog teams pass.

I asked my cousin, "Should I send word to Campion Towers from here? They asked me to send a message to them."

"Aye. They will wish to know you are safe. Where did you stay when you first came to Bristol, Pen?"

"At the Turk's Head in Marsh Street. That is where the Killingtrees wished me to stay. The mistress of the inn is a fearfully respectable woman and a Royalist, too. She misliked me."

"We shall go there," he told me. "Do you think such a reputable woman would permit me to take a cup of wine with my kinswoman in the common room?"

"She would," I said. "Mistress Whidby fancies Cavalier gentlemen, I think," and I thought of how she had despised my visitor, Amyas Moonjean.

We got down at the Turk's Head and Julian took me inside,

but first he left his incredible horse with a boy who stood outside the inn. People laughed at the horse or looked at it in disbelief as it leaned against the inn in the rain, trying to nibble at some drooping thatches.

Mistress Whidby met us at the door. She looked open-mouthed at the horse, then knew me and sniffed. "So ye return to the New World so soon, Mistress Hervey? The *Godspeed* came into port days past. Samuel Enderby was here to take his supper of elvers and to inquire after you. I would not have thought word could travel so swiftly to Worcestershire in these troublous times."

I replied meekly, "General Cromwell orders things well."

This pleased her not at all. Julian grinned at how her face darkened. "Wine for Mistress Hervey and myself," he ordered.

Her eyes took in Julian's sorry costume, his steeple hat, and his lameness. She had no high opinion of him, that was certain, but when he doffed his hat in a low sweeping bow, a bow such as the innkeeper had probably never known, she decided to favor us with a vinegar smile.

"I do not know who you are and I do not ask," she told him, "but you are no Roundhead!" Mistress Whidby turned to me now, nodding. "You keep better company these days," and she hurried off to fetch the wine.

Julian and I sat side by side at the table. "I shall go aboard the *Godspeed* tonight," I said to him. "When you leave, I do not wish to be alone. My friends from Swindon will soon be here if they are not in Bristol now."

Julian cleared his throat. "I suppose one of these Roundhead friends of yours from the New World is a man?"

I felt like teasing him but our time was too brief. Yet, his jealousy had made my heart beat faster. "Amity Wrenn is sixteen and far prettier than I. Pastor Wrenn and his wife, who are her parents, resemble plucked chickens. They are staunch Roundheads and they will be convinced that I shall have gone to the devil in Worcestershire. I must lead a life of great piety for many months to convince them otherwise."

Sir Julian chuckled. "You do not paint a pretty picture, Pen." He put his arm around me as Mistress Whidby came up with a bottle of wine and two pewter cups.

She saw his arm and smiled again. "See," he whispered into my ear, "this is how she expects a true Cavalier to behave. She is not so very respectable after all."

"Julian!" I scolded softly, but he did not take his arm away.

"Bring ink, paper, and a quill," he commanded Mistress Whidby. "Can you find a way to send a message for Mistress Hervey tonight?"

The little woman nodded. "Aye I can," and in a moment she returned with what Julian asked.

"She will read it!" I warned softly.

"Of course! We must carry ourselves cleverly then. Sir Nicholas and Laurel will catch our message." He gave me the quill. "Let it be in your hand, Pen. I shall soon send word from a seaport to them—I trust."

"What shall I say?"

We were silent, thinking. I leaned my head on Julian's shoulder as the autumn rain ran down the windowpane behind us.

He dictated. "I have reached Bristol with our kinsman, Master John Grimstone. My ship lies in port and tonight I shall take passage aboard her. I have conveyed our business successfully for you and consigned our valued goods into the right hands in Bristol. The goods you held at Campion Towers and could no longer store is ready for an early transport." He hesitated, though, and then went on smoothly. "It arrived here quite undamaged by its difficult passage. Master John Grimstone will check further on the condition of your merchandise soon and convey another message to you regarding it. I send my affection to you all."

I finished writing. "How shall I sign it?"

"Sign it 'Pen.' That is enough." He put a silver piece on the table as I signed my name. "They will understand. 'Grimstone' was an imaginary playfellow I had as a small boy at Campion Towers. Laurel will surely remember." Then he took up the quill and added "John Grimstone" under my name. "They will know my hand."

He folded the letter, addressed it, and put the coin upon it. Now he poured the wine, a cup for me and a cup for him. He touched his cup to mine. "To us, Pen Hervey! Until we meet again in the New World."

"To your good fortune," I told him.

And we drank.

"I shall write you from France," he promised me.

"It will be months until I get it," I said, knowing that farewell was very close now.

"Wait for it—wait for me." He put my hand to his face, turned it over, and left a kiss in my palm.

He left me as I finished my wine—without another word—without a backward glance. I could have watched him ride off in the rain through the window, but I did not. This was how he had wished it. We needed no more words between us.

I went to the wharves that night, escorted by linkboys Mistress Whidby found for me, to where the *Godspeed* lay at anchor in the cold rain. I paid off the lads who carried the torches and went up the familiar plank. On the deck I met the same little cabin boy who took one look at me and gulped. Then he darted for the master's cabin.

"She is here, sir!" he cried out. "Mistress Hervey is come!"

Captain Enderby flung his door open himself. Behind him I saw Pastor Wrenn, who rose to his feet.

"You have come!" Samuel Enderby said, sounding muchly relieved. "We expected to wait only three more days. We have had the great news of the battle in Worcestershire. Your trunk came two days past. We wondered what had become of you."

"Aye, that we have. We have been concerned," Pastor Wrenn agreed.

"Were you in danger so nigh to Worcester? Did you have trouble traveling here?" the captain asked.

I took off my rain-spattered cloak. "Not at all," I said. "The countryside is in good order and clear—except for our soldiers who scour about for Charles Stuart."

"They have not found Charles Stuart yet?" the minister from Salem Town asked, disappointed. "Worcester was a great victory for Oliver Cromwell, but he could crown it yet by taking up that young devil. Amyas Moonjean told me they would have him soon."

Wary, I let Pastor Wrenn go on. "I saw Dr. Moonjean again in Swindon a few days past. He told me he had met you here in Bristol, Penitence, and had found you a sober and a godly maid. He wished me to convey his fond wishes to you when next I saw you. He rode on to London then to speak with some members of the Parliament."

Now I let go, taking a deep breath. Dr. Moonjean did not suspect that *I* took Charles Stuart to safety. I had feared that he might ask in and about the neighborhood of Campion Towers and learn that I had gone. Amyas Moonjean was clever and dangerous. But I was safe. The King was safe from him, too, I thought.

"How was your stay in Worcestershire? How did you find your mother's family?" Enderby asked me.

"My grandmother died, but before she died, I learned to know her and to admire her. The others are goodly folk, for all that they are not of our faith. My father would have liked them in time—as I did."

Captain Enderby nodded, approving. "I take it you inherited and you are rich? This may make a difference in your life."

"I believe it shall," I vowed. I spoke to Pastor Wrenn. "Is Amity in our cabin?"

"Aye, probably abed by now. She hoped you would come. Go surprise her, Penitence."

I started for the door but Pastor Wrenn called out to me and I turned to face him. He picked up a round yellow thing from a bowl on the captain's table. "Penitence, do you recall these?" he asked me, his eyes twinkling. "Did you have them in England? As I hear it, both General Cromwell and that tall black devil of a man, Charles Stuart, were not ten miles from you at your grandfather's house. When I learned of the battle, I thought at once of our conversation at Cádiz. The ways of Providence are strange, are they not?"

I curtsied to him. Once more he did me honor to jest with me. I would love to learn what he would say if I dared tell him the full story of my weeks in England. I truly believed that for once I would see little Pastor Wrenn speechless with amazement.

I said quietly. "Alas, I did not sup with Oliver Cromwell." I jested, myself. Pastor Wrenn would not take me seriously, "And with Charles Stuart I did not once sup on Spanish citrons."

And indeed, I had not seen a citron as I rode through England, my arms about the waist of that tall black devil of a man.

Epilogue

LETTERS CAME for me on the *Godspeed* on her midwinter voyage.

It was now 1652. Things were not the same in Salem Town. My money had been put with the goldsmith in Boston and Elizabeth treated me with the consideration Julian had predicted. I had brought my half brother Obedience a fine plume in Boston, purchased from a passerby from Virginia—a fine white plume, not a red one.

I had told my family what I wished them to know—but not a word about the King or the Battle of Worcester other than what I could have gleaned from others. Someday when he was older, I would tell young Obedience, who would understand. I spoke freely though of the Killingtrees and painted them fairly. I showed the emerald and diamond earring to no one, although I talked casually of my kinsman, Sir Julian, who was a merchant in France.

Samuel Enderby sent for me to come to the wharf as before, and as before, Obedience brought me the message. This time I did not hesitate nor did I ask Elizabeth for her permission. This time the captain took three letters from his cuff and held them out. "One from England—two from France," he explained.

I thanked him and took them from his hand. One was from my great-aunt Laurel. I knew the Killingtree coat of arms at once. Could I forget the fleur-de-lis? The second was from Julian. I knew his hand. The third was in a strange black angular script. Which should I open first?

The bitter winds of January caught at my cloak and blew my hair from under my hood in wisps about my face as I stood on the deck of the *Godspeed*, debating with myself.

I broke the seal on Julian's letter. Guarded though his message was, I caught its meaning easily. He was well. The valuable merchandise had come through from Bristol to France in good condition. Julian, himself, did well in his trade and said that in the summer his affairs brought him to Salem Town and from there to Maryland and Virginia. He signed it as I had known he would "with love." I held his welcome letter close for a time, while the wind tried to take it from my hands.

Finally though I put it into my apron pocket. Before he came, I would wear it out with reading. I opened Laurel's letter next. What had happened at Campion Towers in my absence?

Hers was longer than Julian's but as careful. She had received my message from Bristol that I had done their business well. It had pleased her. They had been much occupied for a time at Campion Towers entertaining many guests, some of them great folk, indeed, and she and Sir Nicholas had shown them the entire courtesy of the house. I guessed at her meaning. Cromwell had seen the secret passage! There had been no recent guests. So they had not been molested further.

The red horses were well. Pippin and Cranberry were in foal. The bones in Sir Nicholas' foot had knit at last. Master Meredith had come to live at the manor house. There was not one word about Douglas or Amabel Sutton and I wondered at this. Laurel closed, sending her love and my grandfather's. She asked me to return when I felt the time was right and to write to her soon.

The last letter remained. I broke its seal—the same as Julian's —which was plain red wax without any mark.

The letter was brief:

My dear Mistress Grimstone,

I do not know how to address you. You seem to have more names than even I have used, and I have used a good many. I shall employ the last I used to you.

Your kinsman gave me your princely gift at Trent. You have my deep gratitude for all you have done for me. I assure you I shall not forget.

Your kinsman, my friend, has told me your most unusual history. I trust that the forward behavior I exhibited at times did not lead you to stray from the principles you hold so dearly. I am positive that it did not.

"Henry Will-not" joins me in sending you his greetings. He is not altered in his sentiments and for reasons of his tranquillity of mind he has not been informed as to your identity and religious persuasion.

Have a care for my friend who sails to you ere long. I charge you with his happiness and welfare—as you once were charged with mine. Otherwise, I should not send him to you.

The letter was signed, "Your very affectionate and obedient servant—William Jackson."

I smiled as I reread this letter and put it, too, into my apron pocket with the others.

The King had not forgotten me.

I would not forget him.

Author's Note

CHARLES STUART and Oliver Cromwell, of course, are historical personages. They did face each other in battle at Worcester on September 3, 1651. It is also true that the Roundheads sent spies into the vicinity of Worcester months earlier, for a Royalist shopkeeper in London had been caught and had confessed that the young King would march to Worcester from Scotland.

It is equally true that the people of Worcestershire did not rally to the King and that Cromwell defeated the outnumbered royal forces. We have described the battle as it happened. The King did watch it for a time from the tower of Worcester Cathedral and he personally led the charge on Red Hill—just as Cromwell led the assault across the River Severn.

Cromwell's men searched long and hard for Charles Stuart and his loyal companies after the battle. Actually, three girls braved danger to travel with Charles Stuart. They were Jane Lane, Julia Coningsby, and Anne Wolfe. The King was never captured and made his way at last to a place now known as Brighton where he took ship for refuge on the Continent.

Charles Stuart remained in exile until 1660. After the death of Oliver Cromwell, the Parliament that had beheaded Charles I in 1649 recalled his son to the English throne. Charles II ruled peacefully but not tranquilly until his death in 1685.

Viscount Wilmot of Athlone, Henry Wilmot, was a real person, too. He was a sober, temperate man, well thought of by the Cavaliers but not particularly liked by the King, himself. The faithful Wilmot, who attempted once more to conspire in England in 1655, died in 1658 in exile.

Gentle, scholarly James Stanley, seventh Earl of Derby, was much less fortunate. He was captured by the Roundheads, brought to trial by them on a charge of treason, and in October 1651 beheaded for his devotion to the Stuart cause.

Although he appears only as a name, Edmund Campion, the Roman Catholic priest and Papist martyr, lived and died as we have written. It is known that he was in Worcestershire in the late sixteenth century.

We have depicted our historical persons as they were in 1651. Portraits are very easily obtained of Charles II and of Oliver Cromwell. The characters of Cromwell and of the King are well known. Biographies of both men abound and are readily available at most libraries. The King's fondness for a pretty face is proverbial, but in recent years Charles II has come into his own in the judgment of sober historians as a humane and intelligent monarch. Cromwell's place in the history of England is undisputed. He is one of England's greatest men of all time.

In writing *Campion Towers* we have used many sources— biographies, social histories, political histories, military histories, and others. Often we have worked from mutual memory and from our own historical works in progress dealing with seventeenth-century England.

We found the following books especially useful as well as interesting—*King Charles II* by Sir Arthur Bryant; *Cromwell's Generals* by Maurice Ashley; *The Complete Peerage* by G. E. Cokayne; *Life in a Noble Household* by Gladys Scott Thompson; *The Early Stuarts* by Godfrey Davies; *Illustrated English History* by G. M. Trevelyan; *The Dictionary of National Biography: Oliver Cromwell* by Samuel Rawson Gardiner; and *Oliver Cromwell and the Rule of the Puritans in England* by Sir Charles Firth.

To deal with the language problems, we have relied very largely on C. T. Onions' edition of *The Shorter English Dictionary on Historical Principles* and the vocabulary of the King James Version of the *Bible* as listed in James Strong's *Exhaustive Concordance of the Bible*.

In writing *Campion Towers* we wished to convey the feeling of seventeenth-century written and spoken English but without the complexities and difficulties of usage that strictest accuracy would demand. We investigated a variety of then-contemporary writings, but the *Journals* of the House of Lords and the House of Commons are too cryptic and official; John Milton and John Donne, the major poets of the time, are too involved and grand for everyday use; the letters of Thomas, Earl of Strafford or Algernon, Earl of Northumberland or Edward, Viscount Conway are more down-to-earth, but still too complicated. We finally settled on one principal model, a nonliterary figure but a man who deeply impressed his straightforward, simple personality on the literature of English history. At the age of forty, Oliver Cromwell emerged from the obscurity of a quiet life as a country gentleman and later became Lord Protector of England. He cared little for the usual rhetorical flourishes of his time and his letters are. rather matter-of-fact and abound in simple sentences. In a day before there was any agreement upon such things as spelling, punctuation, word order, and grammar, Cromwell's simple and direct language made it live.

We did, of course, make concessions to the twentieth century. We have not used the current "thee," "thou," or "hath," because these could become tiresome and difficult. In a very few instances we had to use words that Penitence Hervey could not have known since they came into the English language at a later date, and since the use of seventeenth-century equivalents (if they existed) only would have obscured matters. If, however, we made some concessions to our own time, we did make a major effort to recapture this period of English history by writing the novel with much of the language that was available to our heroine. We can claim with some confidence that most of the words used in the novel were in use in England in the middle of the seventeenth century. This may, of course, account for some of the strange sounds that emerge, as when we use "watchword" rather than "password" or "scouting parties" for "patrols." But we hope this will lend a flavor to the book that could not be achieved in any other way. We cannot pretend, however, to have used the language exactly as it would have been then. If we had, the result would have proved too strident to the ear and obscure to the eye to have held anyone to the tale.

John and Patricia Beatty
October 1964